TARNISHED PENNY

Penny Series Book 1

Michelle Bachman

Published by ColorMeRed

Tarnished Penny

Penny Series, Book 1

First Edition Hardcover August 2020

Copyright © 2020 Michelle Bachman

ISBN: 978-1-7346662-1-2

Library of Congress Control Number: 2020903757

This book is a work of fiction. Names, characters, places, and incidents are the product of the author's imagination or are used fictitiously. Any resemblance to actual events, locales, or persons, living or dead, is coincidental.

Photography and Design by Justin Escue

Published by: ColorMeRed

Bristol, Indiana

Printed in the United States of America

Acknowledgments

This book is dedicated to all those who supported, encouraged, and put up with me through the long, crazy process.

To my husband of 20 years, Jeremy, who no matter what, always has my back. You believed in me when I didn't believe in myself.

To my 3 kids, I'm sorry for all the times I drove you crazy talking about my ideas. Even with your eye rolls, I knew you believed in me.

I'd like to thank my Fabulous Princess Manager, Monique Pearson. Without your awesome ideas, this book would've never gone to print. You said we could do it, and here we are.

I'd like to thank my fellow writers at *Bristol On the River* writer's group, for always telling me the truth so I could learn and grow as a writer. Because let's face it, I can be a little intimidating, and you had no problem telling me how it was. You are, "my ladies". I love you all.

A special thank you to Rosemary McDaniel. If it weren't for you, this book wouldn't exist. I truly appreciate all the extra time you took to share your experience and knowledge. You pushed me to become the best I could be. Your encouragement helped me realize my dream, and I don't know how I'll ever repay you for helping me make that dream a reality.

Chapter 1

December 2017

The night was clear, and the wind was howling, as it often did in the city of Chicago. Penelope had been sitting in the dark, watching the street below for hours. Her mind kept spinning, questioning where her husband might be or better yet, who he might be with.

She knew he was with another woman, but continued to tell herself it was her own insecurities. He'd promised to be home before the bars closed, but she should've known better than to believe him. It was already hours after closing and still no sign of him.

She heard a car pull up and wondered if it was Derrick returning home. With her heart pounding from a mixture of excitement and fear, she peeked through the blinds, being careful to only move them a hair.

Between the narrow slits, she could see a black Ford Explorer with dark-tinted windows and a Pink Panther vanity plate on the front. No one appeared to be getting out, so she watched and waited to see if it was him. If so, who was the person driving him home? She knew it wasn't the guy who'd picked him up earlier because they drove a pickup truck.

Minutes passed, and she was about to give up when the passenger door opened. Derrick climbed out, started to walk away, then stopped, turned back, and went to the driver's window. Penelope watched as it rolled down, but from her angle, she couldn't see the driver. After they handed him something, he turned to head inside.

Afraid he'd realize she'd been watching, Penelope hurried to the bedroom. She jumped into bed and pretended she'd been sleeping. Her hands were sweaty, she felt she'd been the one who'd done something wrong and was about to get caught.

I'm crazy, Penelope thought. She had every right to look out her window and wonder where her husband was. He was the one who'd broken his word again, not her.

The sound of the key sliding in the lock and the click of the deadbolt as it released, made her pulse jump and her breath quicken. With her eyes open and ears alert, she heard him slink into the apartment. Not bothering to turn on any lights, he knocked something to the floor as he made his way toward the bedroom.

What kind of mood would he be in, she wondered?

Through nearly closed eyes, she watched as he dropped his coat to the floor. Then used the door frame to steady himself, he leaned over to take off his shoes. Once finished, he headed to the bathroom but tripped on his coat, and hit the floor hard.

"Damn it, woman! Why is this here?" Derrick swore. Grabbing one of his shoes, he threw it at her. "If you'd pick the house up, I wouldn't be on the floor! Why can't you do anything right?" he growled.

Anger surged to the surface, and the words were out of her mouth before she could stop them. "I cleaned today when I got home from work. So, where have you been, and why are you so late?"

Her question was met with only silence. She knew it was going to start another fight, but he shouldn't have thrown the damn shoe at her.

It was too dark in the room to see his eyes. If she could have, she might have kept her mouth shut and fallen asleep instead. He still hadn't said anything, but she could hear his breathing from across the room.

Slowly, he took off his long-sleeve shirt and walked to the bed, holding it. Pulling his left knee up, he leaned over her and placed his hands on either side of her face.

"Excuse me? Do you have something to say?" His breath so strong of alcohol, she had to turn her face away.

Derrick grabbed her by the neck and pulled her within an inch of his face. "Don't you dare turn away from me while I'm talking to you!"

Her pulse rose in her throat, and tears streamed down her cheeks. She couldn't move. The way he'd climbed on the bed tightened the blankets, and now one of her arms was pinned. Frantically, she tried to free herself before he made his next move, but it was of no use. She wasn't going anywhere.

He yanked her up by her hair, and her scalp flamed as though it had been set on fire.

"Let go! Get off me!" she cried.

Using the shirt, he'd taken off, he slipped the sleeve around her neck and squeezed so hard her vision started to blur. The pressure was so intense, she began struggling for air.

I only need a small breath, she thought. Desperate to stay conscious, she feared if she passed out, she might never wake up.

He screamed in her face, his spit spraying into her eyes.

"What? Nothing to say?" Derrick asked, slurring his words. "See, you're all talk! That's what you are. You're worthless, it's no wonder I want to go out with my friends and have a good time. Do you actually think I'd want to stay home with you? What fun would that be?"

He released her neck enough for her to catch her breath, but still held the sleeve.

Thankfully, she still had one free hand; but what to do?

Placing her hand on his cheek, she slowly began to caress it. Barely able to speak, she knew she had to get out of this position. He could do a lot more damage when she couldn't move.

"I'm sorry," her voice cracked in barely a whisper. "You're right. I shouldn't leave things lying on the floor. I'll try to do better from now on. Are you hungry?" she stammered, desperate to appease him. "I could go into the kitchen and make you something to eat? I love you so much. That's all, and I worry when you're not home."

Leaning over, he whispered in her ear. "Do you really think I'm going to fall for that? That I'm going to just let you get up and walk out of here after you talked to me that way? No, I don't think so. You need to be taught a lesson. We both know how much I love to teach you things."

Seizing her free hand, he pulled it tight above her head. "Now, where's your other arm? Give it to me!" His weight on her was almost too much to bear.

Her nostrils were full of the stench of sweat and sex exuding from Derrick's body. Overwhelming her senses, she knew instantly; she'd been right. He'd been with another woman tonight.

"I can't; you've pinned it under the blanket. If you loosen it, I promise I'll leave you alone. You can relax, take a shower, or whatever you want."

"I'm so sick of hearing you talk. Why can't you do what you're told?" Noticing a pair of socks on the far side of the bed, he reached over and grabbed one.

"Here, since you want to keep talking, let's see how well you do with this in your mouth." Rolling it into a ball, he shoved it in her mouth. Roughly, he pulled all the blankets off the bed, grabbed her other hand, and slammed it to the headboard.

Fear rose up in her throat like bile. Maybe there was no way out of it this time. She knew she had to stay calm, breathe, and for God's sake, keep her mouth shut. She knew, the more she struggled, the more enraged Derrick would become.

Tears continued to roll down her face, making it difficult to breathe. But she didn't dare make a sound. If anything, he'd tape her mouth shut with the sock still wadded inside.

Forcing her hands together, Derrick shoved them in the rope he kept attached to the backside of the headboard. Her arms were pulled so taut she thought he might dislocate her shoulders. The more she tried to get a little slack, the tighter the restraints became. Her muscles started to burn and ache; her eyes pleaded with him to stop, to let her go. But he simply stared back with cold, dead eyes.

"Are you sorry for mouthing off to me? Do you want me to let you go? Have you learned your lesson for today?" Not waiting for a response, he raised his left hand and backhanded her.

Pain bloomed across her cheek, like hundreds of bees stinging her at once. Over and over, he continued to hit her, and she screamed in her mind, trying to remove herself mentally from existence.

Penelope assumed Derrick was still yelling, but she'd long ago stopped listening. Biting down on the sock helped to ease her pain. The more pain he inflicted upon her, the more his arousal grew between his legs.

Once he was finished with her face, he started on her stomach, then her ribs. Penelope had no strength left to resist him when he flipped her over onto her stomach and ripped off her panties. He spread her legs wide with his knee, then lifted her core off the bed to give himself better access. She was so weak from all the blows, she barely registered what he was about to do.

Derrick had always liked his sex rough, and she was used to it by now, but something this time felt different. Aggressively he pulled her back by the hips and lined himself up. Quickly becoming alert, she tried desperately to remove herself from his grip. Grabbing her roughly by the hair, he shoved her head into the pillow and slammed into her. Each thrust was sharp and deep, the burning, stabbing pain felt like it went on for hours.

She tried to scream as loud as she could in an attempt to get him to stop, but only a muffled cry came out. Penelope knew she had to get the sock out of her mouth. She'd tried using her tongue to push it out, but it wasn't working.

Her brain was shutting down, she couldn't come up with any more options. Derrick was too strong for her to get free. Biting down on the sock as hard as she could, Penelope rocked herself back and forth in the hope of helping him finish quickly. Finally, she felt him tighten, then pull out releasing himself across her back. She exhaled, not having realized she'd been holding her breath. She felt him loosen her hands, she pulled her arms free and immediately ripped the sock from her mouth.

Letting herself sink into the bed, the blackness finally descended, and she slipped into unconsciousness.

Awakened by light shining through the window, Penelope struggled to open her eyes. The inside of her eyelids felt like sandpaper, and one was almost completely swollen shut. She heard the sound of dripping water and realized Derrick was no longer in bed. It must be morning, she thought but had no idea what time it could be.

The sound was familiar, but she couldn't place it. It was strange, she thought, how when one of your senses stopped working, everything around you seemed to be so much more pronounced.

The air in the room was still, but a sweet scent clung to it, reminding her of coconut. She realized then it was shower gel, which meant Derrick was in the shower. Perhaps she was given a few minutes reprieve to get out of his way.

She attempted to get out of bed, but the throbbing pain in her ribs took her breath away. Even taking a small breath was almost too much to bear. She only hoped they were bruised and not broken this time.

Penelope rubbed her wrists, where angry purple welts had already started to form. Thankful it was winter she could cover up most of the damage without too many questions. Her face was a different matter. Not having seen it yet, she could only go by how it felt, and if pain were any indication, she must look awful. She wasn't sure if her unique concealer was going to be enough to cover it this time, to keep people from noticing. Usually, Derrick didn't leave marks on her face, because he knew people would wonder if he'd been the one who put them there. She could only come up with so many stories or excuses to explain why she was injured and expect people to keep believing her.

Still barely able to move, she heard the water suddenly turn off. There were only moments to make a decision and tried once again to climb out of bed. Penelope clenched her jaw and tried to keep quiet, not wanting to draw any more attention to herself. As soon as her feet touched the floor, she craved to crawl back under the covers and wish it all away. But she knew it wasn't possible, she might as well go make coffee and get on with her day. Her left eye felt the size of a softball. Gently she touched it and realized there was dried blood on her face. Derrick's ring must have cut her open, she thought.

At one time, she'd been happy, and the ring had been a symbol of their love. It was supposed to stand as a reminder for them, of their unity, of how they'd be together forever. Now it only made her think of being trapped forever with this person who did horrible things to her.

How could someone who claimed to love her, be so cruel? How many more black eyes and broken bones would she have to endure in her lifetime?

Standing up was enough to bring tears to her eyes, so bending over to get clothes from her dresser wasn't an option. She noticed the robe from the night before and slowly pulled it on. She knew she had slippers somewhere, so she went in search of them.

Every step she took was unsteady, and she had to hold her ribs as she made her way into the living room. When she found the slippers sitting beside the couch, she took extra care to hold on for support as she slid her feet in. They were so soft and warm, and Penelope had felt chilled to the bone since she woke up. Last night now seemed like a nightmare. She'd take any and all comfort she could get, even something as simple as warm slippers.

Turning around, she headed to the kitchen for a cup of coffee when she heard the bathroom door open. She didn't have it in her to deal with more drama right now. She only hoped he would leave her in peace for the rest of the day.

She was starting to fill the coffee pot with water when Derrick came up behind her. Please don't touch me, she thought, knowing he was about to. Turning her head away, she wanted to avoid any eye contact and braced herself, so she didn't flinch.

Gently he placed his fingers on her neck, rubbing the very marks he'd made. Kissing them lightly, he said, "We shouldn't have let things get so out of control last night. Do you forgive me?"

Penelope knew what he wanted to hear and responded appropriately. "Of course. What's there to forgive?" He placed his finger across her lips and hushed her like a child. Then covering her mouth with his, he kissed her lightly, again taking control of the situation.

He pulled away and said, "Go ahead and take your shower, I'll finish getting the coffee started." Then he turned her around and lightly patted her butt, reminding her of the torture only hours before.

Once in the shower, she let the warm water run over her face and soak into her pores. While she stood under the spray, she couldn't stop herself from crying. She knew he'd be coming in to check on her in a few minutes. He always did, and it wouldn't be wise to let him see her this way. She needed to wash quickly while attempting to clear her mind. She knew the bruises would go away, the physical pain only hurt for a little while, but the mental anguish was much harder to overcome, and the self-doubt seemed to last forever.

Wiping the steam from the mirror, she looked at herself and the damage done. When she was younger, she swore she'd never let a man treat her the way her mother had been treated. But now, looking at herself, it was precisely what she'd become. Her mousy brown hair had a chunk missing from behind her ear. No wonder her head had felt it was on fire. Hopefully, it would cover easily if she styled it differently until it grew back. Her right eye was so bloodshot, she could hardly tell she had green eyes, and all the swelling made her face no longer look heart-shaped. She'd lost quite a bit of weight in the last few years; she'd be lucky to weigh 115 pounds at this point. She hoped, being 5'7", didn't make her look too thin.

Gently touching her right side, a little below her bra line, she felt a bruise about the size of his fist. Could she have been so out of it she hadn't noticed it at the time? Sometimes he hit her so long she mentally shut down for fear she'd go crazy.

Her left eye was nearly swollen shut, and it looked as though she'd taken a softball to the face. She knew the dark purple marks would fade in a couple days. The cuts by her eye and lip didn't seem too deep. Hopefully, they only needed to be cleaned out, and some antibiotic ointment applied.

Lifting the lid on the toilet tank, she flipped it over to reveal the brace she'd taped to the underside for her ribs. The same one she'd had since childhood. Thinking back, she wondered how many times over the years, she'd had to use it. She hated to hide it and be sneaky, but she wasn't willing to take the chance of Derrick finding it either. She wrapped it tightly around herself, then turned and opened the vanity to retrieve her first aid kit. Before tending her wounds, she rewrapped the towel around her to keep it hidden from Derrick. Then got to work on the minor lacerations.

Penelope thought about why he did these awful things to her. She came up with a couple different ideas. Maybe it was stress? He'd always had a bad temper, but it had gotten a lot worse since he'd lost his job a few weeks ago. Or maybe, he wasn't even thinking about her at the time, perhaps his own demons were rearing their ugly heads? The drinking certainly didn't help. He was always much worse after he'd been drinking.

After applying the last of her makeup, making sure to blend it well and cover as many of the bruises as possible, Derrick walked in carrying a cup of coffee.

"Here you go, just the way you like it. I even added a few ice cubes for you." He handed it to her, then leaned on the counter to watch.

"Thanks," she said, trying to finish quickly.

"Oh, it looks like you're almost out of makeup. If you're planning to go out and get more today, I have a few things you could pick up for me," he said.

"Sure, if you want to write it down, I'd be happy to. I promised Baylee I'd take her to get a few things too because her car won't get through all this snow."

"Great, I'll go make my list, while you get dressed. You might want to wear something extra warm. While you were in the shower, the news said the temps are supposed to drop."

"Thanks, for the heads up," she said, going to her closet and pulling out her warmest sweater.

As he left the room to make his list, he pulled out his cell and the small piece of paper he'd stuffed in his pocket the night before. Making sure Penelope was still occupied, he sent a quick text and waited for a reply. He smiled when his phone vibrated almost immediately.

"Can't wait, just tell me when and where" the text read.

Receiving the answer he'd been looking for, he slipped his phone back into his pocket.

Chapter 2

While continuing to get dressed, Penelope heard her phone signal an incoming text message. Thinking it was probably Baylee wanting to know if she was ready to go, she eased into her sweater and grabbed her boots. Remembering where she'd left her phone, she walked straight to the dining room table. But it wasn't there.

"You looking for this?" Derrick asked while going through her phone. "The text was from Baylee, letting you know she'll be down in a few minutes." He tossed her the phone, turned, and walked into the living room to relax on the couch.

"Okay, thanks. I guess I'd better hurry and finish getting ready." Bending over to zip up her boots took the longest, but with the brace holding her ribs in place, she was at least able to move a little without it taking her breath away.

"It's fine, no need to hurry. Just promise me you won't bring her back with you, like last time. I thought for sure, she'd never leave," replied Derrick.

"She's not that bad, but we've been friends since we were kids, so maybe she's an acquired taste."

"She's something, that's for sure. I don't like her, and I don't think you need someone hanging around who's going to be a bad influence."

They'd been through all of this before. Penelope knew how Derrick felt about Baylee, and she thought he understood, she wasn't going to give up her childhood friend. Not wanting to get into another argument, she was happy to be saved by a knock on the door.

Five rhythmic taps and Penelope knew Baylee had finally made her way down the flight of stairs from the third floor and would be standing on the other side. They had made up the little tune when they were kids and still, to this day, always used it.

Hoping Baylee wouldn't make a comment about her face, at least until they were out of the apartment, Penelope opened the door. Baylee stood leaning on the wall, trying to block the wind. All bundled up for the cold and snow, in her black fur hat and matching boots.

Baylee was only four foot something, tiny as could be. If she were lucky, she might weigh ninety pounds soaking wet. She was a feisty little thing, though. Don't tell her she couldn't do something because it would be the first thing she'd go and do. In her mind, she was six feet tall and built like a brick house.

If you were Baylee's friend, she was the sweetest, most loyal, supportive person, around, but if she didn't like you, you better watch out. She didn't care much for Derrick and made it loud and clear almost every time they spoke.

"Hi Bay, come on in. I'll only be a second. I need to grab my purse," stated Penelope.

She noted the startled look on Baylee's face and used her eyes to plead with her to keep her mouth shut. After she gestured for her to take a seat at the bar. It would only be a few more seconds, then Bay could complain all she wanted.

Walking back out of the bedroom with her purse in tow, Penelope held up her hand to signal just a minute. She knew Derrick expected her to give him a goodbye kiss. But when she reached him, he, of course, had to make a show of it and pulled her down into his lap.

"I love you, Baby. Be careful out there and come back safe." Lowering his voice to a whisper, he continued, "I'll be calling while you're out, make sure you answer your phone." When he helped her back up, Derrick's look said it all, you better keep your mouth shut if you know what's good for you!

Penelope struggled into her coat, grabbed her keys, and glanced back at him, lounging on the couch, remembering what drew her to him in the first place.

His dark hair fell slightly across his brow, and when he looked at her with his dark chocolate eyes, she could melt. He didn't work out but was lucky enough to have a lean muscular build. He was only 5'10,", but when he stood over her, he could've been ten feet tall.

When they turned to leave, she let Baylee lead the way. Penelope knew what was expected of her before walking out the door.

"Love you, Honey. See you when we get back." A small part of herself hated saying she loved him after what he'd put her through, but the consequences were steep for not following his rules.

Closing the door behind her, she turned to Baylee. "Wow, it's freezing out here." She said, wrapping her scarf around her neck. "I wish I'd have come out earlier and started the Jeep. He might have had time to warm up a little." Penelope grabbed the scraper out of the back seat and started cleaning the snow off the windows.

Suddenly, feeling as though she was being watched, Penelope looked around. Not noticing anyone, she thought, who in their right mind would be out here if they didn't have to be? Unable to shake the feeling, she glanced up at the window she'd sat by, the night before.

Derrick stood smiling, he sent her a little wave then turned and was out of sight.

Cracking the door enough to get Penelope's attention, Baylee said, "He's creepy. Does he do that all the time?"

"Really, I think it's kind of sweet," replied Penelope staying in character. But on the inside, she was starting to agree. He wanted to make sure she knew he was always watching. "Hey, do me a favor and make yourself useful? Turn the heat on full blast. I'm freezing my butt off out here. You know where the button is."

"I'm all over it," Baylee said.

Scraping the snow off was the easy part, the half-inch of ice under it was another story. Every swipe Penelope held her breath, hoping to relieve some of the burning sensations on her bruised ribs. Not willing to give up and take the easy route, she continued until every window was cleared off.

She hoped the roads looked better than her windows but was thankful her Jeep had four-wheel drive. She knew it wouldn't help much if she started to slide on ice, but her skill could help her then.

Gently climbing back in, she looked over at Baylee playing with the stereo. "Turn on something good, will you? And where to first?"

Baylee paused a moment before replying, "What are you in the mood for? Something angry, mellow, maybe something we can sing too? I vote sing!" She said with a wink. "Maybe you'd feel better if we crank some heavy metal and sing as loud as we can? People might think we're crazy, but who cares as long as no one tells my parents."

"I'm willing to try anything at this point, but no country music today, please. I've cried all I can."

"Got it! No country and no crying." Cranking up Halestorm, she turned and said, "I think we could both use a great cup of coffee from Steams. While we're there, we can talk about what's going on with your face," pointing to her own and circling it. "He sure did a number on you this time. The only reason I didn't confront him earlier, was because you gave me a shut-up look, and I knew he'd take it out on you later when I'm not around."

"Yeah, he probably would. You're right. I appreciate you keeping your mouth shut. I know how hard it can be for you, especially when you go into a mama-bear mode. I realize you only want to protect me, but this isn't something you're going to be able to fix," replied Penelope

"How do you know? Maybe, I can fix it."

Ignoring Baylee and driving north, traffic was all but non-existent, which surprised Penelope a little. Curious if it was the snow or cold temperatures keeping people indoors, she glanced over at the gauge on the dash, it registered only 4 degrees.

Finally, arriving at Steams, finding a parking spot was a piece of cake. Right in the front, which on any normal day would've never happened. Opening their car doors, the wonderful scent of roasted coffee beans aroused their senses. A hint of cinnamon in the air teased and baited them into discovering all the delicious pastries inside.

Walking through the entrance, all the delightful scents intensified. Inhaling deeply, they both walked to the glass case and peeked inside. Everything looked so pretty, all the tiny cakes and cookies with intricate little details.

Baylee located the service bell, pressed it, and waited for someone to come from the back and help them. Looking over at Penelope, she said, "My treat since you were brave enough to venture out with me today."

Just then, someone pushed through the swinging door from the kitchen.

"Sorry about the delay, I was in the back and didn't hear y'all come in. Now, what can I get ya?"

Hearing a familiar voice, Penelope looked up as Baylee started to order.

"It's not a problem, Miss, we understand. I'd like one of those raspberry tarts along with a large vanilla cappuccino, for here, please. Also, if you could box up a dozen of those carrot-cake muffins, that would be great." Turning to Penelope, Bay said, "I'll go grab us a seat."

"That's no Miss," said Penelope with a smile, "that's Erma-Lee Rider. When did you start here?"

Erma-Lee smiled over at Penelope and explained while she worked on gathering up Baylee's order, "Well, Marty was barely giving me enough hours to fill my tank. So, I told him I needed more. He wasn't none too happy about it, but hey, a girls gotta live. Now tell me. How are the roads out there? I'd thought for sure we wouldn't have no customers in today," she said with a southern drawl.

"The snow isn't the bad part; it's all the black ice under it, you need to worry about," Penelope said, pulling off her gloves and rubbing her hands together. "We slid off the road a couple times, but luckily for us, Dime has four-wheel drive."

"I'm sorry, honey, did you just say Dime? Well, isn't that a funny name to call a person. But I'm glad to see y'all made it in safe and sound. Now, what can I get for ya?"

Erma-Lee was right, it would be a funny name, so Penelope thought she'd explain. "Dime is the name of my Jeep. A long time ago my Father said I'd never amount to much and wouldn't have a dime to my name. Hence, I named my Jeep, Dime. But for now, those apple fritters are calling my name, I'll take one of those and go ahead and give me whatever Baylee's drinking, thanks."

"I'll bring it over to y'all as soon as I finish gathering it up. Now, why don't you go on over and sit by the fire a spell? Warm yourself up some."

"I will, thanks." said Penelope as she made her way through the tables and toward the couch where Baylee was sitting. Having already taken off her coat, Penelope could see, Baylee looked as cute as always in her black and purple ensemble. She wished she had a fraction of the fashion sense Baylee had.

Trying to take off her own coat was a bit of a challenge. Every time she moved, sharp pain in her ribs took her breath away. Her muscles would become stiff if she didn't move for too long. So not moving wasn't much of an option either. Plus, she had things to do today.

Noticing Penelope's struggle, Baylee hopped up to assist.

"No," Penelope said, holding up her hand to stop Baylee. "I don't want your help. I got this. Don't you get it? It's embarrassing, not to be able to take off your own coat." Several minutes passed with still no success. Penelope finally stopped trying and turned to Baylee.

Without saying a word, Baylee stood and gently pulled on the left sleeve. Placing her arm on Penelope's shoulder, she gave her a light hug. "It's all right, you know," she said, moving to her right. "To need help once in a while, to allow yourself to be human. I'm here for you, lean on me."

After laying Penelope's coat down, Baylee again took her seat and turned to her best friend. "We've known each other since we were babies, so I'm just going to come out and state the obvious. What the hell happened to you last night? You didn't look like this yesterday."

"It's not that big of a deal. I'm fine, just a couple of bruises; they'll heal in a few days."

"I think you forgot who you're talking to? Hello, I'm a paramedic. I know what to look for in an injured patient. At first glance, I've obviously seen all your cuts and bruises, I couldn't miss them if I tried. But I also see what you're trying to hide."

"Okay, Baylee, drop it, will ya?"

"No, not this time, you wince every time you turn or bend. It tells me you either have bruised or broken ribs. I've noticed you've been very careful every time you sat down, which is a big red flag in my field for sexual abuse."

"All right, you've proven your point, Baylee. I know you're excellent at your job. I wasn't trying to piss you off; I just didn't feel like getting into it."

"Excuse me, sorry to poke in on y'alls little talk," Erma-Lee said, then handed out the drinks and desserts they'd ordered. "If y'all need anything else, you just give me a holler. Enjoy!" Before Erma-Lee turned to head back, Baylee handed her some cash to cover the bill and thanked her for the excellent service.

Erma-Lee hadn't even made it back to the kitchen before Penelope had eaten half her fritter. "These are so good, maybe I should get a few to take home."

"That's why I had her box up a dozen muffins. I'll be jonesing for something from here later, I'm sure. Happens every time," she said, taking her first sip.

Continuing to eat, Baylee turned to Penelope and said, "Now, can we get back to the subject?"

"I'd rather not," Penelope said, enjoying her drink and nibbling her fritter, trying to make it last.

"Pen, I live directly above you, I hear things, not everything, mind you, but a lot. I can't just ignore this. I must have been sleeping by the time it all happened," pointing to all the damage done. "I didn't hear a thing; you know I would've come running."

"I know you would, but I don't want you getting involved."

"How long are you going to keep letting him do this to you?" Baylee sat and waited for Penelope to reply. She assumed she'd once again stick up for Derrick, but she only turned her head and looked away.

Penelope looked so broken lately like she'd given up. Her eyes were hollow, and she kept losing weight. Baylee stared at her and knew something had to change and change fast. Unfortunately, she had no idea what she could do to make that happen.

Baylee knew what she wanted to do. Next time she overheard them fighting and Derrick screaming at her, Baylee would calmly walk to her bedroom closet, pull down the box her father had given her with the nine-millimeter Beretta in it, and go downstairs and blow him away for hurting her best friend. Realistically, she knew she couldn't, but she'd definitely like him to feel pain and suffering. Suffer like he'd made her friend suffer. How would he like it if he had to cry himself to sleep for a few nights? Reality sucks, she thought, because he wasn't worth going to jail over, but she feared the worst. Her fear was one day, if she couldn't get Penelope to leave him, she might be going to her best friend's funeral.

Penelope didn't know what to say. She knew Baylee wouldn't understand. Hell, she didn't understand herself half the time. It felt as though she was in a trance or possessed, and the only thing that mattered was him. The most important thing was making him happy, making him love her. In her mind, she understood what Baylee was saying. She knew what people thought when they looked at her. But what could she do? A person couldn't choose who they loved.

Finally, Penelope sighed and said, "Look, Bay, you don't understand. Derrick isn't always like that. It's only when he drinks too much. He really does love me. I know he does. He's always sorry after and tries to make up for it. What do you expect me to do, leave? I can't do that."

"Penelope, you're right. I don't understand. I just don't get it, but I'd like too. Maybe you could help me see another side to this. I'm afraid for you, we've been best friends since forever, and I don't want to lose you!" Wiping a tear from her eye, she cast a pleading look towards Penelope.

Hating the look in Baylee's eyes, Penelope stared down at the floor. "Do you remember the time, when we were out shopping with our moms, we were probably 7 or 8. Your mom thought they'd lost me in the mall, and mine thought someone had kidnapped me? I can still hear my mom frantically yelling, "Penny, pretty Penny, where are you?" I thought it was funny, hiding inside the rack of clothes until I saw you slumped on the floor crying."

Baylee gave her a sad smile. "Yeah, I remember, I thought for sure I'd lost my best friend forever. I had no idea you were playing around and hiding. All I knew was my best friend was gone." The thought of that day so long ago stirred several old memories. "Once I realized you were gone, I started whispering your name over and over. Telling myself you would be okay, they'd find you. Then I looked up and there you were, standing right in front of me, telling me not to cry."

"You screamed my name so loud, I thought for sure you broke my eardrums."

"How long are you going to hold that over me? I was only a kid. I was so excited; I couldn't help myself. Plus, your hearing is fine, no damage done."

"Baylee, my point here was, you thought you'd lost me once before and everything turned out fine."

"Did it?" Baylee asked, "Not everything turned out fine." Shaking her head, she went on, "It wasn't long after, what, maybe four years that I did lose you?"

"Come on Bay, you didn't lose me, I kept in contact when I could. You know that. Why are you bringing all this back up? The situations are completely different."

Baylee reached over, took Penelope's hand in hers. "I'm sorry, I'm not trying to make it worse, but I don't think you see how similar it all really is. I'm going to tell you something my mom told me only a few years back." Letting go of her hand, Baylee sat back, crossed her legs, and made herself comfortable before continuing with the story.

"My mom was devastated for years over the guilt she had for not stepping up and doing more to help your mom. She told herself if she would have done more, or tried harder, all those years ago, then maybe things could have turned out differently, and Mary would still be alive."

"It wasn't her fault," Penelope said in a clipped tone. "I've never blamed her."

"Thanks for that. I know you didn't, but it's still good to hear. I'll make sure to pass it along. It might help to cheer her up, on one of the bad days. She told me a few stories about how close they were; it reminded me a lot of us." Baylee said, "But once father started rising in the corporate world, I was told your dad, didn't want our mothers being friends anymore."

Penelope nodded her head in agreement. "I remember hearing him yell at her. He'd say, 'Your little rich friend, Ella Reed, was on the news again today. Did she tell you all about it? Did she fill your head with fantasies again? She doesn't fit in our world anymore. Why can't you see that? I don't know why you're so damn gullible; you're stupid if you believe she still wants to be your friend. She just feels sorry for you."

Baylee turned to Penelope and said, "He was lying, plain and simple. I can tell you for certain, my mom never felt sorry for Mary, she admired her and how strong she was. She'd always tell me Mary would do it this way if she were here. I don't know how many times I heard about Mary growing up. How she never gave up, and she was so strong-willed that once she put her mind to something, that was it. So, when your dad told her not to see my mom anymore, it kind of backfired on him. They just snuck around and met at the mall or wherever they could." Baylee paused and took a hard look at Penelope.

"Once the media got a hold of the story about the murders. Father wanted to separate our family from anything connected. Including the information about our moms being friends. When my mom decided we'd have our talk about the past, she could hardly control her emotions. Crying as she explained, how she had no one to talk to, no one who understood. I was told Father wouldn't speak of it, and she was supposed to keep up the appearance that everything was fine. From all outside sources, she was the perfect wife to the up and coming millionaire. But she wasn't fine, and I won't be either if something happens to you."

"So, this?" Penelope motioned. "Bringing up my mom, talking about the past? Do you think it's going to make me leave Derrick? It isn't like he's going to kill me. We're fine, well maybe not fine… but every couple has their problems. It's what you do with them that defines you as a person, and I'm not someone who bails. I stay, I stick, and try to fix what's wrong."

Not letting on, part of her agreed. Penelope was tired of fighting with Derrick all the time, and all the trust issues. She was just so tired of it all. Taking a deep breath, she tried to relax and asked herself the hard question. How long am I going to keep trying to fix this?

"I understand you feel you should stay and work on the relationship, but at what point are you going to say enough is enough and finally walk away? Quit letting him hurt you? I'm not talking only physically, either. I know you and your little brother had it rough growing up, watching your mom being abused by your dad. It doesn't mean it was right, or she deserved it, and neither do you. I can't imagine what it must have been like for you as a kid. I hear it's a cycle. Do you want to have a daughter someday and have her go through something like this too? To watch her hurt and have little to no self-esteem?"

"No, and I don't know why you'd even bring it up. You know I never want to have kids." Penelope said, taking a sip of her drink.

"Because later, you might change your mind."

"No, I won't. I refuse to bring an innocent child into this cruel, mean world. I could never watch a daughter, or a son for that matter, go through half of what I did growing up. Parenting is not part of my DNA. I'd have no idea where to even start; end of discussion."

Penelope's skin felt hot to the touch, and sweat started running down the small of her back as the memories of her childhood came flooding back. Taking a couple slow breaths, she steadied herself and pushed the memories back where they belonged. There were some things a person could never share, things they never wanted to speak of again. She wished the memory itself would disappear like it never existed. She knew better than most how ludicrous the idea was; she'd lost count of how many times she'd relived her torturous childhood through her nightmares.

"I wish there was something I could do to get you out of this." Tears ran down Baylee's cheek as she leaned over and put her arms around Penelope. "You know I love you, right?"

she said, wiping the wetness away and putting on her biggest, brightest smile. "Because I tell you what you need to hear, not what you want to hear."

Lightly hugging her back, Penelope thought, at least I have one thing Derrick can never take away from me. Wanting to sit by the fire a little longer, she asked, "would you get us a refill? I could totally go for another one of those sweet vanilla things you drink." She held up her cup and gave it a little shake. "See if Erma-Lee will hook us up with a couple to-go cups. We still have plenty to do today, and it looks like it's gotten even worse outside if that's possible?"

Apparently, it was, because once they were back outside, Penelope noticed the temperature gauge on Dime said it was now only four degrees. "I keep telling myself to buy a remote start, but I haven't allowed myself the little pleasure yet," she said, smiling.

Shivering, Baylee turned the seats up to high, and all the heaters on full blast. "It's freezing in here. If you remind me next week, I'll buy the stupid remote thing for you; hell, I'll even spring for the installation. Just tell me again why we are out in this weather, and what the hell was so important it couldn't wait," she rolled her hands on the refill Erma-Lee had hooked her up with.

"Hey, come on, a little cold won't kill you. Besides, this was all your idea, not mine, remember? I promise if you give him a few minutes, he'll warm you right up. Dime takes special care of his ladies. Ssh... don't tell Derrick." Laughing, she pulled out of the parking lot and headed east.

"I have to make a quick stop at my bank, it should only take me a couple of minutes. I need to clear up a misunderstanding they have about my account. I'm sure it's nothing," Penelope said.

Lifting an eyebrow, Baylee said, "Good luck with that one. Rarely is it the bank's fault, and unless you are lucky enough to snag one of the few caring tellers, you are going to be in for one long road, my friend."

"Nah," shaking her head, "I haven't done anything wrong, so it has to be on them. Right?"

"The bank doesn't care about your problems. They don't even care if it's their mistake or yours. They only care about one thing." Holding up her favorite fingers, one on each hand, she continued. "The big F word. That's right, I said it! You know you were thinking it too. Banks only care about your financials. In the end, one way or the other, it's always about the green." Rubbing her thumb and middle finger together, she winked at Penelope as they started to slide.

"Hang on Bay! I got this," Penelope said as she turned into the slide and straightened herself out pretty quickly.

"Nailed it!" Baylee exclaimed.

Knowing she should pay closer attention to the roads, Penelope asked Baylee to turn down the music a little. She didn't know everywhere Baylee needed to go today but thought she would allow herself to enjoy the precious time she had with her best friend. They use to hang out all the time, from doing absolutely nothing to basic shopping and partying. Lately, those times were fewer and far between.

It was her own fault, she guessed. Derrick didn't care for Baylee, so it was usually a fight whenever they hung out. It's sad to think, but it was easier to avoid the fight and not hang out, than to hang out and fight for what she wanted.

Penelope was sure there was a saying about fair play, but whatever it was, it had never applied to them. Derrick did what he wanted, no questions asked, and Penelope learned quickly not to ask questions, and do what she was told.

Growing up watching her mom get smacked around, she told herself it would never be her. She'd never let anyone put their hands on her, but somehow it was exactly what she was doing.

She wasn't quite sure how it happened or when it had started, but Penelope knew he hadn't acted this way when they first met. She would have to think about it a while and see if she could figure out what made everything change.

Sweat started beading on her forehead, so she looked over at Baylee to see why she hadn't turned the heat down yet? Still wrapped in her coat and scarf looking as fresh as a daisy, Baylee was going through her grocery list for what appeared to be the fourth time. Penelope knew she would do this a total of five times before they walked into the store. Thinking it was probably an OCD thing, Penelope never mentioned it. She simply smiled at her friend and turned into the bank parking lot.

"I'll just be a couple minutes, you'll see. Hang out and keep the heat on. No matter what happens, don't pick up any trash, do you hear me? I keep bags in the center compartment so I can keep him clean." Blowing Baylee a kiss, she headed inside, knowing full-well Baylee's OCD would never allow her to sit there and not clean."

She should feel a little guilty, planting the seed in her best friend's head, but honestly, she didn't. Baylee was a clean freak and herself not-so-much. She was clean, but not Baylee standards clean. So, knowing her friend the way she did, she knew when she returned, there wouldn't even be a piece of lint on the floor.

As Baylee sat there waiting, she noticed a little shopping center next to the bank with a few businesses in it. Wishing it wasn't so cold out, she would've loved to walk around and see what all there was to see. Then a movement to her left drew her attention. A man stepped out of a big white pickup; he seemed to be talking on his cell. Yet, somehow, he still managed to scope out his surroundings. Being the curious type, Baylee wondered what the man was up to. Thinking back to all the scoping she'd done in the past, it always turned out to be a very bad thing.

But then again, she had just been scoping him out with his ultra-fine physique and light-colored hair. He was tall, and his long, confident strides told her he knew who he was. And who he was, was a hottie! At least from this distance anyway. Then he opened a door and was gone.

What is wrong with me, she thought, here I am getting myself all worked up over some guy I see walking across a parking lot. How pathetic is that? I know it's been a while, but wow, I really need to get ahold of myself. Getting ahold of myself would only exacerbate the problem, she thought. Realizing then how much exacerbate sounds like masturbate, she burst into laughter.

A noise brought her back to reality. She looked around and tried to locate its source. It sounded like a muffled phone, but she didn't see one, so it was probably in something or under something. Baylee opened a couple of the compartments, moved papers around, and still, she found nothing.

Bending over she looked under the driver's seat and there it was buzzing away, she tried to reach for it, but her arm was too short. Deciding to put the seat back, she pulled the lever and back it slid.

"Perfect," grabbing the phone, not bothering to look at the screen, she answered it.

"Hello, Penelope's phone can I help you?" Silence, not a sound from the other end of the line. Thinking she must have missed the call; she was about to hit end.

"Why are you answering Penny's phone? Where is she?" said Derrick.

"Oh, it's you. Why are you calling her Penny? You know her mom was the only one ever allowed to call her that?" She bit the inside of her cheek knowing she needed to be somewhat nice to the prick. "But if you want, I could take a message, she's in the bank right now."

"No, no message, I'll talk to her about it when she gets home."

"Oh, I'm sure you will."

"Excuse me, what's that supposed to mean?"

"I think you know exactly what it's supposed to mean." Apparently, biting her cheek wasn't going to be enough this time, she thought. "How about we don't beat around the bush here? We both know what you've been doing to Penelope, she's my best friend, and I've tried to honor her wishes and stay out of it. I thought I was doing a damn good job of it up until this point."

"Maybe you should find a new best friend. Penelope has me, so she no longer needs you."

"I was here way before you showed up and I'll be here long after you're gone. Let me make myself clear, so there's no misunderstanding. I'm done staying out of it! Do you understand me? You better never lay a hand on her again, if you do, let's just say it will be the last thing you ever do. Am I making myself clear enough for you?" Baylee questioned.

"Just let Penny know I called," Derrick said, ending the call.

Staring out the side window, Baylee wondered if what she had done was smart. Probably not, but there wasn't much she could do about it now. Why couldn't she think things through before she opened her mouth?

Just then, the driver's door flew open, Penelope dumped herself in the seat, slammed her door closed and winced from her still tender behind. Gripping the steering wheel with white knuckles, she screamed at the top of her lungs.

Not really alarmed, Baylee had warned her, she sat and waited for Penelope to explain.

"Why?" Penelope said, "does this always happen to me? I try to be good, try to do the right thing. But it isn't enough, it's never enough. Do I have a sign on my forehead that reads, shit on me?"

"Okay, Pen slow down, first tell me what's going on, then we can hammer out what we need to do."

Penelope's face was all blotchy, her nose was bright red, and her only good eye was swollen beyond recognition. Baylee thought with the look Pen was sporting now, she should consider herself lucky they didn't call the cops and haul her out of there. Saying it wasn't a good look for her was being kind.

Penelope's head was pounding, digging through her purse, she spotted a bottle, flipped the lid off, and downed three pain pills. Then she rubbed her temples and began explaining what the teller had said.

"Someone used the ATM last night and pulled out every cent I had. When they opened this morning, a red flag alerted them to the unusual activity. A few of my auto-pay bills bounced, so the manager decided to lock my accounts."

"I can float you some cash, no biggie there," said Baylee.

"Believe it or not, this gets worse. You'll never guess why I was in there so long."

"There was a hot guy in line behind you? What? Too soon?"

Punching Baylee in the arm, she said, "thanks, I needed that, but could you please be serious for a minute? The manager was going to call the cops on me."

"What? I get it. You look like a crazy person now, but you didn't look as bad when you first walked in."

"Oh, nice. Thanks, Baylee. Exactly what I wanted to hear. The manager said she understood being a little out of balance, but this is considered check deception. The way she looked at me like I was a criminal. I told her I didn't do it, why would I? I had just paid the bills and knew I was cutting it close. I'm still not sure she believed me, but at least I convinced her I was willing to take steps to fix it."

"How much," asked Baylee.

"More than I've ever had in my account at one time. Apparently, the machine kept spitting out money instead of showing the funds as unavailable. So, now I have to cover all of it plus the fees. I have thirty days to pay up, or she'll start the paperwork for court."

"How much Pen? What are we talking here? A couple hundred, a couple thousand not including the fees?"

"I think I'm going to be sick," holding her stomach. She mentally tried to stop herself, "$2,180.00."

That son of a bastard Baylee thought, "Well, first things first, did you keep the printout? You're going to need it when you confront Derrick."

"Wait, confront Derrick? What does he have to do with this?"

"Tell me you're not serious right now? You know as well as I do, Derrick did this. He took the card, pulled out all the money, then went back to partying with his friends."

"Does make sense," said Penelope.

"Need proof? Let's go."

Before Penelope could respond, Baylee was halfway up the steps to the bank. "Bay, wait!"

Once inside, Baylee leaned over and softly asked, "Which one spoke to you? I don't like doing this, but at times like these, it's a necessary evil."

"No, Baylee, don't do it." Pointing to the office, she'd just been in. "I can handle it on my own. She didn't turn me in, but if you piss her off, she might change her mind." Baylee wasn't listening to a word she said.

Following closely behind, Penelope stayed quiet as she watched a master at work.

Stepping over the threshold to an office, Baylee held out her hand.

"Excuse me, Miss?"

Penelope had seen the woman look up during their approach, so she was aware of who was standing in her office. Apparently, she felt the discussion was closed and refused to look up or even acknowledge Baylee's presence. Finally, realizing they weren't leaving and still not bothering to look up or shake Baylee's hand, she said, "I'm very busy, an appointment is necessary to discuss your situation further."

"It's obvious you have no idea with whom you are speaking, Miss." Picking up the nameplate off her desk, Baylee read it aloud. "Miss Lauren Boons. Please, let me introduce myself. I'm Baylee Eleanor Reed, the daughter of William Reed, the owner of Reed Enterprises. I'm here to assure everything is being done correctly concerning my friend's account."

Standing up immediately, Miss Boons said, "Oh, Ms. Reed. Yes, absolutely, I understand your concern, but I believe we have already gone through everything relevant and have agreed on the best course of action. Isn't that correct, Mrs. Williams?" She attempted to pull Penelope into the discussion.

"While I am standing in front of you, I would appreciate it if you would discuss the matter with me. So, if you would run along and gather the necessary forms you need to be signed to discuss her accounts with me, we will wait here for you. Please do hurry, my time is extremely valuable."

"I've never seen her move so fast, and I come in here at least three times a week," said Penelope, after the woman hurried off; Baylee just smiled.

To Penelope's surprise, it only took a few minutes to get the matter settled. Walking out and heading to the car, she turned and asked, "How did you do that?"

"It's not so much what I did, but who I am," Baylee told her.

"Who you are is pretty impressive. I forget sometimes you have clout," Penelope said in her best British accent. "You will always be plain old Baylee to me, and I love you for it."

"Well, that's good, because it's who I really am. Don't get me wrong, I appreciate how hard my father worked to provide for our family. But money and prestige are not everything."

"I agree, but have I said thank you? And wow, I can't get over what happened in there. Getting them to waive all the fees, placing a credit on my account, or as you put it a preventative measure. Plus, you covered everything that was taken out? So, now I owe you one."

"Actually, you probably owe me several, but how about we start with one." Grabbing the keys out of Penelope's hand, Baylee said, "I'm driving."

"Be careful, you know I don't let anyone drive him."

Turning up the music and throwing Dime into reverse, Baylee shouted, "What? You don't want me to show you my cool party trick? I can flip a dime on its side. I never miss." Seeing the fear in Penelope's eyes, Baylee couldn't stop laughing. "You know I'd never hurt your baby, now help me locate the man of our dreams."

"What are you talking about? What, man?"

Pointing to the door, she watched the mystery man walk into, she explained. "Earlier when I was waiting for you, I watched a guy get out of that white truck and walk in there. I just want to do a little drive by and see if I can learn anything."

"What are you hoping to learn? He must have made an impression on you, for him to still be on your mind."

"Right, you would think. But I didn't even talk to him, I only watched him walk in." Shrugging her shoulders, Baylee wasn't sure what to say. "Just help me look, will you?"

"It looks like a self-defense studio," said Penelope.

"Well, it would explain why the guy seemed so focused on his surroundings. Not to mention he was in amazing shape. Too bad, you missed him." Shaking her hand like it was on fire. "Even from a distance, I could tell he was a prime grade A beefcake."

Penelope glanced at the building as they drove by, she tried to picture herself taking classes and laughed. "Thanks, but no thanks. I don't need a room full of people laughing at me while I try to flip a guy over my shoulder," stated Penelope.

Baylee looked at her friend and said, "That's it! We need to sign up for this. You could learn some moves which you seriously need, and it wouldn't hurt me to brush up on mine a little. But the best part; I could get an up-close and personal look at Mr. Beefcake."

"No! I'm not going to embarrass myself, so you can check out some guy. And a real best friend wouldn't ask me too." Penelope tried pouting but knew it would never work.

"Wrong! That's exactly what a friend would do. If anyone needs this, you do; it's an excellent idea, and you know it. Plus, I promise to be right beside you the whole way."

"Let me think about it for a while, I'll let you know. Until then, how about we get the rest of these errands done and get out of all this snow?"

"Sounds like a plan, but I'm not going to drop this." Regretting it before it left her lips, she said, "By the way, your phone rang when you were in the bank, and I answered it without looking. It was Derrick."

"Why would you do that? You know how he is! I should've taken it in with me, but I thought I'd only be in there for a couple minutes. What did he say?"

"Um, to let you know he called, and he would talk to you about it when you get home. I think you'll be ok, though. I told him he better not lay another hand on you, or I'll take care of him myself."

Thankfully they were at a red light because they may not have stayed on the road, Penelope turned to her friend. "I cannot believe you did that. Please, tell me you're joking. He's probably furious you talked to him that way. Now I'm going to have to calm him down when I get home, which I doubt is even possible at this point. Plus, the whole account thing I have to deal with. Could this day possibly get any worse?"

"Hurry! Knock on wood, or you'll jinx yourself," pleaded Baylee, trying to lighten the mood.

"There isn't any wood in here! I'm so screwed. I should start carrying a little piece of wood with me at all times because it seems my whole life is one big jinx." Penelope sounded close to tears.

"Oh, come on, it will be okay. I have an idea of where to get some wood. We could go back to the defense class, I bet Mr. Beefcake would have some wood you could knock on." Laughing, she peeked over at Penelope, who stuck her tongue out at her.

"Well, that's an option too, maybe he'd like some of that instead. You know there are plenty of things a person could do with their tongue, imagine all the possibilities," Baylee teased. Watching her friend's face turn a light shade of red made it all worth it. The light changed, and after checking the traffic, Baylee continued on to their next destination.

Realizing there was nothing to be done about Derrick and his mood at the moment. Penelope figured she'd try to put it out of her mind and enjoy the time she had with Baylee for now.

Chapter 3

Walking into the apartment several hours later than expected, Penelope dreaded the argument she was sure to have with Derrick. When she turned the corner, she was shocked; he was standing in the kitchen cooking dinner for the two of them.

He looked over as she entered and said, "I hope you're hungry because I made enough spaghetti to feed an army. Here, how about we start with a nice glass of wine?"

More than a little stunned, she didn't know what to do other than accept the glass he offered. Then, not missing a beat, he assisted her with her coat and scarf.

"Are you enjoying the wine? I know it's not your usual brand, but I hoped you still might enjoy it."

Taking her first sip, she let the liquid pool on her tongue for a moment before it disappeared down the back of her throat. "Mmm, yes, thank you."

It was a sweet red, her favorite. She didn't drink often, but a glass now and then couldn't hurt, she thought.

Wondering what he was up to, she asked, "Is there anything I can do to help?"

"Sure, I threw a salad together earlier. Could you grab it from the fridge for me," he responded, "I think the sauce is almost ready."

As she went to the fridge to grab the salads, she watched him from the corner of her eye. This was definitely not like him, especially when she'd been gone all day and returned later than expected.

"What did you do all day while I was out? You sure seem to be in a good mood," she said.

"Oh, you know a little of this and a little of that, nothing too exciting. I did have a friend stop by earlier, but something came up, and they had to leave. I was in such a good mood, I thought I'd make us dinner. I know you must be starving since you've been out all day."

"Well, that's nice of you. Everything smells so good; I can't wait to dig in."

The food was delicious, and the conversation delightful. It reminded Penelope of how sweet and charming Derrick could be when he wanted. He had her so relaxed, she almost forgot about the situation earlier at the bank.

After dinner was finished, she stood in the kitchen, loading the dishwasher, when Derrick walked up behind her and grabbed her hand.

"I thought we could watch a movie together, maybe even do a little cuddling on the couch. How's that sound?"

"Sounds great, after the day I've had. How about you go ahead and set it up; I'll only be another minute."

She watched him head into the living room and noticed he'd taken the refilled glasses with him. She usually never allowed herself more than one drink but figured why not relax a little.

He stood and handed her the glass when she walked in. Then after dimming the lights, he headed off for the bedroom. He came back with a blanket in his arms and a smile on his face. She thought it was sweet to see him making an effort to be romantic. She patted the couch for him to join her and smiled back.

"I brought a blanket for us to cuddle in," he told her. Then sat down, pulled her close, and laid the blanket across them. Resting her head on his shoulder, she started to drift off almost immediately.

The movie was an action; of course, it's practically all he'd watch. It wasn't something she would've picked out, but made no comment on it and decided to try and be happy in the moment.

Minutes later, she couldn't keep her eyes open, no matter how hard she tried. It had been a long day, and if she counted the night before, well, she was too tired to count the night before or anything else for that matter.

Derrick noticed her breath was becoming slow and even. He realized it wouldn't be long now until she was sleeping like a baby. If she only knew the things he'd done earlier on that very blanket, she now had pressed against her face. Maybe one of these days, he would get the pleasure of telling her everything she thought she already knew, the things she always wanted him to admit too.

He loved playing little games with her. It was too easy to turn everything around, make her think she was going crazy, or, better yet, make her feel guilty for not trusting him enough.

Most of the time, she was right, but he'd never admit to it. It was more fun to blame someone else for the things she thought was happening. He loved to watch her while he told her these things to try and see the wheels turning in her mind. One of his greatest pleasures was to confuse her, and to do so was a piece of cake. It wasn't like she was the brightest crayon in the box. If she were, she would've known he put a couple sleeping pills in her wine.

Derrick had been sure she would've been able to taste it, but then again, she didn't drink often enough to notice a difference.

Once he was positive she was asleep, he pushed her over so she leaned on the arm of the couch instead of him, then stood and headed into their bathroom. Standing in front of the mirror, he admired himself a moment. Then looked at all the items he'd placed on the counter earlier. He needed to make sure everything was perfect; nothing could be missing he intended to use.

A bag of zip ties, a roll of duct tape, a hot curling iron, a few different sizes of knives, and of course, a large pair of scissors were what he'd assembled.

When he'd found her curling iron, Derrick thought it would be something different he hadn't used on her yet. He couldn't wait to see how she reacted to heat. Turning the curling iron on so it would get hot, he laughed at the thought of getting to try new things.

Hadn't he warned her before she left that he was going to call? He told her she'd better answer. But did she? No, she didn't. Instead, she chose to ignore his warning.

She made her choice, and now he was making his. She needed to be taught a lesson. Secretly, he loved how she never seemed to learn, because he might feel guilty for punishing her, probably not, but he might.

She wouldn't be expecting a thing. Since she thought Derrick was the romantic man, she always wanted him to be. He was so proud of himself for coming up with this brilliant plan; he was starting to feel himself get excited. Anticipation was such a high.

Placing the zip ties and scissors in his pocket, he made his way out to the dining room, where he grabbed a chair and placed it beside the loveseat and coffee table.

He knew he had plenty of time to make sure everything was ready, because poor little Penny was still taking her nap. Laughing, he pulled the blanket back, picked her up, and flipped her over his shoulder. He moved the chair and dropped her in it. Crouching down, he used zip ties to restrain each leg. Then he went to the bathroom to retrieve the duct tape and other items he'd left on the counter.

Derrick noticed the curling iron light was blinking. It was finally hot and ready to go. Not wanting to do it in here, he unplugged it and carried it with him to the living room. Plugging it back in, he wanted to make sure it didn't lose any of its heat.

Yes, this would work fine, he thought.

Glancing at her, he decided to put her hands together in a prayer pose, and zip tied them too. Pulling off a piece of duct tape, he slapped it across her lips, thinking it might be enough to wake her up, but it wasn't.

He slapped her even harder the second time and noticed she started to make noise. Not wanting to miss a single moment, he sat on the floor, crossed his legs, and waited for her to wake up.

Derrick could feel the blood rushing through his veins as he watched for that second, for the moment in time, when she'd realize what was going on. When she figured out she had absolutely no control.

He'd known the moment personally and wondered if she'd feel the same as he had when he was a young boy. Waking up being paralyzed by fear, looking around, only to discover he was no longer in the safety of his bed. His older cousin Jeffery had taught him the importance of structure and rules. Later as a mentor, Jeffery had helped him hone his skills on a few unknown participants.

He wasn't sure anymore what his favorite part was. The control he had or the fear they felt. Maybe it was a combination of both; knowing he held the power to break another person was thrilling all on its own.

Impatient for her to wake up, Derrick took the curling iron and touched her pinkie toe with it. Staring at her intensely, he noticed her eyes start to twitch. She blinked quickly, and there it was, the moment he'd been waiting for.

The moment of pure raw fear.

"I'm so happy you decided to wake up and join me; we can finally get started."

Her head felt heavy, weighted. When she attempted to lift it, the room started to spin. Off-balance, she tried to catch herself. Then realization hit, and she became aware her hands were bound.

Stay calm, don't panic. Penelope started looking around and questioning if there was anything near that might come in handy? She heard the movie still playing in the background, so she couldn't have been asleep for too long.

What had he done, drugged the food? No, that wasn't it; he'd eaten it too. It had to be the wine; he knew she wouldn't notice a difference, and he kept pushing it on her all evening. Curious about what he'd used, but knowing it didn't really matter, she needed to focus on what was important, getting herself untied and out of the apartment. She tried to register everything quickly then notice him standing in the doorway, staring at her with the wicked grin he always seemed to have plastered on his face; until he spoke.

"I'll make this simple for you," he told her. "Answer this question, and I might let you go. Why didn't you pick up the phone yourself when I called? I warned you right before you left the apartment, didn't I?"

Penelope looked up into his bloodshot eyes and knew it didn't matter what her answer was. It was never going to be the answer he wanted to hear. Violently shaking her head, she tried to hum her words through the tape so he could understand, but knowing he couldn't, only made her more frightened.

Frantically, she imagined what he was going to do to her, and how much more would she be able to stand.

"I'm going to take the tape off so you can explain yourself. If you scream, it won't stay off long. We don't need to disturb the neighbors, now do we?"

Penelope shook her head, wanting him to know she understood and wouldn't scream.

Derrick grabbed her hair, snapped her head back, and gripped the corner of the tape, jerking it off in one hard pull. Her skin burned; she wanted desperately to scream; tears threatened to spill out, but her determination held them back. Knowing the familiar taste of copper, she ran her tongue over her lower lip, finding the cut she knew would be there.

She tried to stay calm, took a deep breath, and rushed to explain, knowing it wasn't going to make a difference.

"I'm so sorry I didn't answer when you called. I forgot to take my phone in, and it took longer in the bank than I thought," Penelope tried to explain. "Baylee said she answered because she thought it might be important. She told me you called. Please tell me, how can I make this up to you?"

Never taking his eyes off her, Derrick said, "So you agree, I did warn you?"

When she nodded her head, he raised his hand and backhanded her, the force knocked Penelope still in the chair to the floor. Her head slammed on the hardwood floors; momentarily, all she could see was a bright light. The sharp pain in her temple and a bitter taste in her mouth quickly made her nauseous.

Derrick grabbed her by her still zip-tied hands and hauled her back up, causing the ties to dig deeper into her wrist.

"I swear you must be the dumbest person I know. You could've avoided all of this, you know? All you had to do was listen! But no! You couldn't even do that. Is it really so difficult for you to understand there are consequences for your actions? Do you have anything to say for yourself?"

"I'm not feeling well, Derrick," Penelope stated, as nausea overwhelmed her. "I think I might throw up. Could you please untie me?"

"Do you think I care if you puke all over yourself? Go ahead. I'm not letting you go. One little love tap and you think we're all through here? You're proving my point of how dumb you really are!"

Derrick watched her intently, making sure he didn't miss the instant fear struck. His cousin had always emphasized the fact every action would cause her to have a reaction. The reaction was what it was all about. The more fear she felt, the bigger her reaction would be. The bigger her reaction, the more pleasure he felt. Slowly, he pulled the scissors from his back pocket as he watched her eyes dilate. He tried to imagine what she must be thinking. Was she contemplating all the possible things he could do to her? Sliding the scissors across her cheek, he slowly opened and closed them, hearing the slide of metal scrape against itself, and visualizing the damage they could do. He felt a tremor jolt through her body, like an involuntary chill.

"Don't worry, I'm not going to cut up your face." He turned her chin from side to side and examined the face he'd looked at for too many years. Admiring the J-shaped scar on her left jawline, he continued. "It would cause too many questions, and you know how I hate questions."

The small amount of pleasure he'd felt, as he experienced her reaction was quickly gone, so he knew it was time to proceed. Not wasting a moment, he dropped the scissors back into his pocket and continued on.

Penelope felt his hand gliding down her side, and it made her skin crawl. How could she not have seen how messed up in the head he was? Was she so blind by what she thought was love? There had to have been signs? Thinking back to when it all started, she couldn't pinpoint the exact moment, and nothing, in particular, jumped out at her. It must have been a slow progression, something minor at first, she either missed or simply chose to ignore. His moodiness when things didn't go his way; how it was always someone else's fault. She couldn't remember a single time, he'd taken responsibility for anything; unless of course, he was getting credit for it.

She avoided making eye contact with him, for fear he would take it as a challenge. Now, she sat strapped to a chair, and at the complete mercy of her so-called loving husband of over two years, and thought back to when they'd met.

She remembered the day so vividly. It was an early Saturday morning; the sun had barely peeked over the horizon, and a chill was still in the air. Penelope grabbed her list of supplies and told her boss, Marty, she'd be back as soon as she could.

She had loved the summer months, which allowed her to take the top off Dime and let the wind blow through her hair. Cranking up the radio, she sang along and was at the paint store in no time. She couldn't wait to show her boss how much of a difference a little paint could make.

She'd planned to spend the entire day painting, but everything changed when she stepped foot into the paint store.

There stood a customer all tall, dark, and handsome. Except he wasn't very tall. She "guess-timated" he was around 5'10". He wasn't very dark either, except for the hair. But he definitely had the handsome part nailed. He filled out his jeans nicely, she noticed and wouldn't mind seeing if the rest of him followed suit.

Looking up, she knew she'd been caught as their eyes locked. She should've felt shy or ashamed, but she didn't; what she felt was a tingling sensation rushing through her body. The feeling was unexpected because she'd never felt this before from only a look.

"Do you like what you see?" he asked.

"Umm, excuse me?" Unsure of what to say, she tried to act nonchalant and squeeze past him to reach the paint on the other side.

"No need to be shy now. I saw you checking me out, I was hoping you liked what you saw. Hi, my name is Derrick Williams, and you are?"

"Penelope," she answered softly.

Thinking back now, she wished she would've kept walking, but she couldn't rewrite history. Which brought her back to her current situation. How the hell was she going to get out of this?

Chapter 4

Derrick's touch was becoming more aggressive by the second; he was getting increasingly agitated by the lack of her response. Trying desperately to ignore him, she turned her head away and noticed her reflection in the patio door. Derrick had forgotten to close the blinds, so she used the reflection to assess her damage. It appeared he'd cut away the bottom of her jeans to make the restraints as tight as possible.

When she tugged on each leg, she quickly learned there was no way she was going to wiggle out of this one. She needed to get her hands on those scissors somehow, but trying to focus was becoming more difficult as Derrick continued with his sick game.

The thought occurred to her she might get lucky, and someone could see what he was doing through the door. She knew it was a long shot since they were on the second floor, but she needed to believe there was still a chance.

Holding her body as still as possible, she tried to not flinch when he laid his hand on her shoulder.

"Do you want to know which parts of you I love the most?" Derrick said. Sliding his finger from behind her ear down across the hollow of her throat, he spoke again. "Your long, lean neck where the skin is so soft, it's one of my favorites." Kisses followed where his finger was only moments ago.

Standing abruptly, he grabbed the scissors and quickly spun towards her.

She didn't dare breathe for fear of what he was about to do. She tried to push herself flat against the chair back, only to discover she hadn't moved an inch.

The feeling of cold metal against her neck made her pulse jump; involuntarily, she began to shake. Looking into Derrick's eyes, she could see he was enjoying himself. Her fear was what he craved, and he was doing an excellent job of producing those results.

With one swift move, he sliced down the center of her shirt. Opening it wide, he yelled, "What's this? I don't think you'll be needing this anymore!" Jerking the brace from her ribs, he picked up the largest blade he had and slit it from end to end.

Leaving her exposed except for her bra, he shoved the point of the blade against her skin. As he sliced her over and over, all she wanted to do was scream out for help.

"Please stop, Derrick; you don't have to do this. I'll do anything you want."

"Too late for that," he said. Hate dripping with every word.

She couldn't help but look down and watch as he cut her. The burning sensation was instantaneous; the second the blade broke the skin. She watched the droplets of blood appear, and drip down her body, leaving a puddle on the floor.

Then suddenly, she screamed uncontrollably when Derrick poured alcohol on her fresh wounds. Pulling against the restraints, she tried everything she could to free herself. But nothing worked, all it managed to do was cause the restraints to dig deeper into her skin.

"Shut up, shut up, shut up!" he screamed, "Someone is going to hear you." Slapping his hand across her mouth, he leaned close to her ear. "If I have to do damage control, just know, I'll make sure you suffer for it."

While one hand continued to keep her quiet, he grabbed the roll of duct tape and used his teeth to ripped off a piece and slapped it against her mouth. Walking to the front door, Derrick checked the peephole. Seeing nothing, he continued to the front window and then the back, sliding glass door.

"Sit tight," he smirked, "I'll be right back."

She watched him close the slider door through tear-filled eyes, she knew she had only moments to come up with a plan. The only thing she could think of was getting her hands on those damn scissors. Where were they? She'd lost sight of them.

It's hopeless, she thought. Even if I find them, how am I supposed to pick them up? I need a plan, any kind of plan, even a crappy "there is no way in hell that will work" kind of plan. Because she knew one of two things were going to happen. Either he'd end up killing her tonight, or she would finally start fighting back.

Not much of a plan, but it was all she had. She decided to wait for her opportunity. It would come, she told herself. She knew it would, it had to.

Looking up, she blinked to clear her eyes. Just then, Derrick walked back in, closed the door behind him, and strolled across the room towards her.

"You, Penny, are one lucky girl," he said. "Maybe you are a lucky penny."

She looked up at him, unable to speak, she tilted her head in confusion.

"Do you wonder why? Because apparently, no one heard you scream." Derrick turned and headed into the dining room to grab another chair.

Yeah, lucky me, she thought, then spotted the scissors in Derrick's back pocket.

He set the chair directly in front of her and asked, "Ready to get started?"

Without waiting for a reply, Derrick continued. "Poor, plain little Penny, no one notices her, and no one cares. Isn't that what Daddy Luke used to say when you were a little girl? Did you really think things were going to change for you?" Derrick asked, snapping the scissors an inch from her face, causing her to flinch.

"I have a great idea! How about a makeover? Let's see if I can make you beautiful. We both know I can't make you look any worse."

He really had lost his mind. She could see how much pleasure he was getting from thinking about giving her his version of a makeover. What sane person would think up that sort of thing, let alone do it to someone?

"Now you sit still. You wouldn't want me to cut you, would you?" he said, laughing. Yanking a chunk of her hair forward, he sliced it off.

A tear slid down her cheek, not because it caused her physical pain, but because she remembered a time when she was only seven, and her father had said those same words.

Of course, the circumstances were different then. She had accidentally gotten bubblegum stuck in her hair. Rather than try to remove it with ice, Luke Jones decided she needed to be taught a lesson. And to this day, she still couldn't chew bubblegum. But unlike then, she was no longer seven.

The sharp sound of scissors sliding open and closed, brought her back to reality, as he worked his way around her entire head. Penelope refused to cry another tear or move an inch. She wouldn't give Derrick the satisfaction of knowing how much this hurt her.

"Now the fun can begin; time to curl it," he said sadistically, laying the scissors down on the coffee table and picking up the curling iron. He jerked a piece of hair, positioned it in the curling iron, and rolled it up tight until it rested on her scalp. He never took his eyes off her, again waiting for his favorite moment, the mix of fear and pain in her eyes. When the hair started to smoke, he opened it. Seeing the red welt on her head, he smiled. He loved how he could do whatever he wanted, and she couldn't do a thing about it.

"Oh, I'm so sorry. Did that hurt? I don't use these things very often. I apparently need more practice." He took his time, to make it last as long as possible, and continued to pluck at her hair, curl it, making sure every time left a mark.

Staring at the red welts, a thought occurred to him. It looked a little like what he'd seen on T.V. What was it called? The thing ranchers did to mark their cattle. Oh, yeah, branding.

Derrick was thrilled with the idea and began to think of the best place to put his own mark on her. She, in fact, was his property, after all, certified by the State of Illinois. Hell, he even had the paperwork to prove it. Why shouldn't he sear his mark on her? It would show everyone not to touch what was his.

He circled around to her front and analyzed his work. He could see the progress but still wasn't satisfied with the results. He thought he'd let Penelope see for herself. He knew there was a mirror around here, somewhere. So, he went to search in the bathroom, he began pulling drawers open and dumping the contents on the floor.

Watching him walk away for a few minutes, Penelope realized this might be her one opportunity to get her hands on those scissors. She'd been careful to make sure Derrick hadn't noticed how she never let them out of her sight. She knew exactly where they were; she only needed to reach them. But that would be much easier said than done.

Penelope knew she didn't have long, quickly she tried to scoot her chair closer to the coffee table. As she did so, the legs scraped across the floor, making a scratchy sound. She hoped it was louder to her than it actually was. She tried again, only moving half an inch each time. It was discouraging, but she'd take what she could get. A few more times, and she might be able to reach them.

Aware she was running out of time, but getting closer, Penelope hoped once more would be enough. Digging deep within herself, she moved the chair a tiny fraction and stretched out her hands as far as they would go.

Frustrated by how constricted she was, her fingers barely brushed against the edge of the blade. Pulling her hand back, she noticed a drop of blood drip from her finger. Not ready to give up, she tried again, but she wasn't quite close enough.

Listening for Derrick, she knew she couldn't give up. She might not have another chance. It was her one opening, and she had to take it. Wiggling in her chair, seemed to help turn her a little, and it might be exactly what she needed. She only had seconds left before his inevitable return.

Penelope stretched her arms out one last time, with everything she had. With her zip-tied hands, she managed to touch the tip of the blade with the edge of her fingernails. She wanted to breathe a sigh of relief but knew she didn't dare. Holding her breath, she started sliding them towards her. Closer now, she managed to pinch them between her fingers and prayed she wouldn't drop them on the floor as they made their way to the edge of the table.

Using every ounce of energy she had left, she finally had them in her grasp. Sliding them between her palms, she carefully pulled her arms back toward her body. She heard

Derrick yell bingo and knew she didn't have time to cut herself free, so she decided to hide them instead. She didn't want him to know she'd managed to get them off the table. There was no way of sliding them under herself since she couldn't move that way. Doing the only other thing she could think of, she pulled her knees slightly apart and slid the scissors between them. Closing her legs back, she hoped he didn't try to move them before she could get her arms free.

In the bathroom, Derrick finally looked in the basket sitting on the back of the toilet. Locating the mirror, he took a moment to admire his own reflection. He was good-looking, too good looking in fact, to be with someone like Penelope. He believed he deserved so much more, but usually, the homely-looking ones were grateful, plus they seemed to try harder to please him.

Getting back to the project at hand, he could hardly contain himself from wanting to see her reaction. He headed back out into the living room, but stopped dead in his tracks when he looked around the room. Something had changed.

It still smelled of fear and burnt hair, which might be his new favorite scent.

But that wasn't it, Penelope had moved. How was it possible, he thought? He could tell right away it wasn't far, but he still didn't like it. She needed to stay exactly where he put her. Why did she always have to be such a pain in the ass?

As he crept towards her, he knew the moment she realized he was back in the room, because her body stiffened instantly. He walked around her, then lightly brushed the back of her neck with his knuckles. He bent over, then whispered in her ear.

"Why did you move over here? What were you looking for?" Once he stood back up, he walked around and looked for anything out of place.

Penelope pleaded silently to herself. Please don't let him realize they're missing. Then letting out a long breath she hadn't realized she'd been holding, she watched him look around the room.

It seemed to him, she'd tried to get herself free, but only managed to move a few inches. Stupid woman. Didn't she know by now he'd never allow that to happen?

"So, you actually thought you were smarter than me, huh? You thought you could get yourself loose?" He taunted further. "Then what?"

Oh, my God, he knows! Fear struck her instantly. She needed a new plan and quick, she thought.

"What were you planning to do once you freed yourself? Did you think I'd let you get up and walk out of here?" Placing both hands around her neck, he started to squeeze.

"I will never let you go! Don't you know that by now? You're my Penny tarnished and all but still only mine. I'll do whatever I want with you whenever I want, and no one is going to stop me!"

Her vision started to darken from the lack of oxygen, her lungs tightened, and burned. But she knew if she passed out, it was all over. He would find the scissors she'd hidden, and the knowledge alone kept her fighting.

Derrick chuckled, as he watched her suffer, knowing the pain he was inflicting with his hands, but also with his words. "Hell, your own father would be proud of me! Keeping you in line the same way he did your mother."

"Do you know why men rule the world, Penny? It's because we set the rules, and we make women like you stay in line. It has worked for hundreds of years. Why would we go changing it now?"

She couldn't stop the tears from freely flowing. The mere mention of her mother and what she'd gone through was more than Penelope could bear. Was this part of his plan to distract her, she thought? I can't let him win this time, I need to be strong, stronger than my mother was, she told herself. Straightening her shoulders and looking him dead in the eye, she hummed and hoped he'd remove the tape.

"Hmm, do you have something you'd like to share? Fine, I'll let you speak, but you better remember the rules."

Ripping the tape off the second time was as enjoyable as the first. Her reaction was the same, and he relished in the pleasure he was experiencing.

Not wasting a second, Penelope spoke, "I am not my Mother!"

"I don't know about that," Derrick smirked. "Are you sure? Think back. How many times were there when mommy didn't learn, and how many times did Luke have to discipline her? Are you trying to say you finally understand, and you're willing to learn from your mistakes?"

This is my way out, she thought. "Daddy Luke always said she was stubborn, and one day her stubbornness was going to kill her. I guess he was right. I'm not like her; I'm willing to let someone else have control." Feeling her stomach churning, Penelope didn't know if she could go through with what she was about to do. Sending up a silent prayer for her mother's forgiveness, she went on.

"Daddy Luke also said she was short a few watts, but I'd like to think I'm a little smarter than her. I'm willing to try," she said, hoping her ruse would work. "All I know is, I don't want to end up like her. What do I have to do? Please tell me?" She carefully manipulated her expression in an attempt to appear non-threatening, like a small wounded animal.

This was her only hope. Was she convincing him she was sincere? She knew this was her chance, and she needed to be smart about it. She made her lip tremble and allowed another tear to fall, then cast her eyes to the floor and waited.

Not knowing if he should trust her, Derrick pulled the chair over and sat down.

"I want to believe you; Penny, I really do. The thing is, you've disappointed me so many times. The most important thing for you to understand is, no matter what you do or where you go, I will always be there."

He held the mirror up for her and was excited to see her reaction.

She didn't want to look at his handiwork or tell him the things he wanted to hear, but it couldn't be avoided. Lifting her eyes to the mirror, she saw a stranger looking back. How could he do this, she thought? Reacting without thinking, she bumped the mirror in his hand. Derrick was taken off guard; it slipped and fell to the floor, shattering to pieces. Staring at it, she thought, it's broken like me. I'm merely a piece of what I once was, unrecognizable even to herself.

"I knew I couldn't trust you!" He reached down, picked up the biggest piece, and held it slightly under her right jaw.

With her pulse racing and pushing against the edge of the mirror, she knew it wouldn't take much to open the vein and bleed her dry. She tried to not focused on it, the feeling of her blood pumping against the edge. She needed to focus on something else, anything else.

"You told me once, every time you look in a mirror, the first thing you always see is the scar on your left jaw." Gliding his thumb across it adoringly, he continued. "Does it make you think of the last day? Of the last time, you saw your mother?"

"You know it does!"

"Well, I'm going to give you another one, but on the right side this time." He turned her head to get a better view. "You know? No one would ever know this scar is from a ring, you can barely make out the letter J anymore. I guess that's what time does, it makes things fade. I don't want mine to fade, I want you to think of me, every time you look in the mirror, not of your mother. She's been dead for years. You didn't save her. Get over it. It's time to grow up and move on."

The sharp edge of the mirror cut through her face like it was nothing, barely missing a facial artery. He didn't seem to notice the blood drip from her face because he was too busy admiring his skills with the jagged blade. The letter D was easily recognizable, and he was sure no one would mistake it for anything other than what it was.

"Now every time you look in a mirror, you'll remember tonight, how you lost your temper and made me do this. Every time you see it, you'll be reminded of who's in control of your life."

He stood, patted her cheek, and without another word, turned and walked into the kitchen. Listening carefully, she heard drawers open, things being thrown onto the counter, then him slamming cabinets closed. She heard repeated clinking noises and assumed he was doing something with metal, but what, she had no idea.

When she turned her head, she could slightly see over the breakfast bar. But from a seated position, she could only see Derrick from his chest up.

She watched him bend out of sight and heard what sounded like the toolbox they kept under the sink being pulled out. Panic started setting in; she knew the damage he could do with a hammer or any number of things. When he stood back up, she saw he did indeed have pliers in his hand, and something else.

What was he holding, and why was he bending it around? She squinted to try and get a better look. What was he planning to do next? Starting to doubt herself and her plan, but not having many choices, she decided to keep her mouth shut, stick with it, and follow-through.

From the kitchen, Derrick looked over at her with an evil smile on his face and winked, "It's almost ready only a few more minutes."

What's almost ready, she thought?

Moments later, he came towards her, but she noticed right away; his hands were empty. Why? What had he been doing, and why hadn't he brought back whatever he'd been working on?

He continued past her, then grabbed her chair. Tilting it, so it was only on its back two legs. He started dragging her toward the kitchen. When they rounded the bar, she got her first glance of what he'd been working on. Sweat started rolling down her face as her body temperature soared. Her hands were shaking, and tears threatened to start again.

Her visibly shaking was such a rush for him. Derrick wasn't sure he could give this kind of stimulation up, even if she had promised to change. Secretly he hoped she never did because he enjoyed these teaching moments.

"I bet you're wondering what all this is about? Allow me to explain," he said, with a dark glimmer in his eye. "Earlier while curling your hair, I noticed the marks the iron left on your head. I thought to myself, that's perfect."

Raising her eyebrows so he'd understand she wasn't following; Penelope couldn't take her eyes off the gas burner he'd turned on and what was sitting on top.

He knelt on the floor in front of her and pulled the edges of her shirt up, and tucked them into her bra. Then he unbuttoned her jeans and folded them out of the way.

"I can tell you're still confused, and that's fine, let me explain in more detail. I've created my initials for you, so everyone will know you're mine. Earlier, when I told you I owned you, I meant it. I'll never let you go. I would rather kill you than let you walk away from me. So, I'm going to brand you like ranchers do their cattle, proving to you and everyone else you are indeed my property."

Was he going to permanently scar her for the rest of her life? She was horrified at the thought.

Derrick filled the sink with cold water, then turned and walked to the stove, making sure everything was ready.

Watching him check on the progress, she knew she didn't have enough time to free herself before he did this hideous thing to her. She could only watch as he picked up the tongs and grabbed the letter D.

Derrick turned to face her, holding the scorching red letter D, he could barely contain his excitement. A tiny bead of sweat dripped from his brow, landing on the homemade brand. It evaporated immediately, showing her the temperature of the metal.

With her eyes wide, she watched him walk towards her. She was paralyzed by fear, knowing the terrible things he'd done in the past. Nothing had come close to this.

Visibly shaking, a scream caught in her throat, she knew what was about to happen. When Derrick touched the brand to her lower abdomen, she screamed. He covered her mouth with his hand, but it only slightly dampened the sound.

The searing pain exploded within her as her nostrils filled with the scent of burning flesh. She thought he was trying to burn it straight through. Jerking back into her chair, she attempted to pull herself as far from the heat as possible, but he only continued to push harder.

After what felt like an eternity, he finally pulled the brand away and dropped it into the sink of cold water. It sizzled at first then died off, tears continued to stream down her face.

She watched him walk to the stove and glance back at his handy work. Picking up the next letter, he knew as soon as he touched it to her, she was going to scream like a banshee again, and that wouldn't be a good thing. So, he sat it back on the flame and went in search of the duct tape. Thinking he'd left it in the living room, he went to search there first.

She only had moments. Penelope knew she had to move now before he came back to finish the job. She quickly pulled the scissors from between her legs. Bending over slightly, she cut her left leg free, then her right. Hearing him heading back, she swiftly tucked the scissors back between her legs. She left her hands resting on top and hoped it blocked them from his view, but it also gave her easier accessibility.

Derrick spotted the tape on the floor halfway under the couch. He quickly grabbed it and headed back to Penelope, pulling a piece off as he went.

Once he reached the doorway, he stopped and took in the view of her sitting there waiting for him. He could feel himself becoming aroused at the mere thought of what he was about to do. Reaching down, he adjusted himself slightly. Then he continued through the door and slapped the tape across her mouth once again. He bent over a tad and kissed her now silent lips.

She felt bile rise in her throat as he kissed her, and tried to look away. Please, let me get out of this before he brands me again, she thought. She knew he was about to get the other letter he'd made and decided she couldn't wait any longer for an opening. She needed to move now. Taking a chance, she pulled the scissors out and gripped them between her bound hands, she waited only a second for him to grab the brand and turn towards her.

Slamming the scissors into his stomach, she pulled them out. Barely registering her blood-covered hands, she stabbed them into him a second time.

Derrick grabbed her hair in an attempt to restrain her once again, and when she looked into his eyes, she saw pure evil. With her hands still bound, she reached for the coffee pot sitting on the counter. She spun around and slammed it into his head. Instantly, he released her and fell facedown straight onto the scissors she'd left in his gut.

Not knowing if he'd stay down, she quickly pulled a large knife from the butcher block sitting on the counter and slid it between her wrists, cutting the zip ties away. With one last look, to see if he'd started to stir, she pulled the tape from her mouth. Still holding the knife, she crouched down and whispered. "Don't call me Penny; only my mother was allowed to call me that." She stood and took off in a run, desperate to make it out of the apartment alive.

Chapter 5

"Help! Please help me," Penelope screamed, running up the stairs to the one person she knew who'd do anything to help her. Almost to the third landing, she heard a door slam, fearing it might be Derrick coming to finish the job, she didn't dare look back but kept going.

A scream erupted from her throat when a hand clamped around her forearm. Looking down, she instantly knew who the hand belonged to. The bright purple nail polish gave it away every time.

"Oh my God, look what that bastard did to you!" cried Baylee, helping her friend into her apartment.

"We need to get you to the hospital. I can only do so much from here, and from the looks of it, you need more than I can provide," said Baylee. Leading her friend to a chair, she tried to survey all the damage Derrick had done. She kneeled down and picked up Penelope's blood-covered hand and held it for a few seconds.

"Where is he, Penelope? Where is that son of a bastard? I'll kill him for this, I swear!"

"That may not be necessary," whispered Penelope.

"What do you mean? I don't understand, he definitely deserves to die for this. Look at what he's done."

"Oh my God," screamed Penelope. "I think I might have killed him." Covering her mouth, she ran, trying to make it to the toilet in time.

Baylee followed and tried to comfort her friend. She handed her a cold washcloth, while Penelope lost everything she'd had in her stomach.

Finally, Penelope leaned back, grateful for her friend. She tried to smile up at her but just couldn't bring herself to do it. "Thank God, you were home and opened the door; I was so scared," Penelope tried to explain. "What if I made the wrong choice to go up instead of down? What if you were gone? What if you didn't hear me? What would I have done then? There would have been no way for me to escape a second time."

"Try to calm down. Stop all the what ifs. I know you've been through a traumatic experience, but you're safe now. Derrick isn't going to be able to get to you again," said Baylee.

"I think I'll be fine. What I need to do is call the police, because I might have killed him. All I know is, he wasn't moving when I left him lying on the kitchen floor," Penelope told her.

"No! What we need to do is have you looked at. I'll call the police, but first, I'll run down and grab your keys. While I'm down there, I'll take a look myself and see if he's dead. If not, maybe I'll finish the job."

Baylee grabbed her sneakers and walked to the door. While looking through the peephole, she slid her feet into the shoes and made sure they were secure in case she needed to run.

"Looks to be all clear, so I'll be right back," Baylee promised. Turning the deadbolt to unlock the door, she twisted the handle and slipped out.

Penelope watched the door softly close and worried because she knew Baylee didn't understand how strong Derrick could be, or what he was capable of.

Slowly and softly, Baylee made her way down the steps, trying to be as quiet as possible in case Derrick was lurking around. Finally, reaching the landing, she peeked around the corner to check the next level of stairs. Again, being all clear, she kept going.

Almost to the second-floor landing, she could see the door wide open on apartment 2B. Assuming Penelope left it open when she ran out, Baylee quickly crept towards the door. Looking around to make sure no one could sneak up behind her, she stepped over the threshold into the apartment.

Holding her breath, she listened and tried to see if she could hear any sounds coming from inside. But the only thing she heard was the beating of her own heart. She took a few steps in, and peeked around the corner of the entryway, noticing right away the place was in disarray, but she didn't see Derrick anywhere.

Cautiously, she moved in a little further. From there, she could see into the bedroom and knew Penelope always left her purse in the nightstand. Gauging it to be around 20 feet away, Baylee, quickly but quietly, tiptoed into the bedroom.

Upon entering the bedroom, she noticed the light was on in their bathroom. Listening, she hoped he wasn't in there and carefully made her way across the room to the bedside table. When she slowly reached into the top drawer and pulled out the purse, she heard a door slam.

Oh no, I'm trapped! Crouching down beside the bed, she hoped Derrick wouldn't find her. She stayed down for what felt like hours, then realized she hadn't heard anything for a while. It had been only the one time actually; maybe it was the wind, she thought. Slowly standing up, she made her way to the bathroom door, slightly ajar, she used her foot and tapped it lightly. Gradually it opened, and she peered inside. There was nothing except a mess to clean up.

She headed back towards the entryway but looked down the small hall that led to the kitchen. Taking a step in that direction, she felt something unusual under her shoe. She bent down and saw something on the wood floor. After she swiped her finger through it, she noticed it was sticky. Pulling her hand back, she rubbed her fingers together and held it up to the light for a better look. It appeared to be blood, and by the looks of it a lot.

Not knowing if it was Penelope's or not, Baylee knew she was going to follow it and see where it would lead. Hearing a crunching noise, she again looked down and found broken glass all over the floor.

Baylee noticed more blood the closer she got, and it made her pulse jump. Curious to discover exactly what she was about to find, she stopped herself only inches from the doorway. If I find him not dead but in pain, will I help him? Hell, No! Baylee thought and turned the corner.

Stopping dead in her tracks, she was shocked by what she saw. Blood covered almost every inch of the floor; it was on the counters and even on the ceiling. The sink was overflowing with water, and the burner on the stove was still on. After turning the water off, she tried to not step in blood as she made her way over to extinguish the flame. The only question now was, where was Derrick?

Oh no, could that have been him who slammed the door earlier? What if he knew she was there? It would tell him exactly where Penelope was? Spinning around quickly, she took off at a run for her own apartment.

Whispering to herself, "Please let me be wrong, please!"

Chapter 6

Once she reached her apartment, Baylee told herself to be alert, stay focused, and above all else keep her emotions in check. Don't let the job get personal. How many times had she heard that? Endless lectures, but no matter how well she knew it to be accurate, she was having a hard time following the advice.

Daily, she'd witnessed awful and unimaginable situations. The type of thing that made her wonder how anyone could survive. But she'd come to realize when appalling things happen, the strong stand. She lived her life to help others, to be a strong woman, and someone who could separate the people from the problems. She was often told she had a calming effect, and there was something special about her. She was easy to talk to. Hoping it was true, she inhaled deeply, opened the door, and went inside to search for her best friend.

The chair she'd left Penelope in was now empty, where could she be? Baylee thought.

Surveying the open space quickly, nothing seemed out of place. The curtains swayed slightly at the sliding glass door, she assumed from the furnace running. Her leaky kitchen faucet dripped every couple seconds, but other than that she didn't hear a thing.

"Penelope, where are you? Are you okay?" she yelled, rounding the corner to her bedroom. There she was, lying on the bed.

"Oh, thank God. I was so worried when I saw the chair out there empty, I thought for sure…" Dropping the end of her sentence so Penelope wouldn't worry, she quickly moved on.

"You thought for sure what?" asked Penelope.

"Nothing for you to worry about, I promise. Plus, it's a moot point, seeing as you're right here." Patting her lightly on the leg, Baylee continued. "Now stay put while I go grab my field kit. I know I don't have everything you'll need, so we're still going to need to take you in and have a doctor look at you."

Penelope didn't like the idea of going to the hospital, but she would do as she was told. Waiting for Baylee's return, she hoped her friend at least had some good pain meds. Her adrenaline had long ago subsided, and reality was starting to kick in. She could really use something to take the edge off.

She decided to try and pull herself back together, hoping it might take her mind off the pain. Tugging at her shirt, she pulled it back out of her bra and held it closed while looking down at her pelvis. She knew she wouldn't be able to close her pants or put anything near the area for some time. She wasn't sure what she should do because the pain from the burn was excruciating. Sensing Baylee's return, she looked up just in time to see her walk back in.

"Don't worry Pen, I got this." Setting the kit on the bed, Baylee turned and pulled something out of her closet. "How about a pair of comfy yoga pants? You can let them ride low so they won't touch the burns."

"I think you might be forgetting something, Bay, I'm a lot taller than you. How's this going to work?"

"Again, you doubt me, when will you ever learn? I know you're taller than me, but if I cut the cuffs off, they should work." Pulling a pair of fabric shears from a drawer, Baylee eyeballed them and snipped the cuffs off. "See, what did I tell you, now a super cute pair of yoga capri. Which are totally in right now, by the way. Now back to business, let me get a look at you."

"They look a little shorter than capri's, more like Bermuda shorts but they'll work, thanks. Wait! You didn't say what you found downstairs. Baylee, what aren't you telling me, what happened?"

If looks alone could tell a story, Penelope knew something had Baylee scared. She tried to sit up and asked again. "Baylee, tell me what's going on. Is Derrick dead? Did I kill him?" Starting to panic, she couldn't take it any longer, she leaned forward, grabbed Baylee's hand, and tried to get some answers.

"I can handle it, I swear, just tell me!"

Maneuvering her friend back into a lying position, Baylee said, "I can only tell you what I know. Derrick wasn't down there. I didn't see him anywhere."

"Wait, what?"

"I did see a lot of blood, and I mean a lot. I'm not sure how far he could get without seeking some kind of medical attention."

"What do you mean, he wasn't down there? Where else would he be?" Penelope replied, confused.

"Maybe he's smarter than he looks and knew he'd get arrested once the police showed up, so he took off. That's my guess anyway. Sucks too, because I could think of a few things I'd have liked to have done to him. Since he's gone, I'm going to go call the police and paramedics. I know you're ready for some painkillers. I can give you a couple Tylenol. But that's about it since I'm not on duty. They keep pretty close tabs on the pain meds since some went missing, and they sure don't let us bring the good stuff home." Baylee handed her a couple of Tylenols and a bottle of water.

"While we wait, I want you to hold this cold compress against your head. It should help a little with the pain and swelling."

Penelope watched Baylee talk on the phone to the police and hoped her friend was right, and Derrick did leave. It wasn't like him to give up, though. He thought he always had to win, and for him to simply walk away wasn't a win in her eyes. She knew he'd feel the same. She had a feeling this was a long way from over.

"Okay, they're on their way. Now, let's see what I can do until they get here," Baylee said, coming back into the room.

Autopilot took over, and once Baylee opened a bottle of saline solution, she started cleaning the minor cuts. Then removed a packet of ointment, carefully placed a small amount on some of the wounds and bandaged them up. She left the large areas open so the paramedics could get a clearer picture of her injuries.

Penelope watched as her friend skillfully did her thing. "Thanks for this. I don't know what I'd do without you."

Baylee stopped and looked straight into Penelope's eyes. "Listen up. We're family, don't you get that?" She held up her hand to quiet, unspoken words and went on. "Not the messed-up kind of family you came from, but the real deal. We're the all-in kind of family, the kind who always has each other's backs. No matter what, even if it's to help hide a body. And you better remember this, because if it ever does happen, you're going to be the first person I call."

A knock sounded at the door. Penelope's muscles instantly tensed. Her mind told her it couldn't be Derrick, but the what-ifs continued to play on her emotions.

Lightly patting Penelope's leg, Baylee rose to go answer it. Being extra cautious never hurt, so she leaned in to check the peephole. She was relieved to see it was the paramedics, one of which she knew quite well.

She was glad to see April Bade, her old partner from a couple years ago. She hadn't seen her in how long, she thought? Must have been back when the top brass at the hospital decided changes needed to be made on how they partnered up. Teams were now made up of one female and one male on every route, no exceptions.

Opening the door, Baylee said, "April, it's been too long, I was wondering who'd be on call tonight. I'm glad it's you; it's good to know she'll have the best working on her."

"Thanks, not sure I'm the best, but I did learn a lot from my old partner a few years back." Following Baylee into the apartment, she asked, "So who's our patient?"

"A close friend of mine. Follow me, and I'll take you to her. I cleaned and applied ointment to a few of the smaller abrasions, I also gave her two Tylenol to help with the pain until you arrived".

"Okay, thanks for the heads up. I'll go get started on her now. Call me sometime; we'll do lunch. It's been too long." Snapping her gloves into place, she walked into the bedroom and kneeled down beside the bed.

She placed her field kit on the floor, and said, "Hi, my name is April, I'll be taking care of you tonight. I hope that's all right? Sorry, we couldn't meet under better circumstances, but let's see if we can get you feeling better, okay?" Crouched down, she opened her case and retrieved a few needed supplies.

"Hi April, I'm Penelope."

"Well, Penelope, first things first. I'm going to give you an injection to help with the pain. I need to take a look at those burns on your scalp. The cut on your jaw looks pretty deep; it might need stitches. It looks like your friend already did a pretty good job on the smaller cuts on your torso. But I'll keep you informed on what I'll be doing as we go along."

Tuning April out, Penelope focused on the man who'd arrived with her. Standing in the doorway, he took up every inch of space the frame would allow. He made no move to enter the bedroom or to retreat. He had no smile displayed across his face, no kindness vibe coming off him in waves. There was something about him that didn't fit in her mind, as what she referred to as, "Baylee" type people.

April must have noticed Penelope was uncomfortable with the male presence in the room because she nodded towards him and took on a playful voice.

"See him over there, that's Jeremy, he's my partner. I know he can be scary looking, with the big bald head and long goatee, but that's all a façade. Don't let him fool you." She winked at Penelope and kept on working.

"A façade? Hmm, do tell," Penelope said, as the sedative worked its way through her system.

He must have overheard. It wasn't like April was being subtle, Penelope's only hint was the slight rise of his brow, which she almost missed. Other than that, he paid no attention and kept his head buried in his electronic ledger.

The medicine must have been flowing smoothly through her veins because the next thing she heard was April talking in mid-sentence about onions.

"Some people use onions in metaphors, but I hate onions. So, let's use candy; who doesn't love candy, right? Think of him as an M&M, hard outer shell with a chocolatey center or better yet a tootsie pop. He's the sweetest guy ever, but really hard to get to know."

"Yum, tootsie pop. How many licks to get to the center?" Penelope said.

Baylee and April looked at each other and couldn't keep from laughing. Then Baylee said, "Wow, I needed that! Too bad I didn't think to pull out my phone." Still giggling, she turned to Jeremy.

"So sorry for my friend here, she is clearly under the influence of some very potent drugs. That's not something she would normally have said. Me, on the other hand, well, that's a whole other story."

Finally, looking up, he said, "It's cool, I have a few 'pervy' friends too." The corner of his lip perked up, almost into a smile. He took a few steps back, pulled out his recorder, and started speaking into it. "Female looks to be in her middle twenties, bruising on her face and torso, as well as her throat. Some appear to be a day or two old. Minor lacerations on the face, as well as wrists and ankles. A deep cut on her right jaw and a few smaller cuts on the torso. Severe burns on seventy percent of her scalp, as well as the lower pelvic area."

Penelope lay listening, as he recorded her injuries, but his words seemed to be trailing off. He was getting further and further away. She could see his lips moving, but it looked more like a silent movie than reality. She became unaware; was she dreaming or awake? Maybe at this point, it was a little bit of both. She felt so detached from everything, weightless even.

Becoming frightened, she looked to Baylee for support, only then realizing she'd been holding her hand all along.

Looking into her friend's eyes, as she had hundreds of times, Penelope saw something she hoped she'd never see again. She knew the look; she'd seen it countless times growing up. People would always look at her mother in the same way. Sometimes they'd make snide comments thinking she and her younger brother wouldn't hear, but they always did. Penelope had promised herself long ago she'd never see that look directed at her again.

Until today, she thought she'd done a pretty good job living up to the promise. But the look on Baylee's face had just proved her wrong. The look spoke volumes as it screamed to her that she had failed.

Not wanting to be a failure at life as well as love, she needed to find a way to break the cycle and learn to finally stand up for herself and what she believed in. The weightlessness was fading and becoming more of a dream. She knew it was useless to fight it, so she let herself fall into the darkness of sleep.

The strong scent of antiseptic hung in the air, yet not quite powerful enough to hide the stench of urine, dried blood, and whatever other pungent smell, she'd yet to decipher. Opening her eyes, Penelope saw curtains dangling from small hooks on three of the four walls. Curious about how long she'd been there, she started looking for a clock, which of course she couldn't find. Why is it they never put clocks in Dr. offices and emergency rooms, she thought?

Suddenly, the curtain swung open, and Baylee walked in, holding a coffee in each hand.

"How are you feeling," she asked. "You had me worried there for a minute." She took a seat on the corner of the bed and handed over one of the coffees. She tried not to stare, but it was hard not to notice all the bandages covering Penelope. "Sorry, it's not very good. It's from vending, so our only choices were… what am I saying? There weren't any choices."

"Thanks, I'm sure it's fine. Now tell me what's going on, and how long have I been here? What did the police say? Do you know how long the doctors are planning on keeping me?"

"Whoa, slow down, you just woke up, you nut. There's no need to rush into all of this. Plus, I can only tell you what I know, and it isn't much."

"Not much is still more than I know, so spill it."

"You've only been here for a few hours, and they did blood work, X-rays, and bandaged you up. As for the results, you're going to have to wait and speak with the doctor."

"Whatever. I know you Bay, so don't act like you didn't sneak a peek at my results."

"I may have peeked a little, but I'm still not telling you. You know how strict the policies are around here. And if I get called into Mr. Karp's office one more time, I can't be held responsible for what I might do."

"What you might do? Isn't he in his sixties?" Penelope asked, not trying to hide her amusement.

"He's in his fifties, and I don't care how old he is. That man will be sexy even when he's dead. Think of a mix between a young Sean Connery and Johnny Depp. He's so yummy I could eat him with a spoon."

"You can stop daydreaming now, or wet dreaming, whichever you want to call it. Focus. Let's get back to what is really going on. What else do you know?"

"Don't freak out," Baylee said.

"Yeah, because that's a good way to keep me calm. By telling me not to freak."

"Well, I wanted to at least give you fair warning; because if you do, just know I'm going to have them knock you out again."

"Fine, I promise not to freak, but tell me what you know," Penelope replied anxiously.

"The police, as far as I know, haven't found Derrick yet. I stayed at the apartment until they finished their initial walkthrough. They gathered all the evidence they could, took my statement, and wanted me to tell you they would be by later to get yours."

"Thanks for taking care of it."

Ignoring Penelope's thanks, she went on. "They believe he probably took off for fear of being caught and arrested. I say, of course, he took off. Being the piece of garbage, he is. He isn't man enough to stand up and take his punishment. He's more like a puppy that pisses on your carpet whenever he gets caught chewing on a new pair of shoes."

Penelope's eyes got huge and started to water. "So, he's out there somewhere, waiting for me?"

"I'm right here, Pen; he's not going to hurt you again, okay? We're going to make some changes. Maybe that will help to put your mind at ease. I already called the apartment manager and explained everything; the locks will be changed by the time we leave here. We just need to stop and grab the keys."

"I'm glad you're on top of it, Baylee, because I don't know what I'd do if Derrick were able to get back in, especially without me knowing about it."

"Oh, remember the self-defense place we saw yesterday? As soon as you're healed enough, we're going to be all over that. The sooner, the better, I think, but I'm sure the doctor can give us some kind of time frame."

Baylee stood, walked over to the curtain, turned back, and said, "Before I forget, there's one more thing. I'm taking you gun shopping. I should've done it a long time ago. Looking back, I'm sorry I didn't, maybe this could've all been avoided." Shaking her head in disgust, she went on. "I'm going to go find a nurse and let them know sleeping beauty finally decided to wake up." Not waiting for an argument, Baylee winked and quickly slipped out.

Looking around the tiny room, Penelope noticed the television was on, but muted. She had no idea where Baylee put the remote so, she watched it in silence for a couple of minutes. The monitors beside her bed were beeping quietly with a steady rhythm in the background. Turning, she glanced briefly but had no idea what all the different numbers meant.

The much-needed sleep the medicine had given her, was bliss. She didn't even remember having any dreams; all she could remember was it had been peaceful and relaxing. She couldn't remember the last time she'd actually slept through the night without waking from a nightmare.

Wishing Baylee would hurry back, she sipped the coffee, realizing she hadn't been lying about how awful it was. Starting to get impatient because there was absolutely nothing to do in the room except think, she decided to close her eyes, lay back, and listen to the sounds around her.

The beeping of the monitors, a child crying, and of course, a few nurses trying to console him. Then there were footsteps right outside her room, and a couple speaking in hushed tones. Penelope strained to hear what was being said, but couldn't make it out.

The curtain drew back, causing Penelope to open her eyes. She watched Baylee stroll in, and once again take a seat on the edge of the bed. Following shortly behind her, was whom Penelope presumed was the Doctor, wearing a white lab coat with a stethoscope hanging from her neck, she adjusted her glasses, looked up, and smiled.

"Hello, Penelope. My name is Dr. Laura Morris; I'll be your attending physician while you're here at Edward Memorial Hospital," she said, looking over the top of the tablet she was studying. "I need to go over some results with you privately if you wouldn't mind."

"Hello, Doctor, anything you have to tell me, I'm okay with Baylee hearing," said Penelope.

Smiling and nodding the Doctor said, "Then let's continue, I want to inform you we took x-rays of your ribs, and luckily they are only bruised. We taped them for you, but it will hurt to breathe and move until they have had some time to heal. Also, we performed an MRI of your head to identify any swelling. There is some swelling, which is very slight; this would be conclusive with a concussion. The burn area on your head has second-degree burns, which means your hair should grow back fine with very little to no scarring. However, the burn on your lower abdomen is a third-degree burn and will have heavy scarring. You need to be aware it will take quite some time to fully heal. I closed the cut on your jaw with a special incision glue we use during surgery. I will be sending you home with a special ointment for the burns, extra tape for the ribs, and possibly a rib brace. Do you have any questions?"

"Yes, are you going to send some pain medication home with me? I feel like I've been run over by a bus. Also, could you give me an estimate of when I could resume normal activity?" replied Penelope.

"I'm sending you home with some Tylenol with codeine, please be careful using it. It can make you tired. As for normal activity, it could be a couple weeks, or it could be a couple of months. Go by how you feel. If you feel okay at the end of the day, then try to do a little more the next," stated Dr. Morris. "If there are no more questions, I'll send your nurse in to check your vitals one more time while I get your discharge papers ready."

Dr. Morris turned to leave, looked back, and said, "You should be thankful your injuries were treatable. Remember you may not be so lucky next time."

"I understand, thanks. I promise you won't see me again, at least not for the same reason," replied Penelope.

Moments later, the curtain opened again, and a girl with bright pink hair walked in. Smiling, she looked at Penelope and said, "Hi, I'm Alicia, nice to finally meet you. You've been asleep all the other times I've been in your room. I hear you get to go home as soon as I check your vitals and go over all the paperwork."

Trying not to stare, Penelope smiled back, the girl couldn't be old enough to be a nurse, she thought. She was wearing black scrubs, which set her pink hair off even more. She looked a bit out of place but seemed friendly enough. Penelope just didn't expect her nurse to be a preteen with neon hair.

"Great news, your vitals look good. Now let's go over all the home instructions, then you can get dressed and head home."

"Excuse me, sorry to interrupt. Do I have time to run out and grab the clothes I brought for Pen while you guys go over all that?"

"Sure, sounds like a plan. I'll try to get through it before you get back," said Alicia.

Leaning over, Baylee gave Penelope a quick kiss on the cheek, whispered something in her ear, and slipped through the curtain.

"Ready?" Alicia asked, and getting a thumbs-up, she went on. "First thing, you need someone to stay with you for the next 24 hours, making sure to wake you every two to three hours. This is only a precaution to keep an eye on you because of the concussion. Can I assume this won't be a problem?"

"I'm sure Baylee will be all over it. I probably won't be able to get a minute alone."

"Okay, great. Second, you need to clean and dress your wounds twice daily. I'll be giving you a bag with all the supplies you'll need. Next, Dr. Morris is starting you on antibiotics to prevent any infections. You need to take them until they are gone. Any questions?" asked Alicia.

Balancing herself on the edge of the bed, Penelope smiled and said, "Nope, I got it."

"I also have information on a few local woman's shelters, as well as battered and abused groups. I hope one of these can help, and you'll find yourself in a better situation soon. Take care, you were the easiest patient I've had all week." She handed over the bag of supplies and smiled at Baylee, as she passed her on the way out of the room.

Baylee came into the room, holding a small suitcase.

"Are you all set and ready to go? I'll help you get dressed, and then we can take off. If you're hungry, we can stop and grab a bite to take back to the apartment. I thought maybe I would stay with you for a few days if that's all right? If nothing else, it will ease my own mind knowing I'm there."

Chapter 7

Baylee knew it wouldn't be easy for Penelope to walk back into the apartment only hours after the attack. So, she stayed close and watched for any sign her friend might need her.

Standing by her side the entire time, Baylee watched Penelope walk from room to room, trying to take it all in. Baylee waited for the moment it came crashing back, but to her surprise, it never happened.

Penelope had been resting since they had arrived back at the apartment, which gave Baylee plenty of time to clean. She loved listening to music anytime she cleaned, which was quite often with her OCD. So, she plugged in her earbuds and got to work. She hoped it would help Penelope a little, not having a visual reminder of what had happened. She only wished there was something she could do about the mental reminder she was sure Penelope would have for the rest of her life.

Hours later, Baylee stood on the kitchen counter and held onto the top lip of an open cabinet, as she reached for the last specks of blood on the ceiling. She adjusted her left foot slightly and lifted her right foot off the counter, which gave her the extra couple inches she needed to finally reach the last spot.

Penelope walked into the kitchen in time to see Baylee pull some crazy maneuver she assumed only a short person would understand. Not wanting to scare her and make her fall, she wasn't sure how to get her attention. Then noticing a towel on the counter, Penelope picked it up and tossed it into the air close to her friend's head.

What was that? Baylee thought, then dropped straight down, landing on the balls of her feet, and moving instantly to a fighting stance. She relaxed immediately once her brain registered; it was only Penelope.

"Oh, my God, how did you do that? It was like one of those superhero moves they do in the movies. I've never seen you move that way!" exclaimed Penelope.

"I have many talents, some of which even you may not be aware of. It's really not a big deal. I'm just on edge lately," Baylee told her. She walked over and threw her rag into the bucket. "I hope you're feeling better; it's nice to see you up and around. If you're hungry, I can make you something to eat." Opening the fridge, she leaned in, pulled out a bottle of water and took a sip.

"I cannot believe you cleaned this whole place while I was sleeping!" Penelope said, turning around in a slow circle. "You're amazing! I clearly haven't told you that enough." She leaned in and kissed Baylee's cheek, "Thank you. I don't know what I'd do without you, and I hope to never find out."

"Sweetie, I love you too and no worries; I'm not going anywhere."

Hearing a knock on the door, Baylee turned to answer it but first checked the peephole, as she always did. She saw the same two police officers standing on the other side from only hours before. "Hello again. Please come in," she offered.

"Thank you. Is Mrs. Penelope Williams available?" Baylee saw him nod slightly in positive acknowledgment of the new locks as she led him into the apartment.

"Hello. My name is Detective Don Black, and this is Officer Smith. We have a few questions we'd like to go over about what happened at this location earlier this morning."

"Okay, where do you want to start?" questioned Penelope.

"Let's start with the basics. Your full name is Penelope Mary Williams, correct? Your mother was Mary P. Jones, maiden name, Fitch? Your father was Luke P. Jones? Both deceased?" asked Detective Black.

"Yes, that's all correct," Penelope said. "Won't you please take a seat?"

"Yes, thank you," answered Officer Smith.

The Detective nodded his head, took a seat, and continued with the questions. "Sorry, but I needed to make sure we are looking at the correct information in our system. Now, if you'd go through the events in as much detail as possible, I'd appreciate it."

Minutes passed as Penelope went through the details of what had occurred within the last twenty-four hours. She watched them make several notes on their tablets during her statement, stopping only briefly to answer additional questions along the way.

Once she finally finished the play-by-play, Penelope said, "I have a few questions of my own, if that's all right?"

"Go ahead, we're happy to answer all the questions we can."

"Have you found Derrick?" she asked.

"No ma'am, we haven't as of yet. A canvass was done of the area, and there have been no sightings. The blood trail we were following ended abruptly, and with the recent snowfall, it's making it more difficult for the dogs to pick the scent back up. All the area hospitals and medical facilities have been notified to be on the lookout. We will find him Mrs. Williams, but until then, I feel it's quite necessary you take out a restraining order as soon as possible."

Detective Black stood and signaled for the other officer to do the same. Handing Penelope his card, he turned to leave.

"I'll walk you out," said Baylee, following closely behind them.

"One more thing," he called out. "Please be extra cautious; always be aware of your surroundings. If anything feels odd or out of the ordinary, don't hesitate to call."

"Okay, thanks, I will," said Penelope.

Closing the door behind them, Baylee bolted it and slid the new chain across the slide.

"I'll make us some tea," Baylee said, turning toward the kitchen. "It might help you relax a little after having to relive all of that again."

Going back through it all for the police had been exhausting, Penelope realized. All she wanted was to take a couple of pain pills and crawl back into bed. She hoped the meds would be strong enough to ward off her nightmares, or at least not make them worse.

"Tea sounds nice, but I have a better idea. I vote we order some takeout and have it delivered. I think Chinese food sounds about perfect." Penelope told Baylee.

Reaching for the blanket on the couch, Penelope stopped and stared at it, remembering when Derrick wrapped it around her to cuddle, or so he claimed. Immediately she tossed it to the floor and said, "I should burn this and everything else in here that's his."

"Cool, I'm down with that," Baylee responded. "Want me to start a pile in the bathtub? You know I'm always happy to help."

"I know you are, and it's why I love you so much. Maybe later, after we eat. Right now, I'm starving."

Baylee hurried to the bedroom to grab a different blanket off the bed. After she handed it to Penelope along with her tea, she sat on the opposite end of the couch.

"I'm hungry too, now that you mentioned Chinese, it sounds so good. Don't forget extra crab wontons; you know they're my favorite."

Penelope signaled she understood and was almost done ordering on her phone.

Not sure how to re-start the conversation, Baylee figured she'd be blunt as usual. Otherwise, Penelope would think she was avoiding the elephant in the room. "I know it must have been hard for you, reliving all of that. I'm here if you want to talk."

"You'd think it'd get easier to talk to the cops, but it doesn't. Looking back now, it seems they've always been a part of my life, almost from the time I was born. I can still remember talking to them when I was little. They came to the house; the neighbors had called about the noise again. They split my little brother Philip and I up and asked us a bunch of questions. They wanted to see if our stories actually matched."

Taking a drink of her tea, Baylee listened carefully; this sounded like a story she might not have heard yet.

"I wish you wouldn't have had to go through all of that as a kid. Can I ask, which time are you talking about, was it the last time you were at that house?" Baylee turned in her seat to face Penelope while they talked.

"No, not the last night, even though the cops did the same then too. Splitting us up and asking questions. This was a few years before we were taken and thrown into the child protection system. I think I remember it so well because it was the first time in my life, I actually had hoped someone was going to help us." Covering her feet with the blanket, she continued.

"There are things you learn growing up in a house like mine. First, keep your mouth shut, because if you don't, it will be shut for you. Second, do what you're told, and don't hesitate. And finally, try to stay out of the way, because you never want to bring attention to yourself. Those were the golden rules Philly, and I lived by." The rules that never helped, she thought, pausing a moment before going on. "Have you ever heard the saying, be careful what you wish for?"

"Yeah, hasn't everyone? But it's only an old wives' tale, isn't it?" Baylee asked.

"For so long, I wished someone would come and take the monster away and make him stop hurting my Mom. That day finally came, but it was also the day they took my Mother out in a body bag. Then Child Protection Services arrived, and they split Philly and me up. We were put into separate foster homes, and that was the last day I saw him."

For a moment, she remembered the things she'd been forced to do in those foster homes. Unimaginable things a little girl should never be forced to do. She'd always hoped her brother had gotten lucky and ended up in a better place, with people who actually loved him. But she supposed she'd never know. She'd never been able to find him.

Trying to pull herself from the past, she stood up and made her way toward the T.V. "Since the food should be here any minute, what do you say to watching a movie?"

Baylee realized Penelope had been deep in thoughts she hadn't wanted to share. And knowing her friend was done talking, she hoped it would help to lighten the mood, so she replied, "How about a comedy? I think we could both use a laugh, don't you? Do you have anything with Jim Carrey?"

"Of course, I do. My favorite movie ever is "Me, Myself and Irene." I bet I've seen it fifty times. I'll get it all set up."

"Sounds like a plan; I'll go grab plates and everything we need from the kitchen." Once Baylee came back and put the plates, napkins, and drinks on the coffee table, Penelope started the movie.

Later hearing the knock on the door, Baylee paused it and went to grab the food. Thinking a nice quiet evening might be just what they both needed.

After handing Pen a fork and her carton of Chop Suey, Baylee popped a crab wonton in her mouth, winked, and said. "This was the best idea you've had all day."

"You know I do have them once in a while," Penelope said, shoving in another bite of Suey. Eyeballing Bay's wonton's, she gave her best puppy-dog eyes.

"Here," Baylee said, tossing her one. "But you know I'm only sharing because of what you've been through lately."

"I know how you are with food. That's why I was hoping to get some sympathy. See how well it worked?" she asked, and shoved the whole thing in her mouth at once.

"Don't count on it working a second time," Baylee said, laughing, picking up the remote and restarting the movie.

They happily stuffed themselves while watching Jim Carrey, and mutually laughed over the funny parts.

Penelope's eyelids were heavy, but she tried to keep from giving into sleep. She knew she needed it. Baylee was always telling her how sleep helps the body heal faster. But with the nightmares, she always woke more anxious than relaxed and well-rested.

Without realizing she'd closed her eyes; she was immediately pulled back to when she was 12 years old. "Daddy, please don't hurt her! Daddy, stop!"

Daddy Luke turned his head, looked at her with his bright red face and bloodshot eyes and vein protruding from his temple. "Shut up, Penelope! Or you'll be next."

"But you're killing her!" Penelope cried, running toward her mom lying on the kitchen floor. She reached out her arms, wanting to protect her, but was stopped only inches away. Penelope pulled with everything she had and tried to break free from the grip Luke had on her shirt.

"What did I tell you, little girl?" he yelled. Yanking on her shirt, he pulled her back a couple of feet. Still looking at her mom in a pool of blood on the floor, she didn't see his upraised hand coming at her.

He backhanded her, she flew across the room and landed in a heap on the floor beside his favorite recliner. Not able to move for a few minutes, she continued to watch him kick her mom in the head and ribs. She knew she had to do something before it was too late, she struggled to her knees and crawled closer to the chair. Not noticing the blood dripping from her left jaw from his ring.

She slid her hand between the cushion and the seat; there she felt the cold, hard metal. With shaky hands, she pulled it from its hiding place and stood. Then with everything she had, she yelled. "Stop!" But with his laugh ringing in her ears, she pulled back on the trigger.

Chapter 8

"Pen, wake up!" Baylee yelled while gently shaking her friend.

Penelope opened her eyes, thankful to see her, then pulled Baylee into a hug.

"It was only a dream! Derrick isn't going to hurt you. I promise," Baylee urged, hugging her tight.

She knew she should correct Baylee's misconception about her dream, but it was easier to let her think Derrick was the subject of her nightmare. "Thanks for waking me up. It was so real."

"It wasn't real, it was only a dream. Nobody's going to hurt you as long as I'm around," Baylee assured her. "Now, let's get you to bed. Maybe you'll sleep better there than out here on the couch."

Baylee helped her to her room, and Penelope glanced at the clock on the nightstand. Realizing she only had two hours left before she had to get ready for work, she knew she wasn't going to get any more sleep.

"I think I'm going to take a shower. I only have a couple hours before work anyway. But go ahead, you rest. I'm sure you're tired from taking great care of me, and I know you haven't slept much," Penelope told her.

"I'm okay, really. Go ahead and take your shower, I'll stay nearby in case you need any help. Once you're finished, I'll head upstairs and get some stuff done before my own shift starts."

"Okay, sounds good," Penelope said, walking into the bathroom. After she turned on the water to let it warm up, she carefully undressed and pulled the supplies from the bag the hospital had given her.

After she covered her head with a shower cap, she pulled the curtain open and stepped in. Gasping instantly from the sting the water caused by touching her cuts, she quickly adjusted the water to a lower temperature, hoping it might help ease the pain.

"You okay in there?" Baylee called from outside the door.

"I'm fine. I won't be long." Gently washing, she watched the soap suds disappear down the drain. Finally finished, she wrapped the towel around herself and stepped out.

Opening the bathroom door, she stepped into her room and saw Baylee sitting cross-legged on her bed. Baylee had opened her laptop, while she drank a cup of coffee and ate leftovers from the night before, Penelope raised her eyebrows in question.

"What? I was hungry and didn't feel like cooking. At least I made a fresh pot of coffee. Want some?" Baylee asked.

"Sure, I'll take a cup," Penelope said, walking to her dresser and selecting clothes for the day. "But I thought you were going to go upstairs to your place?"

"Why the rush? Are you anxious to get rid of me?" Baylee asked, walking to the kitchen to get another cup.

"Of course not, don't be silly. I just know you have things you want to do today. That's all."

Penelope carried the clothes she'd picked out and turned back to the bathroom as Baylee walked in, holding a steaming cup of coffee.

"Here you go, Pen. I hope it's the way you like it. I guess I'll take off. I really don't like you going to work so soon, but I guess you are going, no matter what I say. So, first, I want us to have a buddy system. Whenever you go anywhere or leave one location to go to another. Text me, and I'll do the same. How's that sound?"

"All right, we can do that," Penelope said, using the coffee Baylee had given her to swallow her meds. "Sounds like a good idea to me, then we'll know right away if something isn't right."

"Cool, I'm glad you're on board. I didn't want to have to put a tracking device on you." Smiling, Baylee leaned over and kissed Penelope on the cheek. Grabbing her leftovers and her cup of coffee, she headed back upstairs to her place.

After locking the door behind her, Penelope returned to the bathroom and placed her clothes on the counter. She re-bandaged her wounds and secured her rib with the new rib brace. Once she was finished, she dressed for the day.

After she applied a little makeup to cover some of the bruises, she was ready for work. She locked the door and headed to her Jeep. The thought of working a thirteen-hour day was daunting, and she wasn't sure if her body would be able to make it through. It wasn't like she had a choice, the bills still needed to be paid. She patted her pocket and was thankful she'd brought more painkillers with her, just in case.

Penelope's knuckles were white on the steering wheel and started to ache from all the effort it was taking to stay on the road. She was more than ready for summer to begin, so she could take Dime's top off and let the sunshine on her face.

Finally, pulling into the parking lot, she was glad to find her usual spot empty. While gathering up her stuff to take in, she still had to hold her ribs. She was thankful the hospital had replaced the brace Derrick had ruined. She couldn't imagine trying to work without it. It still hurt, but she told herself she could handle it. She was tough, she'd had to be her whole life.

While walking inside, she thought, it's a good thing I know my job as well as I do, I could almost do it blindfolded. She'd never counted how many outlets she'd wired in a day, but it had to be somewhere in the hundreds. Of course, that wasn't counting all the lights, appliances, and electrical wiring that needed to be done while building a recreational vehicle.

She'd worked hard for five years to become the group leader in the electrical department, and had a great group of guys working under her. She felt they all respected her and knew she was good at her job. Not that they'd all felt that way in the beginning, of course. It had been a struggle to be accepted by an all-male department, but she'd been determined to see it through, and she had.

None of them would ask about her personal life because they knew she wasn't at work to flirt or gossip. She felt she was paid to do a job and to perform it well, not to stand around and talk all day. So, though a few might wonder to themselves about her bruises, they knew better than to ever ask.

She couldn't imagine what her group of guys would've thought if she hadn't worn a stocking cap today. What would they have felt when they saw most of her hair missing, and the little that was there was fried? She told herself it didn't matter. As far as she was concerned, they would never find out. Penelope knew she couldn't hide the bandages or the fact she was moving slower than usual, but she would keep her mind on her job and expect the same from her workers.

Relieved, when the day was finally over, she realized she might have time to run home for a quick shower before heading to the gas station to start her shift at her second job. Penelope clocked out and walked as quickly as she could across the parking lot to her Jeep. Noticing even before she got there, the driver's side door was hanging wide open. She was almost sure she'd closed it.

I was exhausted, so maybe I forgot, she thought. But having an uneasy feeling, she decided to look under and around the Jeep, to be sure. She sighed and was certain she was paranoid. She climbed in, started it up, and headed for home.

After unlocking the apartment, she made her way straight to the shower, knowing she didn't have any extra time to spare. The water still stung but helped to ease her sore muscles a little. When she'd finished, she reached for the faucet, turning it off, she opened the shower curtain. Suddenly, she froze and chills instantly shot up her spine as she read the message written on the foggy mirror.

"I'll love you always."

Caught off guard, she started to panic, fearing somehow, he might be in the apartment. Had she locked the door when she came in, she thought? She pulled the towel around her, and grabbed a heavy shampoo bottle, and made a mental note to make sure she always had something with her for protection.

Tiptoeing out of the bathroom, she peeked into the living room. Then seeing nothing out of place, she decided to check the entire apartment just to be safe. Going to the front door first, she was speechless when she found the door unlocked. How could I be so careless after everything that's happened, she asked herself. Locking it and sliding the chain, she continued to search the apartment. This time, she'd gotten lucky; but she knew she needed to be more diligent because next time, her luck could run out.

Stepping back into the bathroom, the steam was now gone, but the image remained in her mind. She decided Derrick had probably written it days ago, and she just hadn't noticed. Bending down carefully, she pulled the glass cleaner and paper towels out from under the counter and quickly cleaned the mirror. Once she was done, she breathed a sigh of relief, glad she had finally wiped a small part of him out of her life.

Penelope walked out of the bathroom and went to her closet, pulled down an old box, and lifted the lid. Inhaling deeply, she breathed in the scent from years ago, taking her mind back to when she was little. She knew exactly what she was looking for, so, she slid a few pictures out of the way, and found it; a blue cashmere scarf that had been her mother's. Gently, she removed it and placed the box back on the shelf.

Penelope knew she needed to hurry, or she might be late. Knowing her boss, Marty, wasn't a patient man, it wouldn't be a good idea to be late. So, as quickly as she could, she slid a tank top over her head and pulled on a pair of jeans, making sure the bandage was still secure over her abdomen. She shoved her arms into a long-sleeved flannel shirt and was almost ready to go.

Then, holding the scarf in her hands, she hugged it to her face and remembered a time when her mother had worn it. The wind would catch the corner, and Penelope was captivated as it danced around, until her mother would tuck it, along with a few strands of hair that had escaped, back into place. Smiling at the memory, she wrapped it around her own head.

Ready to leave, Penelope picked up her keys and purse while shuffling out the door. She needed to text Baylee, and let her know she was on her way to her next job, although she'd forgotten to text when she'd left the factory. Penelope had promised to keep her updated on her whereabouts by trying her new buddy system with phones. She just needed to remember to do it. Baylee had a crazy schedule most days since she was a paramedic, and she never knew what her day would hold. So, this new system would work great for helping them both stay safe.

Less than a block away from the gas station, Penelope noticed a light had burned out behind one of the letters in the overhead sign. It was now reading Mary's Gas instead of Marty's Gas. Looking up as she pulled into the parking lot, she knew it would be the first task she needed to complete.

Not wasting any time, Penelope locked the Jeep and headed for the front door. Hearing a few people call out "Hello's," she waved to them as she made her way inside. Happy to see Erma-Lee would be working with her tonight, she said "Hi," then went to the back, grabbed her smock, clocked in and located the supplies she needed to fix the sign.

Erma-Lee was a short wisp of a woman somewhere in her middle sixties Penelope guessed. Her white and grey hair was a short crop, you could tell she'd taken the time to style it. She had on a pretty pink sweater, but it was mostly hidden by the ugly smock they were required to wear. Refusing to give up her cowboy boots, she swore they went with any attire. Penelope didn't always agree, but it proved Erma-Lee was a true southerner at heart.

"Erma-Lee, are you all right in here by yourself for a while? I need to go out and change a bulb in the sign," asked Penelope.

"I sure am, but are you sure you're up to it? You be careful out there; with the winds picking up, it sure don't seem like a safe thing to be doing."

"You're probably right, but I'm tougher than I look. Marty once told me when he was little, kids use to call him Mary to make fun of him, and he hated it. So, if he comes in and sees Mary instead of Marty up there, heads will roll."

"Well, get on up there then, girl, because you and I both know half of the regulars in here wouldn't think twice to poke fun."

"Then Marty has already left for the day?" Penelope questioned, pouring herself a large coffee. She was glad to be able to take full advantage of the free coffee and fountain drinks the employees were allowed.

"He was here earlier; hollered, he'd be back later as he slammed out the door. I ain't sure where he took off to. But I overheard him on the phone, grumbling about something to do with them permits. I figure he went over to the other store he plans on opening," said Erma-Lee.

"I better go out there and get it done before he gets back. Could I leave my smock and coffee with you until I'm finished?"

"Sure thing, sweetie."

"Thanks."

The extension ladder was bulky and awkward; it made her ribs burn to pull it out from where Marty kept it. Finally, after setting it into place, she watched it sway back and forth while it leaned on the pole holding the sign. Penelope wasn't afraid of heights, but it didn't seem to ease her fear of climbing the ladder in this kind of weather.

"Well, it's not going to fix itself," she said, stepping on the first rung. Just hurry up and get it done before you freeze to death, she told herself. She made the bulb change, carefully climbed down the ladder and dragged it back to where she found it.

Her teeth chattered when she stepped back into the store. Thankfully, there stood Erma-Lee looking like an angel holding out her cup of coffee. Taking a sip, it felt like a warm splash of heaven sliding down the back of her throat.

"Thanks, I feel like a popsicle, but this should warm me up pretty quick. Could you do me a favor? Next time I attempt something like that in this kind of weather, just lock me in the freezer, will ya? I might still freeze, but I don't take the chance of breaking my legs too. I swear, at one point, I thought the wind was going to pick me and the ladder up and carry us both away."

Penelope pulled off her coat and spotted her smock sitting beside Erma-Lee's register. Carefully sliding the smock on, she took another sip of her coffee and headed to the back to put her coat in her locker.

Erma-Lee followed her and reached for a piece of the headscarf that had come loose. "Here, let me help ya with this," she said, noticing the burns the scarf was trying to hide.

"Oh, you poor sweet girl, what's happened to you?" She asked, tucking the scarf back into place, and leaning in to give her a gentle hug.

"Nothing, I'll be fine. It will heal."

"Now don't you be acting like it's no big deal. I noticed the bandage on your face, and you seem to be hurting when ya moved. But I was trying to keep my nose clean and mind my own business."

"And I appreciate that. I promise I'm going to be fine. Don't worry about me." Penelope said, trying to avoid getting into it any further.

"I hear ya, and I understand ya not wanting to talk about it. But if ya ever need a whole slew of fellas to whoop somebody, ya let me know. My family back home would be happy to help."

"Thanks for the offer, I'll keep it in mind," Penelope said. "Now, could you do me a favor? Stick a note on Marty's door telling him he needs more lightbulbs because I used the last one?"

"I sure will, and I reckon he should be appreciative he's got an employee that's willing to risk their life and limbs, so he ain't made fun of," giggled Erma-Lee. "Even though I think it ought to be a maintenance man's job to change them lights up there, not us."

Waiting for Erma-Lee to be out of eye-shot, Penelope popped a couple more pain pills, and said, "What maintenance? The maintenance around here consists of only Marty. He's been so busy trying to get everything ready to open the second store that I didn't want to add more to his plate," said Penelope.

"See, that's the reason he wants you running the other store. Because you do what's needing to be done. You don't ask; first, you just do it. So, have you made up your mind yet, about running the other store?"

"No, I haven't," Penelope admitted. "With everything that's been going on, I haven't had time to really think about it. But he gave me two weeks to decide, and if I decline, he'll still have time to find someone else.

"Well, if you ain't gonna take it, I might throw my hat in the ring. I know I ain't worked here as long as you, but I think I've got what it takes," Erma-Lee told her.

"Good to know. Now I don't have to feel guilty if I say no because I have full confidence in your capabilities to handle any situation," said Penelope with a smile.

Penelope wasn't sure what she wanted anymore, but she knew she needed to start making some decisions. All she could think about was the words Derrick had taunted her with. Did she really think things would ever change? He thought it was a joke, laughing when he said it. Hating to admit even to herself, he had a point. Why do I hope things would turn out differently for me than my mother? For something to change, don't I need to change? I can't expect to have a different outcome if the pattern stays the same.

"I need to shake things up," Penelope said aloud, staring out into space, not noticing a customer standing right in front of her.

"Excuse me?"

"Oh, I'm so sorry, Fred. I didn't see you there. I must have been thinking out loud." Feeling awkward, someone had heard her inner thoughts, she went on. "How's it going? Did anything new happen over the weekend?"

"Nope, same old, same old. Nothing new happens to me," he told her. "I go to work, stop by here and then head home. But don't you worry about thinking out loud that way; it happens to me all the time," he said. "It's the answering yourself back you should worry about. If you start having a two-sided conversation, then you might want to go get yourself looked at."

They both laughed.

After handing Fred his change, Penelope started bagging up all the junk food. "Thanks, I'll keep that in mind," she said and pushed the bag across the counter to him.

She watched him head out and climb into his old rusty VW Bug. She knew he'd be in again tomorrow; some things never change, she thought. But that brought up thoughts she'd rather not think about right now, so she hollered back to Erma-Lee.

"Hey Erma-Lee, I say we stock all the shelves, clean everything we can, and relax until it's time to close. What do you say, any preference?"

"I'll be the stocker; you be the cleaner. That way, I ain't worrying about them dang gloves when I need to be helping a customer."

A few hours later, everything was done, and Erma-Lee stood behind the counter, waiting on another customer. As Penelope watched. She thought; Erma-Lee was really good with people, and Marty was lucky to have her.

"Heads up," yelled Erma-Lee, "Marty's walking in, and he sure don't look happy."

"Does he ever?" Penelope asked.

Marty liked to yell, but he wasn't mean, Penelope thought. He was extremely focused. He'd come from nothing, and he started out as the guy who worked on the pumps or fixed whatever else might be broken. But now, he was the owner of this station and about to open his second location.

Stomping through the door, his face as red as his hair, Marty headed straight to his office. Hoping she could help, Penelope filled a large fountain cup and followed him. Tapping lightly on the open door, she entered and handed him the cup.

He took a long drink, looked up, and said, "Girl, you are a godsend; this Pepsi is exactly what I needed." Sitting down behind his desk, he continued. "Well, that and maybe something to make the zoning and permits board listen. They called me earlier and claimed I didn't file the proper paperwork needed to put my tanks in the ground. They claim I need to file a separate form for the diesel since it exceeded the maximum capacity I originally had planned."

He rubbed his hand over his head, making his hair stand on end, and sighed in annoyance. "He acts like I'm a pup like I have no idea what I'm doing. I've been doing this since that boy was still in diapers. I have copies of everything I've filed, but do you think he'd look at them? He claims my copies aren't proof they've been filed. Well, how about I stick a boot up his ass? Think that would be proof enough?"

Standing up, he started to pace, but could only take two steps in either direction before bumping into a wall.

"I'm sure you'll get it all worked out," Penelope said. "Like you said, you have worked in this field practically forever; you know all the ins and outs. He probably lost the form and is trying to place blame."

"Maybe you're right, but it still doesn't help me meet my timeline. The guy was talking about pushing the whole project back a month. Can you imagine? I can't allow that to happen, I need to get this done and back on schedule." He sat back down at his desk and kept going through the papers he had stacked in piles.

Penelope sat in the chair across from him, always baffled by how he could find anything in the mess he called a desk. He always told her he had a system. She knew it must be true because he was able to pull out any paper or form he needed in mere seconds.

"So, what do you need? I know it's something because I can count on one hand how many times you've come in here and actually sat down," Marty asked, scratching his beard and considering what else could possibly go wrong today.

"Can we talk about the promotion you offered me?" Penelope asked.

"Sure thing, I'm so pleased you've decided to take me up on my offer. I know the new place will be in good hands." He stood up and reached across the desk to shake Penelope's hand. "Finally, I hear some good news today."

Grimacing at his words, it wasn't going at all as she had hoped. There it was again, that word: Hope. She decided right then and there, that word was no longer going to be allowed in her vocabulary.

Marty noticed Penelope refused to shake his hand, so he pulled his back and sat down, not looking happy.

"I've been doing a lot of thinking the last couple days," Penelope told him. "I need to make some changes in my life. I'm not certain yet what those will be, but I felt I needed to be honest with you. I know you didn't ask for my opinion, but I think you should offer the position to Erma-Lee." Her hands felt clammy, was she making a big mistake, she thought? No, she was just nervous, making changes wasn't going to be easy.

Sitting back in his chair, he bit down on the toothpick he always seemed to have in his mouth, and asked, "Is it the money? Do you need me to raise the salary I was offering? I thought you were happy here?"

"I think you're misunderstanding. I love it here. I'm not saying today will be my last day or anything. I'm just taking some time to figure out what I want out of life, like what are my life goals?" Pulling a loose thread from her smock, she looked up at Marty and continued.

"I honestly believe you'd be happier in the long run with Erma-Lee as your new store manager. She's really creative and freethinking. The regulars all love her, and she can handle your temper tantrums with the best of them," smiled Penelope. "I just don't know where I'm headed right now; maybe I'll still be here in a month, maybe I won't, but to take a page from Erma-Lee's book... changes, they are a-coming."

"Yeah, sure sounds like something she'd say. Are you sure? If you decide in a month from now you want it, I'm sorry to say it'll be too late."

"I understand," said Penelope.

"I can't say if I'll offer it to Erma-Lee or not. I need some time to think about it. But whatever happens, I want you to know I believe in you. You're a hard worker, and that promises you an endless amount of possibilities. Dedication and hard work are what it takes to reach your goals, and I believe you'll succeed in whatever you decide to do."

Standing up again, he walked around his desk and rested his hand on her shoulder. Giving it a small squeeze, he said, "now why don't you go ahead and take the rest of the night off?"

"Absolutely not!" she said, standing back up. "I still need to clean the coffee makers and take out the trash."

"Well, what are you standing around for? Go get it done!" He yelled but smirked as he made his way back to his chair.

Finishing up much sooner than she expected, all that was left was to lock up and count down the drawers.

Less than half an hour before closing, Erma-Lee turned to her and said, "now you get on home, girl, I can lock up."

Feeling confident Marty needed to see Erma-Lee do just that, Penelope decided she'd take her up on the offer. Happy to be going home early, she was glad she'd remembered to fill her coffee before breaking down the machines. She took one last look around, grabbed her stuff, and headed out.

On the way home, only a few miles from the store, she heard sirens. She couldn't tell which direction they were coming from, but a quick glance in the mirror told her they weren't right behind her. She turned up her tunes and continued the rest of the drive home.

Finally, arriving at her apartment, all she wanted was a warm bowl of soup and a hot bath. Turning off the engine, she looked up and noticed a light was on in her apartment. She pulled out her cell and called Baylee, but there was no answer. Confident she hadn't left any lights on when she'd come home to shower, she continued to sit and contemplate what to do.

The smart thing would be to call the detective who'd given her his card. But the faster thing was to check it out for herself. She climbed out, walked around, and popped the back open to her Jeep. Lifting the carpet, she seized the tire iron and quietly closed the door.

She held the tire iron over her shoulder like a baseball bat, because she wanted to be ready in case someone came running at her.

She headed up the stairs and tried to position herself as close to the wall as possible. Testing the knob, she slowly turned it. Locked? Thinking it was a good sign, she took out her key and unlocked the door.

Chapter 9

Penelope opened the door, stepped into the apartment, and was instantly blasted by music and someone singing a little off-key. Knowing the voice, she dropped the tire iron to the floor and walked in.

A thump in her feet and vibration in her chest made her wonder why the neighbors hadn't complained yet. Or maybe they had, and the cops were already on their way.

She located the remote to the stereo and turned down The Rolling Stones while Baylee walked in from the kitchen, singing her heart out.

"Hey, you're killing my buzz, dude. Turn it back up, I love this song. Come on, sing with me, you know you want to." Baylee pulled Penelope into the middle of the room, spilling half her beer in the process. "Remember when our moms use to listen to this, and we'd all sing and dance?"

"Yeah, I remember," Penelope said, smiling at the memory of so long ago. "Those were good times, weren't they?"

"Hell yeah, they were the best. So, come on, grab a beer, and join me."

"Looks like you have a head start on me," Penelope said, grabbing Baylee's beer and taking a swig.

"I said grab a beer, I didn't say grab mine."

"Well, you should be more specific next time, huh?" Laughing, Penelope walked to the kitchen, grabbed two beers, and handed one over to Baylee.

"Just so you know, you almost scared me to death. I thought someone else was in the apartment. When I pulled up, I saw the light on, and I was sure I'd turned them all off when I left," said Penelope.

"Well, someone is in the apartment, silly, me. Wait! You thought someone was in here, and you just walked in?" Reaching over, she grabbed the remote for the stereo. "What's wrong with you? What if it had been Derrick?" Baylee pushed the button and silenced the music.

"Geeze, relax, I had it covered." Penelope walked back to the front door, bent down and picked up the tire iron, waving it around she said, "See?"

"No, I don't see. All he would've had to do was take it away and use it on you. You really need to be more careful."

"Okay, Mom, tell me something else I need to know," teased Penelope.

"Fine, I will. This weekend I'm taking you gun shopping at Midwest Gun. Lucky for you, I can teach you everything you need to know, and I can get some target practice in at the same time," Baylee said.

"Whoa, whoa, slow your roll; you know how I feel about guns!" Frowning at Baylee, she continued, "You know I haven't picked one up since… that day." She trailed off, lost in her own thoughts.

Baylee snapped her fingers, trying to get Penelope's attention, and went on, "Will you at least think about getting some pepper spray? I'd feel better knowing you had something just in case. You know my father always told me, 'It's better to have your gun and not need it, than to not have it, and wish you did."

Hitting the button and turning the music back up, Penelope grabbed Baylee's arm, pulled her into a twirl, and said, "No promises, but I'll think about it."

"Well, go shake your ass on into the kitchen because I cooked us a light dinner."

"Awe, Bay, you didn't have to do that, but I'm so glad you did. It smells delish." Lifting the foil off the Pyrex dish, Penelope sniffed the scent rising from the Salmon and wild rice.

"Let's dig in. I thought I'd be nice since I have to work a double shift tonight. I have to make up the time I missed, you know. God forbid I get any special treatment, because what would people think?" Baylee laughed because she knew it was true. Anytime she did anything extra, whether it was good or bad, it all came back to her last name and her father's money or prestige.

"You think you'll be all right here by yourself?" Baylee questioned.

"I'll be fine, even though I'll admit it will be strange being here alone." Penelope hadn't realized how hungry she was until she looked down and noticed more than half of her food was gone.

"I think you missed your true calling," said Penelope, stuffing another bite into her mouth.

"Watch it," Baylee teased. "Don't say that too loud, my mom might hear. She always wanted me to go to culinary school, as she did. I enjoy cooking, but it isn't my passion. You know? My passion is to help people to make a difference in someone's life. That's why I went to medical school."

Through a mouth full of food, Penelope replied, "You could save them with food." Finally, swallowing, she smiled, "People gotta eat."

"Let my mom feed them; I'm good with that." Baylee stood and started cleaning up.

"Leave it, I'll get it later," Penelope told her.

Inhaling sharply, Baylee sighed. "You know I can't do that. Oh, how many times I've thought that I wish I could."

Penelope only smiled and hugged her friend.

Once the kitchen was clean and leftovers were Saran-wrapped, they chatted until it was time for Baylee to leave for work.

Hours later, feeling unsettled, Penelope knew she needed some rest. But first, she had to double-check all the windows and doors, making sure everything was locked uptight.

Finally, she climbed under the covers but was unable to turn off her mind. She kept thinking about what Baylee had said earlier about passion. She knew she needed to figure out what she was passionate about, it sure as hell wasn't being an electrician at the factory. No matter how much she enjoyed working at the station, she didn't feel it was where she was supposed to be either.

She closed her eyes and tried to make herself go to sleep, but the more she tried, the less it seemed to be working. Checking the clock for the hundredth time, she decided it was no use. She wasn't falling asleep so, she might as well get up and climbed out of bed.

When she stepped into the hallway, she thought maybe a cup of warm milk would help. So, off to the kitchen, she went. While the milk was heating up in the microwave, she noticed her purse sitting on the counter. Moving it over closer, she started pulling everything out. How had she let it get so disorganized, she thought? There were receipts, gum wrappers, and something she wasn't quite sure about.

Then she saw the card the nurse had given her at the hospital. Holding it in her hand, she decided it was time to make a list of her own. Baylee would be so proud, she thought. She opened a drawer, dug for a notebook and pen, and carried them both back to the bedroom. Forgetting all about the milk she'd left in the microwave. She climbed back into bed and started on her list.

She inspected the card for more information and wrote down the name Dr. Grace Wyatt, who was a psychiatrist specializing in abuse. The card also listed a website, so Penelope reached for her laptop sitting on the nightstand and quickly pulled up the site. She read how everything was private, confidential. You could choose to have either individual or group therapy.

After she finished her list of possible life goals and passions, she decided to make another column to show steps in reaching those goals. Feeling she'd started in the right direction; she closed the laptop and notebook. She reached for the bottle of water and pain pills on her nightstand. After swallowing a couple, she laid back and quickly fell asleep.

Later she woke to music playing, and instinctively she reached out and hit snooze on her alarm clock. Slowly realizing music had woken her, she froze. Her alarm had never been set to music. Penelope knew she always set it on the loudest, most annoying beep setting it had. Reaching over, she turned on the light and saw someone had mounted her MP3 player to her clock. Staring at it, trying to wake up, she was caught off guard when the music started playing again.

The song was eerie, a guy's voice sang about a spell. She wanted to know what he was saying, so she let it continue. Listening carefully, she realized the song was about the singer wanting to make someone his. Repeating himself several times, I love you. Not being able to stand hearing it anymore, she pulled the MP3 player off of the clock and threw it to the floor. Silence fell over the room, and all she could hear was the sound of her own breathing and the hum of the laptop still lying beside her on the bed.

How had it happened, she thought? Could Baylee have hooked it up the other day while she'd been cleaning? But if that were true, why hadn't it played music yesterday morning?

Dazed from the lack of sleep, she climbed out of bed and went in search of Baylee. It didn't take long to realize she was alone in the apartment.

What should she do? The thoughts kept swirling in her mind.

Grabbing her phone from her purse, she started to call Baylee but remembered she had to work a double shift. She decided to call the only other person she could think of, Detective Black. He'd told her to call if anything seemed unusual.

She looked through her contacts for his number, but couldn't seem to find him. She remembered she'd added it, so where could it be? She finally gave up and located his business card from her wallet.

Dialing she second-guessed her decision, and when the phone started to ring, she almost hung up.

"Black here," he answered, sounding half asleep or perhaps distracted.

"This is Penelope Williams. I'm not sure if you remember me?"

"I do, yes. What can I do for you? Has something else happened? Did Mr. Williams show up?"

"No," Penelope answered, now wanting to crawl into a hole. She was so embarrassed. How was she going to explain all of this without sounding crazy and paranoid? "I'm calling because you told me if anything seemed off, to call you. I had a strange thing happen this morning, and I'd really appreciate some advice."

"No problem, I'm good at giving advice. How about I head over to your place, and then you can explain everything so we can decide from there the best course of action."

"Um, there's no need for you to come all the way here. I shouldn't have bothered you," said Penelope.

"It's no bother, really. I actually live in the same apartment complex as you do but on the opposite side. It will only take me a few minutes to get there, but keep the doors locked until I arrive," he said, ending the call.

Penelope stood in her bedroom with nothing more than a tee-shirt on, she decided she better hurry and get dressed. She knew since he lived so close, he would be here soon. She had to go to work as soon as he left, she decided she might as well go ahead and get ready for the day.

She took a couple of pain pills and hoped they'd take effect quickly, so she could get dressed without being in too much pain. She pulled a pair of clean jeans from her dresser and slid them on, then picked a sweater from her closet. As she put a knit stocking cap over her head, she heard a knock on the door. Hurrying to open it, she stopped and remembered to check the peephole. Satisfied it was him, she opened the door.

"Thanks for coming over like this. I bet you don't get many calls at this hour."

"Actually, you might be surprised, but I've only been home a couple of hours. So, tell me everything, I'm here to help."

She relayed all that had happened only moments before.

"You said it didn't play music yesterday morning? Are you positive? I'm not trying to discredit you, but haven't you been taking some pretty strong meds lately? Could it be you just didn't notice?" He walked around the apartment, checked all the windows, then opened the sliding glass door, and stepped out onto the small deck.

"I'm telling you, I'm positive," then poured water into the coffeepot. She set it in place and hit start. "Plus, the song it was playing, I didn't put on my MP3 player. I don't know how he did it, but I'm sure it was Derrick."

Still standing on the patio, he bent over and picked something up from the floor. "Where's the MP3 player now? Can I take a look at it?" he asked, closing the door and locking it behind him.

"Sure, let me go grab it. I left it on my bedroom floor." Making her way towards her room, she said, "I put a cup on the kitchen counter for you if you'd like some coffee. It's fresh."

"Sounds great," he said, as he leaned on her bedroom doorway.

Looking over at him, a chill ran up her spine. When he leaned on the door casing, it had sparked a memory from not long ago. She shook her head to clear the thought, stood up, and handed over the music player.

Their fingers touched slightly during the exchange. Penelope felt her heartbeat quicken. She immediately pulled back from the contact but looked up into his face, and their eyes locked for a long moment.

Then, saying nothing, she walked past him, straight to the kitchen.

Following her, he spotted the mug she'd mentioned. While pouring himself a cup, he spoke, as if to clear the air.

"Did I do something to offend you?" he asked. Leaning back against the counter, he took his first sip.

"No, of course not, why would you ask?" Penelope told him.

"I'm a detective, you know. I pick up on these things." He smiled, and for the first time, she noticed he had dimples.

Feeling her face start to flush, and not wanting it to get worse, she rushed to explain.

"It's not you; it's me," she began.

"Oh, here we go; the whole it's-not-you thing," he said, with another smile.

Penelope laughed without meaning to or even realizing it. "Give me a second to explain," she said. "A few minutes ago, in the bedroom, when you were leaning against the doorframe. It took me back to a darker time in my life. I guess it all left me a little, edgy."

"Oh, I'm sorry. I didn't realize," Black said.

"How could you? It's fine, really. Sorry, I forgot to ask, would you like any cream or sugar?"

"No thanks, I take mine black, like my name. I'm not a complicated guy." Again, the dimple appeared as he smiled. "Now let's see what's on this," he said, turning it on and scrolling through the contents.

"What's wrong? Did you find something?" she asked, noticing that he continued to raise his left eyebrow every few seconds.

"Oh, no, sorry, I was just surprised to see you have such a wide array of music on here. But you say that the song you heard was not something you downloaded?"

"No, I didn't. I like Marilyn Manson's music. Well, some of it anyway. But I know I didn't download that particular song, and I never set it to wake me up to music."

"And you did change the locks?"

"Yes, well, Baylee had it done. But, it's not the music that worries me. It's how he managed to get in to dock it and set it as my alarm."

"I have to admit I'm not sure how it happened yet. But like I said, figuring out things is what I do."

113

Penelope started gathering up things she needed for work and explained she only had a few minutes before she needed to leave.

"If you don't mind, I'd like to take the MP3 player with me and give it to my tech guy at the station. Maybe he can find something useful on it. I'll let you know as soon as I find anything out."

"Sounds good," Penelope said, pulling her coat and scarf on.

"One last question before I leave. Do you smoke?" He asked, pouring the remainder of the coffee down the sink he placed the cup in the dishwasher.

"No, but Derrick smoked two packs a day. Why?" she asked.

"It might be something I want to look into. I'll let you get to work, and I'll call if I hear anything. Have a good rest of your day, ma'am."

"Please, call me Penelope or Pen, all my friends do," she said, walking out and locking the door behind her.

"Okay, Penelope, it is then. You can call me Black if you like, or if you prefer to keep this strictly by the book, call me Detective Black." Chuckling, he continued, "I'll walk you out and make sure you get to your vehicle safely."

"Thanks," Penelope told him. She climbed into her Jeep, locked her doors, and gave him a thumbs up to let him know it was fine for him to leave.

The day at the factory seemed to drag on, and she thought for sure it was never going to end. Two of her guys had called in sick, which left her shorthanded. With no one else able to perform the job, she was left handling the work of three people. The lack of sleep and a pounding headache did not help her mood.

Finally, able to clock out, she was running short on time to get to the gas station. Knowing Marty hated when his girls were late, she stepped on the gas, hoping to make up a little time.

Going a little faster than she realized, something caught her attention from the corner of her eye. Turning her head slightly, she glanced into the back seat to see what it was. She froze immediately, and all the fear came rushing back.

Then hearing the sound of a blaring horn, she turned her attention back to the road and screamed, "Oh my God!"

Chapter 10

Penelope slowly opened her eyes. The last thing she remembered was hearing a horn and finding herself in the wrong lane, heading straight for another car. She tried to piece together what had happened, but the details were coming back fuzzy.

Her head was throbbing, so she reached up and patted it gently, then let her hand fall back into her lap. She noticed her fingers were covered in blood and assumed she'd hit her head on the steering wheel. Turning her head carefully, she looked out the side window and tried to see exactly where she was.

It looked like she'd slid about ten feet off the road. She'd hoped no other cars were involved but then noticed a tiny car not far from her. She only hoped whoever was in it was okay and not injured.

Hearing sirens in the distance, she realized someone must have called 9-1-1. With nothing left to do but wait, Penelope decided to lean back in her seat and rest her eyes.

Back at the fire station, having heard the accident over the radio, Baylee didn't think much of it. After all, responding to them was her job. But once she arrived on the scene, she noticed the Jeep looked a lot like Penelope's. Jumping out of the ambulance, Baylee felt she couldn't run fast enough, fearing her friend's life depended on her.

Finally, reaching the vehicle, the first thing Baylee saw was blood on Penelope's face. Reaching for the handle to open the door, she soon realized it wasn't budging. It was either locked or damaged from the accident.

So, she used her fist, banged on the window and yelled, "Unlock the door, Penelope, so I can help you."

With no response and the possibility Penelope could be unconscious, Baylee wasted no time. She pulled her dispatch microphone off her collar, and hammered it on the window, shattering it instantly.

Ignoring the broken glass, Baylee leaned in, hit the unlock button, and opened the door. Resting her fingers on Penelope's throat, she felt a strong pulse. After counting the beats, Baylee looked up from her watch and straight into Penelope's eyes.

"How are you feeling," Baylee asked?

"Baylee? How are you here, where am I? I hit my head and have a killer headache," Penelope replied. Lifting her hand up, she noticed tiny squares of glass.

"Really, Bay? Did you have to break my window?" she asked.

"Yes, I really did. I pounded on the glass and yelled, but you didn't respond. What was I supposed to do, wait and see?"

"I guess not," Penelope said, and tried to smile but failed miserably. She sat up straighter and attempted to nudge Baylee out of her way.

"No, you don't, you stay put until I have a chance to look you over. There might be internal injuries you're not aware of, and it's better to err on the side of caution," Baylee told her.

"Nope, no internal injuries here," Penelope said, trying to move again. "I think I'm okay. It's only my head that hurts. Give me a couple aspirin, and I'll be good to go."

"Well, seeing how I'm the paramedic and you're not. I think I'll be the one to make the call. Now sit still! Why are you trying to make my job harder?" said Baylee.

Penelope looked up at her friend, feeling like an ungrateful fool, she said. "I'm sorry, I'm not trying to make things harder for you. I promise I won't move again until you tell me it's okay."

Moments later, Baylee's partner ran up carrying a red duffle bag. "Hey, Baylee, how's it going, do you need anything?"

"No, I'm good here. How do the passengers in the other vehicle look?" asked Baylee.

"I came over to let you know I've called for backup since we can't carry three at a time. By the looks of mine, I assumed yours would need to go in too," he said.

"Probably, wouldn't hurt. At least for observation, the patient has a pretty deep gash above the right eye," said Baylee.

Knowing they were talking about her; Penelope couldn't help herself and spoke up. "I'm fine, it's just a scratch. I have to get to work, Marty will wonder where I am."

Baylee looked at her, without saying a word, shook her head, and took a couple steps away so Penelope wouldn't be able to continue to overhear.

But sitting still and waiting for Baylee was becoming harder every second. All Penelope wanted to do was jump up and run over to the other vehicle and make sure everyone would be all right.

Baylee finally came back after talking to her partner. She immediately started checking Penelope's vitals, flashing a light in her eyes, making sure they dilated properly. She kept asking, on a pain scale from 1 to 10, where would you say your pain level is, waiting for Penelope to respond each time.

While Baylee continued to poke and prod, Penelope asked, "Can you please tell me about the family in the other car? I thought I overheard something about a child being hurt, is that true? Please tell me something, I don't want to be responsible for hurting a kid," cried Penelope.

Baylee looked at her and shook her head. "You know I can't tell you. Patient confidentiality still applies even out here. I wish I could; I really do, but there isn't any way around it. The only thing you should be worried about right now is the police officer heading this way."

Great! Why did things keep going from bad to worse, Penelope thought? Why couldn't she catch a break?

"Ma'am," tipping his hat as he spoke, "I'm officer Davis, I need to see your license, registration, and ask you a few questions."

"All right," said Penelope, opening the armrest storage compartment and handing over the information he'd requested. She noticed he looked sick, his face was flushed, his eyes swollen, and bloodshot. His nose looked raw, and she assumed it was from blowing it all day.

"Thank you, Mrs. Williams, and sorry that I'm a little under the weather today." Excusing himself to blow his nose, he followed up with, "So, what had you so distracted that it caused you to cross the center line and almost hit another vehicle head-on? If you hadn't swerved in time, this could have had a very different outcome."

Suddenly remembering what had happened to cause the accident, she said in an anxious tone, "You have to help me find it!" Pushing Baylee out of the way, she attempted to turn around and climb into the backseat.

Pulling his gun from his holster, Officer Davis yelled, "Remain in your seat, and keep your hands where I can see them."

"No, you don't understand, I can't just sit here, I need to find..." she said, trailing off, unable to finish her sentence when the Officer pulled her from her vehicle.

"Excuse me, Officer," Baylee spoke up. "Maybe I could help deflate this situation."

"And how do you plan on doing that? Didn't you just arrive on the scene?"

"Yes sir, I did, but I'm also Penelope's best friend, and I think I might be able to help."

"All right, let's move this over to my squad car, then I'll listen to what you both have to say."

Turning to Penelope, he asked, "Mrs. Williams, do you understand the reason I pulled you from your vehicle? As an officer, I can't take a chance whether you have a weapon of some sort in your vehicle or on your person."

Acting like a crazy person probably didn't help him think otherwise, she realized. "I'm sorry, you thought I might have a weapon. It never even occurred to me."

He directed them both to his patrol car. Then he opened the back door and motioned them inside. "You're not under arrest at this time, it's just cold out, and my car is warm," he told them with a faint smile, pulling another Kleenex from his pocket and getting into the front seat.

Penelope and Baylee nodded their heads in agreement and climbed in.

"If we can start from the beginning, it might make all of this go a lot smoother," said the officer.

"I'll start," said Baylee. "Penelope's husband, Derrick, is crazy. I'm talking needs meds, padded-room kind of crazy."

Looking at Baylee through his rearview mirror, he nodded for her to continue.

"I mean, look at her," Baylee told him.

His eyes slid over in Penelope's direction, and again he nodded.

"I'm going to assume, seeing as you're an officer of the law, that you've seen this kind of thing before and can tell at first glance that her face didn't get this way, just from today's car accident," Baylee said, pointing to Penelope's face.

"I see your point, both old and new bruises," Officer Davis responded.

"Right."

"Baylee," Penelope whispered, nudging her friend in the leg and giving her a shut-the-hell-up look. "Ignore my friend here, I'll tell you what you need to know," said Penelope.

"Okay, start with, where were you headed?" he asked.

"I was on my way to my second job and running a little late because a couple of my guys at the factory didn't come in today, and I was delayed leaving."

"So, you were probably speeding, is that what you are saying?" the officer asked.

"Um, I don't know. Is it going in your report?" Penelope asked.

"No promises, one way or the other just yet. Give me a little more information, and we'll see where we end up," he told her.

"I might have been speeding a little, but here's what happened. While I was driving, something caught my attention out of the corner of my eye in the rearview mirror. So, I very carefully turned and glanced in the backseat to see what it was."

"So, you're saying you were distracted?"

"Please, just listen, then maybe you'll understand. I couldn't believe what I was seeing! There on the seat, tied with a big, bright pink ribbon was a lock of my hair." Visibly shaking, she continued. "I was so shocked, I forgot I was still driving until I heard a car horn, and that's the last thing I remember."

"Oh my God, you poor thing!" Baylee hugged her friend and forgot about the Officer still watching them from his mirror. "I can't imagine how you felt once you realized what it was."

"If you could, then you'd know why I literally ran off the road and caused the accident."

Baylee pulled Penelope tighter and whispered in her ear, "This does prove Derrick's still around."

"Excuse me, ladies, am I missing something?" the officer asked.

Baylee piped up, "That's an understatement."

"Baylee, quit," said Penelope. "After all, the Officer came in on the tail end of this."

"Well, we can hope it will be the end of it," Baylee stated, matter-of-factly.

"Officer? Sorry, I didn't catch your last name," asked Penelope.

"It's Davis," he said, "Officer Davis. Now can you explain what's going on here?" he asked.

"I'm sorry, Officer, it's a very long story. But the detective on the case is Don Black. Do you know him?" asked Penelope.

"Yes, I do," he replied.

"If you would contact him, he could explain it all to you. So, could we walk back to my Jeep and see if we can find what frightened me?" Penelope pleaded.

"I'm sorry, ma'am, but that's not possible. I've already contacted a removal service, and they're in route as we speak to retrieve both vehicles."

"What? I'm almost sure I can get it back on the road again as it is," Penelope told him.

"What about the broken window?" asked Baylee.

"The window isn't a huge deal. I can turn the heat on full blast until I can get someone out to replace the glass."

"Really? Not a big deal, huh?" Baylee said, raising her eyebrow. "Earlier, you would have thought I torched your Jeep, the way you acted when you saw the broken glass."

"I've had time to think about it, and it could be replaced pretty quickly."

Turning around, they watched through the patrol car window as a wrecker pulled up, and a big burly man climbed out.

Opening his door, Officer Davis said, "I'll be right back." He stepped out of his patrol car and walked over to greet the man.

Moments later, the big guy hooked up her baby and dragged it back up to the road. In her rather anxious state, Penelope almost giggled, because he reminded her of the Jolly green giant, from the package of green beans in her freezer. But although the giant part fit, the jolly part apparently didn't.

She took control of herself and considered precisely how she was going to sweet talk this guy into letting her keep her Jeep out of impound. She watched as he went to retrieve the other vehicle. Then glanced over and saw Officer Davis was now talking to someone on his cell phone.

Penelope turned to Baylee, "My phone's in my Jeep. Could you call Marty's Gas for me and let them know what's going on."

"Sure, I can do that," said Baylee.

Pointing out the window, Penelope said, "I'm going to try and talk the Giant over there, into not towing my Jeep. What do you think my chances are?"

"Honestly?" She leaned around Penelope to get a good look, then replied, "Slim to none." Then she pulled her phone out of her pocket to make the call.

Penelope tried to get Officer Davis's attention by knocking on the window, but whoever he was talking to, distracted him from her tapping. She gave up, leaned back in the seat, and eavesdropped on Baylee's call, just as it ended.

"Great!" said Baylee, "I'll let her know. Thanks, I'm sure she'll appreciate it." Hanging up, she relayed to Penelope that Marty wasn't upset with her and was even giving her the rest of the week off with pay.

"Wow, that's really generous of him. I'm almost speechless. How did you get him to do it?" Maybe things are starting to turn around for me, her lips curved, almost into a smile.

"Isn't it about time? You are the best employee he's ever had, I'm sure," said Baylee.

"I need to ask you a question. It might sound strange, but please, humor me. Did you mount my MP3 player to my alarm clock last night?" Penelope asked.

"No, I didn't. Why do you ask? Did something else happen I don't know about?" With a concerned look, she waited until Penelope had finished explaining everything that had occurred before she responded. "Now, it makes sense you'd ask since I cleaned the apartment the other day."

"Honestly, I'd really hoped it was you because the alternative scares the hell out of me. At least Detective Black lives close. I called him, and he insisted on stopping by. I just hope he's able to get back to me soon if he finds something out," Penelope said.

"I'm sure he will, but what else am I missing here?" questioned Baylee.

"What do you mean? I've told you everything. I can't think of anything I left out."

"I'm not sure. I can't put my finger on it. Something seemed different when you were telling me about what happened this morning. Oh well, I'm sure it will come to me later," Baylee said.

"Different, how?" asked Penelope.

"I don't know yet. Well, look who just showed up?" said Baylee, pointing to the car out the window.

Turning to see, Penelope watched Detective Black slide out of his car and walk toward them.

Opening her door, Detective Black said, "Are you all right?" At the nod of her head, he motioned for them to exit the car. "Let's go over and talk to Officer Davis."

"Why don't you two go ahead. I need to be getting back to my partner and see if he needs any help," Baylee said. She leaned over, gave Penelope a gentle hug, and asked, "Are you sure you don't want to go in and get checked out just to be safe? The accident on top of everything else worries me."

"No, I'm okay, I promise."

"Okay then, I'll see you after my shift." Baylee turned and walked back to where her partner was.

Detective Black asked if Penelope was ready, then escorted her over to where Officer Davis and the tow truck driver were standing.

"Hey, Red, how's it going, staying warm?" Detective Black asked the other man.

"It's going pretty good. I love this weather, and all the ice out here sure keeps me hopping, and my bills paid," Red replied.

"Can't ask for more than that, can you?" said Black.

Officer Davis turned to the Detective and said, "Looks like you have everything under control here, so I'm going to take off." He dropped Penelope's keys into the Detective's hand, shook the other, and turned to go.

"Thanks for calling me. I'll send you a copy of the report once I'm through," Black told him.

"Sounds good, Detective," Officer Davis replied. Stopping by his car door, he yelled back to Penelope. "Good luck, Mrs. Williams. I hope things work out." He climbed back into his patrol car and took off.

Turning her attention back to the conversation between the Detective and tow truck driver, Red, Penelope wondered what they were laughing about.

Detective Black crouched down, looked under her Jeep when he asked Red, "Has it been inspected for safety? We wouldn't want anything to happen to her on the way home."

"Yes sir, I checked it myself. It's a tough old bird. It would take more than a little run off the road, to take this baby out of commission. I have one myself and believe me when I say, this model can take a licking. I beat the hell out of mine, and she hasn't failed me yet," Red answered.

Walking alongside Black, he spoke. "She really is a beauty. Someone must really love her. Sure is a shame about the dent, though." He patted the fender and made his way back towards his wrecker.

Penelope watched Red flip a lever and unlatch her precious baby. Climbing back into the cab, he prepared to tow the other car, then turned back and yelled, "See you around the next bend Detective."

Shocked, Penelope turned towards Detective Black.

"It's all yours," he said, dropping the keys into her hand.

"Thanks so much for this. How did you do it? I thought for sure they wouldn't let me have him," Penelope said.

"Red and I go way back, so as long as it was safe, I knew it wouldn't be a problem to let you have it. Now tell me exactly what happened."

While explaining everything to him, fear gripped her once again, by the mere thought Derrick might still be around, just waiting to finish what he'd started.

Once he'd heard it all, Detective Black asked her to show him exactly where she had seen the ribbon. He explained once they found it, he'd take it in and have it analyzed. If they were lucky, it might give them a clue about what Derrick was up to.

Penelope climbed into the back of the Jeep, hoping it might have fallen under the seat during the accident. She slid her hand under and tried to locate it. But no luck, it wasn't there. Yet, with the Detective searching in the front, she was sure they would find it eventually.

Finally, she saw something between the seat and the passenger door. "I think I might have found it," she called out.

"Don't touch it!" He ordered, and pulled an evidence bag out of his front pocket, he used a pair of tweezers picked it up and placed it in the bag.

"Now we have something new to go on. It could take a few days to get the results, but I'll let you know what we find out."

"I don't want to seem ungrateful, and you've done so much for me already, but is there any way you could find out what happened to the people in the car I hit? I'd feel better if I knew they were going to be okay."

"I'll see what I can do, but no promises. Since we're all through here, how about I follow you home?"

"Okay. Give me a few minutes to go tell Baylee, I'm leaving." She located Baylee and told her the Detective would make sure she got home safe.

Chapter 11

True to his word, Detective Black followed her home and made sure she was safely inside before he left.

Penelope still felt some of the after-effects of the accident and thought it would be a good idea to take a couple more of her pain pills. She hadn't taken any since that morning before work.

It was still early, so she decided to take a step toward those changes she'd been thinking about. Pulling a business card out of her purse, she dialed the number and waited for someone to answer.

"Hello, you've reached Choices Make Changes. This is Grace, how may I help you?"

"Hi, I'm not exactly sure how to do this," said Penelope.

"That's all right dear; how about we start with your name?"

"My name is Penelope Williams."

"It's nice to meet you, Penelope. My name is Grace Price, and I'm a counselor here. Anything you say is completely confidential. We here at CMC believe it must be our top priority. Once people realize it's a safe environment, it's usually much easier for them to open up. We think building trust is essential to the healing process, as well as personal growth."

"I'm only looking for a little information at this point. I've done some research online about your organization; I understand you have individual and group therapy. Would I be allowed to sit in on a group session and observe, or is it required to speak?"

"Absolutely, you can sit in on any of our group sessions, you're not required to speak. Our goal here is to be your support system; you'll never be pressured to do anything you're uncomfortable with. We have a meeting starting in a couple hours if you'd like to attend?"

"Thanks, I might. I appreciate you taking the time to talk to me and answering some of my questions," Penelope said.

"Anytime, dear. That's why we're here. Let me give you a little information, in case you want to come by. All of our group meetings are held in the Comfort Hall. It's located on the north side of the building. There's a sign above the entrance, but the easiest way to find it is to look for a bright purple door, purple being the color representing domestic violence survivors. You really can't miss it. It was a pleasure speaking with you, and I look forward to meeting you in person."

"Thanks, you too," replied Penelope as she hung up the phone.

Feeling positive about moving forward with her plan to make some changes in her life, she decided to call Baylee. She wanted to let her know where she'd be this afternoon and give her a head's up that she might be a little late getting home.

Baylee was glad to hear from her, and after promising to be careful, Penelope hung up and went to take a quick shower and redo her bandages. Then, she went to the kitchen for a small bite to eat. She decided to warm up leftovers; they seemed her best option, and after opening the microwave, she discovered the cup of milk she'd forgotten about the night before. Replacing the cup with her bowl, she hit start.

Proud of herself for taking the first step, she decided to do something she ordinarily wouldn't. Checking the clock, she knew she had enough time to make a quick stop before the meeting.

Penelope placed her empty bowl in the dishwasher, grabbed her keys, carefully slid on her coat, and pulled the door tightly closed, making sure to lock it behind her. She was excited to see where this new chapter in her life would go.

Driving to her first destination, she thought about how her life had turned out. She felt she was finally starting to make the right moves. She knew her life wasn't suddenly going to turn around. But she could say for the first time, she was feeling somewhat optimistic.

Penelope pulled into the familiar lot, quickly parked, and walked into the bank. Her cheeks heated while she passed Miss Boon's office. She walked to the next open teller with cash in hand to correct her accounts. She could've made a scene, but everyone knew where the money had come from, and she wasn't proud of that fact.

Penelope knew Baylee's family had a lot of money, but it didn't mean Baylee did. Aware her friend wanted to make it on her own, Penelope felt guilty. She suspected Baylee would now have to ask her father for help this month.

Penelope had promised to pay her back, but Baylee shrugged it off and said their friendship was worth more to her than money. Baylee insisted she could handle her dad, and he wouldn't be a problem. Even if she didn't mean to, Baylee could lay on a guilt trip with the best of them when necessary.

Walking out of the bank, Penelope felt a little better, knowing the issue was cleared up for now. She looked across the parking lot, and her eyes focused on the self-defense studio Baylee had pointed out the other day. Not wanting to chicken out, she stepped off the curb and walked directly over.

Penelope pulled the door wide open. She suddenly knew; this was where she was supposed to be.

Penelope didn't know what to expect, so she stood in the doorway, with her hand still on the knob in case she changed her mind and wanted a quick escape. Her first thought was the place was a lot larger than it appeared from the outside.

It was covered with tan and green mats, with a few splashes of red here and there. The mats covered most of the floor and all of the walls. Somehow, it looked more like an Army recruiting station than a self-defense training facility. But what did she know?

Noticing a display of pamphlets on a counter, she headed that way. Reading through some of the information, she discovered they had several different types of classes. Each instructor apparently specialized in their own area of expertise.

She heard footsteps approaching and lifted her head, instantly captivated by ocean blue eyes. This had to be the "Mr. Beefcake," Baylee had talked about.

"Hi there, and welcome. I thought I'd come over, introduce myself, and see if you had any questions," he said with a smile.

She could see why Baylee considered him some serious eye candy. She guessed he was over six feet tall, with strawberry blond hair and a body straight out of a magazine. It was no wonder Baylee had been impressed seeing him from across the parking lot the other day.

Feeling like a shy schoolgirl, she wondered if she'd been staring at him long. Had he been holding his hand out this whole time?

Quickly she shook his hand and forced herself to focus on his words instead of his looks. Realizing she'd missed half of what he'd said already, she responded, "I'm so sorry, could you repeat part of that. I didn't quite catch it all. You've owned this facility for three years?"

"I have, yes. How about I give you a tour of the place, then I can answer any questions you have along the way."

"Sounds good, but can we make it a quick tour? I have a meeting I can't miss. So, I won't be able to stay long," she said.

"That's not a problem; follow me. We'll start in the back and work our way up front." He led the way to the rear of the building, pointing out things along the way. "Let me show you our locker room first. We have separate facilities for males and females, along with showers. We also have a large steam room, which everyone shares," he said, pointing to his right.

"Believe me when I tell you, the steam room will be your best friend after a long training session. Over in this corner is where we work with the weights." Circling back towards the front, he continued. "And finally, the majority of our space is here in the main arena, where I'm sure you've noticed all the mats."

"Yes, I was impressed by how well-arranged everything was. Thank you for the tour. I'm definitely interested in taking some classes. When does the next session start?"

"That depends on whether you want private or group sessions? Let me give you my card, along with some information on both, then you can make a more informed decision. Again, my name is Emerson Burns, and I'm the owner of Inner Strength. If you have any questions, please feel free to give me a call."

She said goodbye and walked back to her Jeep, amazed at everything she'd just seen. The atmosphere was friendly, but more importantly, the instructors were apparently excellent at their jobs. Which was by far the most important thing.

She sent Baylee a quick text of her whereabouts, then realized it was later than she thought. Not wanting to make a bad first impression, she threw Dime into high gear and quickly but carefully made her way to Choices Make Changes.

Arriving there with only minutes to spare, Penelope got out of the Jeep and hurried toward the building. Grace had been right about not being able to miss the large purple door. She pulled it open, walked through, and bumped straight into a girl about her age.

"I'm so sorry, I really should pay closer attention to where I'm going," said Penelope.

"No, you're fine. I shouldn't be standing right in front of the door. I don't believe we've met, you must be new here," the girl said.

"Yes, this is my first time here," Penelope replied.

"Let me be the first one to welcome you," she said, grabbing Penelope's hand in a firm handshake. "I'm Abby."

"Hi Abby, I'm Penelope. Nice to meet you."

"Follow me, Penelope, and I'll show you the ropes. I've been attending meetings here for around six months, and almost everyone here is really great. Of course, there are a few, not so nice ones, but I'll let you form your own opinion," Abby told her, smiling.

As they continued down the hall, Penelope noticed a few people standing around chatting, who stopped mid-sentence as she passed. It made her wonder if they were the "others" Abby had been talking about.

Counting doors as Abby led the way, Penelope wanted to make sure she'd be able to find her own way next time. But once they arrived at the room, she realized it was also the only purple interior door.

Inside, Penelope saw a group of very comfortable chairs placed in a large circle. Fortunately, they looked nothing like the chairs she remembered from her school days.

Pointing to the only red chair in the room, Abby said, "That's where Grace sits; she's the lady who leads the group. We've got a couple minutes before the meeting starts, so why don't we drop our stuff here and go grab some cookies."

Following Abby's lead, she grabbed a bottle of water and one of the cookies Abby had bragged about. While looking for a napkin, Penelope heard someone announce the meeting was about to begin.

Spotting an older lady handing out pencils, she leaned in and asked Abby if it was Grace.

"Yup sure is. You're going to love her, wait and see," said Abby.

They went back to where they had dropped their stuff, took their seats, and waited for the meeting to begin.

Grace greeted more people as they came in, giving encouraging words here and there. When Grace leaned in to hug someone, Penelope noticed hot pink toenails peek out from underneath her long blue dress.

Initially, Grace reminded Penelope of a little old grandmother, or maybe a librarian, but those bright pink toenails told another story. Penelope decided there might be more to Grace than meets the eye.

She wanted to go introduce herself but decided it was best to wait until after the meeting. Then a moment of fear struck her. Why had a man walked into the room? She hadn't realized men would be attending the meetings. She wasn't sure she liked having a mixed group.

Surprised by the number of people walking in, it made her wonder if there really were that many people going through the same type of thing she was? But she decided to wait and see how the meeting went, so she made herself comfortable and quietly listened in.

"We have a few new people joining us today, I'd like to welcome you. My name is Grace Price. I'll start by giving you a little information about myself. I'm one of the counselors here, and for those in need, my door is always open. I have twenty years' experience and have my master's in psychology. I also, on occasion, have been a consultant for the Chicago Police Department with a few cases."

Grace handed papers to the girl sitting next to her, and they were passed around the room.

"Please help yourselves to the refreshments as we begin. For our newcomers, we have only one rule, but it's the most important. What's said here stays here. If you prefer to stay silent and observe, that's fine, but everything has to stay completely confidential," Grace told them.

People started nodding in agreement.

"Here at Choices Make Changes, we want to be a safe haven. Now, who would like to go first?"

A lady with hollowed eyes stood on the other side of the circle. "I think I'm being watched," she whispered, her eyes nervously darting around the room.

Penelope sat there and watched the tears flow down the woman's cheeks as she continued.

"I might be going crazy."

Handing her a tissue, Grace asked, "Why do you think you're being watched, Allie?"

Dabbing at her eyes, she continued, "I don't know. That's part of the problem. I just keep having a feeling someone is watching me."

"I understand your fear, and we're all here to support you," said Grace.

"I know it sounds crazy, but is it possible that Bobby is coming back for me?" asked Allie.

"You know it can't be Bobby, Allie. He can't hurt you anymore. Do you remember why?" Grace spoke in hushed tones encouraging her to sort it out.

"I remember, and I know dead people can't come back. I thought once he was gone, once it was all over, I'd feel better. So why don't I feel better? I don't know what to do with myself. I don't know how to make my own decisions. Bobby always told me what to do. Will you help me, Grace? Will you tell me what to do, and help me feel better?" Waiting for a reply, she took her seat.

"Allie dear, give yourself some time. What you're experiencing is normal, we all get complacent. Sometimes even awful things can become habits. You are used to living under a microscope, always having to ask permission, being told what to do, watching everything you said. This is all new to you. It's only been a couple months."

"So, you don't think I'm crazy?"

"I know you're not crazy. And I promise as you keep moving forward, things will get better. Look towards the future, and see all the possibilities it may hold."

Penelope just sat there, curious about what the girl she'd just heard had gone through. She understood what Allie said about being watched. She had the same feeling.

Moments later, Abby stood up. She had been so friendly to Penelope when she'd first arrived. Hoping to make more of a real connection with her, Penelope listened in.

"I wanted to share what's been going on with me these last few days. It doesn't seem to matter where I am, whether at home, work, or sitting in my car. I feel anxious all the time." Stuffing cookies in her mouth, she continued.

"I don't know what he'll do if he catches me here. As some of you already know, he thinks I'm at my sister's house while he's working. He has no idea I come to a support group."

"We understand you're scared, and you must be careful. It's nice of your sister to drop you off. It shows how much she cares about you and she doesn't want you to miss a meeting," said Grace.

"Yes, and I love her too. She's the best thing in my life, well, her and my nieces. She told me I might be setting a bad example for them. Do you think it's true? I'd hate to think someday, they'd put up with someone treating them this way."

"I don't believe you're doing that. I think you're doing the best you can. Kids see more than parents think. Yes, they probably have seen you go through some rough times. But they also see you're not giving up, and that's a powerful thing. Life is hard, people make bad decisions all the time, but it's persistence that wins in the end," Grace assured her.

"It's so hard listening day in and day out, how worthless I am. How much more weight can I gain? Is it even possible for me to still be a woman as fat as I am? Between the daily abuse and ridicule, sometimes it seems too much," Abby said, nearly in tears.

Penelope watched as several people stood and hugged her. Others gave words of encouragement. One person said, "You're stronger than you think." Another told her she would have her back if she needed it.

Penelope sat there, taking it all in, realizing, they might really understand what she was going through. Once the group hug was over, and Abby sat down, Penelope squeezed her hand to show support.

After listening to several others speak, even the man who was having issues at work with his female boss. Penelope stood, hardly realizing what she was about to do. Looking out over the room, she cleared her throat and began.

"Hi, my name is Penelope, this is my first time here. It's overwhelming to see and hear so many of you going through something similar to myself. I wanted to introduce myself, and let you know, I'm here to support you. I think we all need someone in our lives who understand us and helps us through the tough times. Don't you? My best friend Baylee, helps whenever she can, and I don't know where I'd be without her, but some things she just can't understand, because she's never been there, but you guys have, so you get it." She took her seat, and Abby squeezed her hand.

Penelope continued to listen as others stood and spoke. Slowly, she came to understand this might really be a safe haven. She felt some of the weight of the last few days slip away.

Once the meeting was over, and people started to leave, Penelope made her way over to Grace to introduce herself.

Before she could say a word, the older lady smiled and pulled her into a hug. Wincing, from the still bruised ribs, she inhaled the sweet scent surrounding Grace.

"I was surprised you dared to stand and speak your first time here."

"I didn't want anyone to think I didn't understand what they were going through," said Penelope.

Grace gathered up all the papers and notes she'd taken during the meeting and said, "Penelope dear, we try not to judge here, we've all been through our share of hard times. Some of us have made it through to the other side and come to encourage others. To show them, it can be done. While others, sadly, are still amid the abuse and are trying to gather enough courage to leave. Unfortunately, some never make it out. Some give up and quit coming to the meetings, thinking it's easier to live with it than fight."

"How do you know, they just quit coming?" questioned Penelope.

"I try to check up on them, but I know if the abuser finds out, then they will be punished severely or worse. Did you get the paper I handed out tonight?"

"Yes, I did thank you. I noticed it had the dates and times of the next meetings. I also saw you put your personal number on it."

"I was glad to see you and several other people I had spoken to, showed up tonight. Please remember, I'm always available if you need me. Although I must say I am not the police, and if you are in danger, please call them first. Let's say I'm more of an emotional emergency contact."

"Thanks, I'll make sure to put your number in my phone. I'll need it when I have my next mental breakdown." Smiling, Penelope told Grace goodbye and slipped out the door.

Reaching her Jeep, she stopped briefly to send Baylee a quick text, letting her know she was on her way home.

While driving, she thought about all the people she'd met and their stories. She was starting to feel proud of herself for the choices she was beginning to make. It was a strange feeling. She couldn't remember the last time she'd been proud of herself, if ever.

Walking up the steps to her apartment, Penelope pulled out her keys but stopped short of the door. There was a bright pink sticky note she couldn't miss stuck to it. It read: Peek-a-boo I still see you!

She pulled the note from the door and quickly turned around, feeling she was being watched. She didn't see anyone, but it didn't mean Derrick wasn't out there, somewhere watching her. Pressing her back against the door, without delay, she used her key and hurried inside, hoping he wasn't already in there.

Chapter 12

The following day after working at the factory, Penelope stood in the shower covered in soap and wondered why her phone kept ringing. What could be so important to make someone call five times in a row? Whoever it was, they were certainly determined to get a hold of her. Reaching for a towel, she carefully stepped out and went in search of her phone.

She found it on her bed and tried to answer, but whoever it was had already hung up. Frustrated, she carried it back to the bathroom and sat it on the toilet lid, so she could reach it when it inevitably rang again. She stepped back into the shower and had barely pulled the curtain closed when it started back up.

She flung open the curtain and answered in an annoyed voice, "Who is this?"

"Hello, is Penelope Williams available?"

"This is Penelope," she answered, thinking it better not be a sales call or someone's head was going to roll.

"Hello again, this is Emerson Burns, from Inner Strength. I was calling to let you know I have an opening tonight for the self-defense class. A couple I had scheduled has decided to go a different route, so they canceled their standing appointments. So, if you and your friend would like to take their time slot, I have it open."

"Oh, that's great, what time? I need to call my friend and see if it works for her."

"It's at six o'clock. I understand its short notice, but if you'd like, I can save you the spot."

"Sounds perfect, how about I'll call you back only if the time doesn't work. Hopefully, you won't hear from me, and I'll see you at six."

"Okay, sounds good, hope to see you then," said Emerson.

Hanging up the phone and pulling the shower curtain closed, Penelope smiled. Her plan to change her life seemed to be coming together so far, she only hoped everything else would work out as well.

She dried off, then texted Baylee to her call her back. Instead of waiting around for the call, Penelope decided she'd go ahead and get dressed, and maybe even start some of her overdue laundry.

Later, Penelope stood in the kitchen, cutting up carrots and potatoes for dinner when her phone finally rang. Checking the number, she answered, "Hey, Bay, I was hoping it was you. Guess what? The hottie from the defense class called. He had a cancellation and wanted to know if we were interested. It starts tonight at six, are you up for it?"

"Absolutely! I'm so glad you're doing this. I'll be home in about an hour. I'll shower, change, and head down to your place."

"Okay, sounds good. I'll have dinner ready, so we can eat before we go." Wiping her hands on a dishtowel, she hung up and got back to cutting up the veggies.

Almost an hour later, Penelope heard the water turn on upstairs. Good, Baylee must be home, and in the shower, she thought. It was strange how she could hear everything that went on up there, from the shower turning on to the toilet being flushed. Of course, there were those awkward times when Baylee brought home a man. At least, Baylee always gave her a head's up, saying she needed her fix of sweets, and it was time for her to go hunt up some eye candy.

Noticing the light blinking on her phone, she picked it up and realized she had a new voicemail. While she waited for the message to start, she heard the dryer signal her laundry was done.

Penelope held the phone to her ear and walked over to remove the dry clothes and start a new load. Music started playing on the voicemail, and she froze. Standing there holding a pillowcase in her hands, she couldn't pull her ear away from the phone. Suddenly, the music cut out, and a familiar voice broke in, "You're mine forever, Penelope."

At that moment, something touched her shoulder. Screaming, she dropped the phone, spun around, and instinctively put her hands up to defend herself.

"Whoa, whoa, it's me," Baylee said, holding her hands up in a sign of surrender.

"Oh my God, Bay," Penelope said, and pulled her into a hug, refusing to let herself cry, "Is it ever going to stop?"

"What happened?" asked Baylee.

Penelope took a deep breath, knelt down, and started tossing clean sheets out of the basket.

Baylee feared her friend had finally reached her breaking point. She took Penelope's hands and pulled her back up. "What are you doing? Let's go sit down so you can tell me what happened."

Pulling out of Baylee's grasp, she leaned back down and continued her search in the basket. "I'm looking for my cell, it had a message on it. I must have dropped it when you startled me."

"Well then, let me help you. What was the message that had you so scared?" Baylee asked as she dug through the basket. Locating it, she held it up like a prize.

Penelope snatched the phone out of her hands, "I'm going to delete it. I can't let Derrick keep doing this to me!" She opened it and was about to push delete when Baylee snatched the phone out of her hands.

"No, you can't. We need to call the police, this could be evidence," Baylee said.

"Don't you get it? I don't care anymore," Penelope's words poured out in a rush. "I don't want to wait for the police; they never do anything! They can't even find him. Derrick is the one in control. He's the one with all the power. He knows it, and so do I. I've played by his rules, but what has it gotten me?"

Falling to the floor, she pulled the scarf off her head. "This…this is what I got for trying to play by his rules, and I just can't do it anymore!" She finally broke down into tears as she rubbed her hand across her scalp.

Moving to her side, Baylee sat down and pulled Penelope into her arms. "I'm not going to say I know how you feel. Because we both know I don't. But I've seen a real difference in you lately. You've stopped second-guessing yourself all the time, and you're making better choices. This is just a little hiccup. I know you can get through it." She pulled Penelope back so she could look into her eyes and said, "You are so much more than you think you are, and I believe in you."

Baylee stood, reached down, and brushed the tears off Penelope's cheek. "Come on, we can make a plan while we eat. Whatever you made for dinner smells delicious," Baylee said.

She went into the kitchen, and Penelope followed. As Baylee loaded their plates with food, she kept the conversation going.

"By the way, I heard some good news today. The people from the other car involved in the accident are all okay. They were released from the hospital and doing fine. But that's all I'm going to be able to tell you, so don't ask. After we eat, I'll call the Detective about the message you just got, and then we can go to our first class on butt-kicking."

As they ate, Penelope told Baylee about the meeting at Choices Make Changes (CMC), and all the different people she'd met. She explained how Grace explained she would be an emotional emergency contact, so she'd added Grace's number to her phone right away.

"I think I'm going to like CMC and being around others who have been through the same thing or something similar. Being around people who are trying to better themselves seems like a great way to start my own personal journey," said Penelope.

"I'm so happy you've found somewhere you think will help. And from the way you talk about Grace, she seems like a smart lady, who will do whatever it takes to help you reach your goals," said Baylee.

Once they were finished eating, Penelope put the leftovers in the fridge, as Baylee put the last dish in the dishwasher.

"Thanks, I feel a little better since we talked it all out. You're right, of course. Giving up only lets Derrick win," Penelope told her.

Pulling her yoga pants out of the dryer, Penelope wiggled out of her pants and slid them on. She dug through the laundry basket in search of a sweatshirt. Finding one she liked with a four-leaf clover, she tugged it on over her tank top and was almost ready to go.

Penelope glanced at her watch and realized they only minutes before it was time to leave. Hurrying into her bedroom, she snagged her tennis shoes from her closet and was tying the last one when Baylee came in.

"Are you ready to go, Lucky?" Baylee teased, pointing at her shirt.

"Yeah, hold on a sec," Penelope said with a smile. "Don't you need to run upstairs and grab anything before we leave?"

"Nope, I'm ready to go." Baylee pulled down her sweats a little to show Penelope she had yoga pants on underneath. "I'm pretty excited we get to do this together," Baylee said as she did a little happy dance. "Plus, my gym bags by the door."

"Well, we may be stinky, sweaty, and miserable after the workout. But I'm happy for you, but we both know you're only excited about the possibility that 'Mr. Beefcake' could be our instructor," Penelope said, laughing.

"Well, duh, why else would I be excited? I even wore my sexy workout clothes," Baylee confessed.

"Of course, you did." Penelope rolled her eyes to show Baylee how crazy she thought she was. "No one but you would get all decked out to go to a self-defense class, in hopes of snagging the instructor."

"Got to keep my options open, you never know when 'The One' is going to show up. It's better to always look your best just in case." Baylee did a hair flip and turned to go.

"Hey, are you going to call Detective Black," asked Penelope.

"I thought you might want to since I noticed a wee bit of a spark between you two the other day."

"Are you serious? A spark? I think attracting a guy is the last thing I need to do right now, don't you," Penelope asked.

"I didn't say you needed to start a relationship with him. Did I?" Baylee tilted her head, smiled, and batted her eyelashes. "But he could be a nice little distraction, something to take your mind off things. It doesn't always have to be serious, you know. It could be something light and friendly."

"Wow," was all Penelope could say. She tugged the knit cap on her head, motioned for Baylee to follow her to the door, and locked it behind them.

Penelope let Baylee drive and attempted to call Detective Black while they were on their way, but the call went straight to voicemail. She left him a vague message, saying she'd be back home later, and asked if he'd return her call. She didn't say why she'd be gone or mention the class she was about to walk into. She didn't want to sound like she was doing it because she couldn't take care of herself, although the Detective was already aware of what had happened since he was the first on the scene the night of the attack.

Baylee parked beside a little yellow car and shut off the engine. "Are you ready to do this?"

"Nope, I didn't think there would be this many people here, did you?" Penelope said in a hesitant voice.

"Stop it! It will be fine, let's just go in," Baylee told her.

"You can say that because you're in really good shape. You won't be the one to look like a fool. You know I get winded just walking up the stairs to your apartment."

"Again, stop it! You'll do fine, maybe since it's our first time they will take it easy on us, and let us mostly observe," said Baylee.

"Do you really think so? Wow, that makes me feel a little better, I'm a good observer," Penelope said.

"Seriously? GET OUT! It's time to go in. You're not going to learn anything sitting out here. Remember why we're taking classes, we are here so you can learn to kick butt, and how to stick up for yourself. Now let's go."

"I know I'm lucky I have you to push me. But just remember, after this, you won't be able to push me around much longer." Laughing, Penelope climbed out of the car, and they headed inside.

"Laugh now, Pen, my Dear, because I guarantee you won't be laughing once I get my hands on you." Baylee tried to be serious, but couldn't hold in her laughter.

Still laughing, the wind caught the door as Baylee tried to close it behind them. Finally getting it to shut, she turned and stood in disbelief as the man she'd admired the other day in the parking lot, stood only a few feet away, talking to someone at the desk. She looked over at Penelope to get her reaction, but she only rolled her eyes, which wouldn't be any help, Baylee thought.

He wore a pair of shorts and a tank top with large red letters across the chest that read: Inner Strength. Smaller words underneath said, 'It's what's on the inside that counts.' She'd definitely have to buy one of those shirts, she thought. She loved her morning runs, and she was sure they had that in common, by the look of his calf muscles.

Her temperature started rising, and a bead of sweat formed on her brow, as he turned, saw them and walked in their direction. She found herself staring directly into his eyes.

Baylee had seen blue eyes before, but these were different. They were a "tragic blue"; they made you sit and wonder what all he'd seen, and what things he'd been through.

Blinking quickly, she focused on his hair, it was shorter than she usually liked. But it looked so soft, it made her want to run her fingers through it.

Suddenly she felt her arm being pulled and looked over at Penelope with a confused look on her face, "What?"

"I was just about to ask you the same thing. Are you feeling okay?" asked Penelope. "You look a little flushed."

"I'm fine, cut it out," Baylee whispered, as he got closer.

"Hello, Penelope, it's good to see you again." Turning to Baylee, he continued, "I'm Emerson Burns, the owner of Inner

Strength. You must be the friend Penelope mentioned earlier. I'm glad you were able to make it tonight."

"I'm Baylee," she managed to get the words out.

Not seeming to notice Baylee's awkwardness, he smiled and said, "Nice to meet you, Baylee. How about we go ahead and get started. I like to accomplish as much as possible in the first session."

Following him along the back wall to the mats, Penelope whispered to Baylee, "What was that all about? I don't think I've ever seen you act that way."

"Nothing, I'm fine, no big deal. I hope I didn't make a complete fool of myself."

"Oh, no. I'm sure he barely noticed," Penelope smiled, as she took the towel, he offered each of them.

They started with stretches, and once they were warmed up, he asked who was ready to try something new. Still a little dazed, Baylee nudged Penelope.

Penelope walked over but was taken off guard when he grabbed her and put her in a headlock. He told her to try to get free, so he could analyze how much training she was going to need.

Baylee jumped up instantly when she saw the look of horror on Penelope's face. She was confident that in Penelope's mind, she was back in the apartment, where Derrick had enjoyed torturing her.

The instructor was distracted by the lack of Penelope's response, so Baylee ran up behind him and took stance. She knew he'd be hard to bring down since he was over 6 feet tall and built like no one she'd ever encountered, but Penelope was in distress. All she could think of was setting her free.

Her adrenaline was running high, so first, she kicked him in the back of his knee, which took him off balance. Then she attempted her version of a roundhouse kick. Placing her hands on the floor, she pushed off, locking her ankles around his neck and swung herself counter clockwise, landing on the mats in a somewhat graceful roll. Not taking a chance to let him get the upper hand, she rounded on him and placed her heel over his groin.

Emerson lay on the floor and stared up at the tiny girl who had managed to bring him down. Without saying a word, he slowly moved Baylee's foot from his crotch and stood. Then he went over and kneeled down to check on Penelope.

"Are you all right?" he questioned. "I think your friend here went a little crazy and attacked us." Still seeing no response from her, he looked over at Baylee.

"What's going on here, and why won't she answer any of my questions?" Getting more frustrated by the second, he stood up and walked over to Baylee. "Are you going to answer me?"

"Sure, I'll answer you, even though you're the most unprofessional person I've ever met. Give me a minute to check on Pen, then I'll answer anything you want. After that, we'll walk out of here and promise to never come back."

Emerson sat and watched Baylee slowly and carefully make her way over to her friend, who was now rolled into a ball. She reminded him of a wounded animal, or perhaps an injured soldier. Why hadn't he noticed before the session started that she was damaged somehow? He'd seen enough when he'd been in the military, and knew the signs to look for. But he'd been distracted by her friend, instead of keeping his focus on Penelope.

Baylee sat on the mat with Penelope and pulled her close, telling her everything would be okay, and she was there for her. But Penelope just sat there, not responding or even reacting to Baylee. She'd never seen her so traumatized.

Usually, all she had to do was talk to Pen, and she'd come around.

Looking over her shoulder, she saw Emerson watching them. "Find me her purse and bring it over here, quickly," Baylee said.

"I didn't mean to scare her. I was trying to determine how much training she would need. I could have warned her first, but I usually get a more accurate reading when it's a surprise. Is she going to be okay?"

"I told you, I'd explain it all after I take care of her. So go get her purse. Now!" Baylee demanded.

Shocked by her tone, he wasn't used to being talked to that way by a woman. Only one had ever even tried. He stood up, went over to the benches, and retrieved the purse. Then handed it over to Baylee.

"Now, could you go get her some water, please. I need to make a call." Baylee opened the purse, but not wanting to waste time going through it, she dumped the contents onto the floor. Once she located Penelope's phone, she knew there was a number in it for a woman from the center named Grace. She only hoped she'd be able to help.

Locating the name in the contact list, she quickly pushed the button and prayed the woman would hurry and answer.

"Hello, this is Grace, how may I help you?"

"Thank God you answered, you don't know me, but you know my friend Penelope, and I need your help," said Baylee.

"Oh, dear, of course, I'll help. Tell me what's happened," said Grace.

Baylee explained what had taken place and the state Penelope was in now. "I've never seen her like this, could you please tell me what to do?"

"Where are you? I'll come straight there. I believe she might need a sedative, which I can bring along. Once she's relaxed, I'll be able to talk to her, and hopefully, resolve the situation."

Baylee told her the location of Inner Strength and was surprised when Grace said she knew exactly where it was located. She wasn't far and would be there in a few minutes.

Hanging up, Baylee continued to rock her friend and stare down Emerson, who had done this to her.

She spoke to Penelope in quiet, even tones, and never took her eyes off the front door. Emerson tried to talk to her a few times; once, he'd brought the water for Penelope, but she felt there was nothing more to say.

A short time later, the facility door finally opened, she watched a tiny older lady walk in. She wore a long blue dress with printed snowmen all over it, and her gray hair was pulled back into a messy bun. Baylee waved her over to where she and Penelope were sitting.

Emerson jumped up to escort Grace over to the two women.

It seemed to Baylee that Emerson and Grace seem to know each other, which struck her as odd. But she pushed it to the back of her mind and turned her focus back to Penelope.

Grace crouched down and turned Penelope's head so she could see into her eyes. Then, using a small flashlight, she checked for proper pupil dilation. Pulling a syringe from her apron pocket, Grace told Penelope there would be a slight pinch, then slid the needle into her arm.

Baylee watched and realized she hadn't noticed Grace wearing an apron when she'd walked in. It reminded her of her own grandmother a little because she'd always worn an apron over her clothes, too. Baylee couldn't remember a time when she'd ever seen her without one.

"Thank you for coming, I really appreciate it, I was so worried," Baylee said.

"It's fine, it's what I do," Grace stated with a smile. "Now if you'll help me get her to my car, I need to take her home and get her to her bed. I know her address. You can check on her later."

Surprised, Baylee wasn't sure how she felt about letting a stranger take her friend anywhere, even if she did remind her of her own grandma.

"It's fine, sweetie, I promise to take excellent care of her," Grace said. "I love how you're so protective. You must be Baylee, she thinks the world of you, and has stated, she isn't sure where she'd be if it weren't for you."

"Yes, I'm Baylee; we've been friends forever. I feel the same about her. I don't know you personally, but Penelope has spoken highly of you; I guess I'm okay with you taking her home. But I have to ask, how are you planning to get her inside once you arrive?"

"No worries, my dear, I'll manage," Grace replied.

Baylee pulled Penelope into a standing position, but before she could take a step, Emerson Burns came over and started to pick Penelope up.

"Wait a minute!" Baylee said to him. "What the hell do you think you're doing?"

"It's all right, dear," laying her hand on Baylee's forearm, Grace broke in. "I know Emerson; let him carry her to my car."

"When he was the one who freaked her out and put her in this state?" Baylee growled.

"I'm so sorry," Emerson said. "I didn't realize…"

Grace cut off his words of apology. "Whatever happened wasn't done in malice, I'm sure. Let's not deal with this now; what's important is getting her home and in bed. Wouldn't you both agree?"

Baylee nodded and allowed Emerson to pick Penelope up and carry her out the front door, following close behind.

"I could have handled it myself. I've taken care of Pen for years," Baylee said under her breath, but Grace overheard.

Grace smiled and gently laid her hand on Baylee's shoulder. "He really isn't a bad guy; you should give him a chance. He made a mistake. He knows that now, but he really is a gentle soul. He has his own demons; he fights daily. He would never have harmed Penelope intentionally."

Now that they were outside, Grace turned from Baylee and watched Emerson open the passenger door and carefully place Penelope inside. Then Grace climbed into the driver's seat, started up the old black caddy, backed out of the parking spot, and was gone before Baylee could say another word.

Turning around, she realized Emerson wasn't outside any longer. Not sure what she was supposed to do now, Baylee stood there for several minutes. Finally, she decided to go back inside, gather up all their things and see what the jerk had to say for himself. And maybe even give him another piece of her mind.

Chapter 13

Emerson Burns had gone back inside Inner Strength and knew Baylee wouldn't be far behind. When she walked in, she started poking her well-manicured finger into his chest.

He thought it was funny, but kept a straight face. He probably should've been listening to what Baylee was saying, but realized she wasn't ready to hear his response, or how badly he felt about the entire situation.

He nodded his head, as though agreeing with whatever it was she was saying, while he thought back to when she'd managed to take him to the floor. It had been quite impressive; this tiny girl who stood before him could take him down. How had she managed it, he thought, she couldn't be taller than five feet.

"How tall are you?" he asked abruptly, forgetting he was supposed to be listening to her, instead of analyzing what had happened earlier.

"Excuse me?" Baylee stopped her tirade to say. "I'm talking about how irresponsible you are as a business owner, and you have the audacity to interrupt me and ask how tall I am? How does that possibly even fit into this conversation?"

It made her even angrier that he apparently hadn't been listening to a word she'd said. She turned, walked away, and started gathering up her and Penelope's things.

But then Baylee changed her mind, circled back around, and continue her thought. "Please, enlighten me," she said in a superior manner. "Explain how my height has anything to do with the fact you scared the hell out of my best friend, who only came here because I talked her into it."

Emerson couldn't stop himself from smiling. There was something about this girl and the way she stood up for her friend. It reminded him of the camaraderie he'd felt for his fellow soldiers, while in the army. A couple of those buddies worked for him now as instructors.

"So, let me see if I have this straight, you're the reason Penelope came in and checked us out? It was you who pressured her into learning some self-defense moves?" Emerson asked.

"Yes, I explained all this to you earlier, but you decided what I had to say wasn't important enough for you to pay attention," Baylee insisted.

Ignoring her statement, he replied with one of his own. "But why did you talk her into coming here, when you could have taught her yourself? Apparently, you have had some substantial training. You didn't seem to have a problem taking me down," he said as he walked around the studio, picking up dirty towels and wiping down equipment.

"Don't walk away from me while I'm talking to you. Owner or not, you seem to need to learn a little thing called professionalism." Baylee was steaming and not going to let him just walk away. "How you've managed to keep this business up and running is beyond me," she finished with a final insult.

"Well, I guess it's a good thing you've promised to walk out and never to return. Then, there will be no need for you to worry about how I run my business, or anything else," Emerson said in an off-handed manner.

Baylee was furious she was being spoken to that way. She made a defiant hand gesture behind his back and walked over to the spot where she'd dumped Penelope's purse out on the floor.

Gathering up all the stuff, she quickly realized she had to carry not only her things but Penelope's too. Baylee thought she might have a travel bag out in her car, so she threw the pile back on the floor and headed outside to grab it.

Why did everything have to be so damn difficult, she thought? All she wanted to do was gather everything up and get the hell out of there. Was she asking too much?

Pushing through the door, she popped the trunk on her car and started searching through all the stuff looking for her bag. It was bright pink, so you'd think it would stick out like a sore thumb. Pink was not her favorite color by any means, but the bag was pretty bling, and it had been free with one of her recent purchases. She couldn't bear to throw it out.

Finally, seeing something shiny, she leaned in a little further and found it. Dragging it out, she slammed the trunk closed and turned to go back in. She told herself she'd go in, grab the stuff, and get out.

When Baylee reached the door and pulled the handle, it didn't open. She tried again and it still wouldn't budge. Looking through the glass, she could see Emerson leaning on the check-in counter. She pounded on the door to signal it must be jammed, but he only smiled and pointed up.

Baylee looked up, but couldn't see what he had pointed at. She took a couple steps back, and it hit her like a slap in the face. The jerk had waited for her to step outside, and once she was distracted, he'd locked the doors and turned the closed sign on.

"Is this really how you want to play it?" Baylee yelled as she kicked the door even harder. "You coward, let me in. Are you afraid I'll take you down again?" When he didn't respond, she quickly changed tactics. "Please, I don't even have my coat, and Penelope's things are in there too." She watched him as he pushed off the counter and thought to herself, "Got him!"

Ever so slowly, Emerson walked over to the door and placed his hand on the lock. "I'm sorry. We're closed for the night if you'd like to come back tomorrow during regular business hours?"

Baylee was tired of the game. "All right," she said. "Stop kidding around, I'm freezing out here." She pulled her hands into her sweatshirt and wrapped them around herself.

"I'm just trying to be a professional business owner, and it's way past closing time. Being the responsible person I am, I must make sure the building is secure before leaving for the night," he replied. He reached over and flipped a couple switches that turned off the lights.

Baylee watched him walk towards the back of the building, but she was sure he'd turn around any second and come back to open the door. Instead, he disappeared through a pair of swinging doors. She only had a moment to decide what to do, should she stand out here and freeze to death, get in her car and leave everything here, or run around back and hope he was exiting from the rear door.

Choosing the last option, she took off at full speed for the back, but took the last corner a little quicker than she should have. Unable to avoid a large patch of ice, she tried the only thing she could think of to keep herself from sliding face-first into the pavement. Her only option was to drop to her knees, and she regretted her decision almost immediately.

The gravel and ice cut through the thin material and dug itself into her skin. With no time to waste, she stood to locate the rear door. Quickly, she realized there wasn't one; she'd been tricked!

Well, two can play that game, she thought. She let out an ear-piercing scream and laid down on the ground. Counting to herself one, two, three, she looked up, just in time to see Emerson turn the same corner she had at full speed. Quickly, she closed her eyes.

He dropped to his knee and leaned over her. "Baylee, are you okay? I heard you scream." He felt sudden guilt. Why had he been so childish? "I'm so sorry! This is all my fault. If I would've just opened the door and let you get your stuff, none of this would've happened."

He could see the rip in her stretchy pants and the blood covering her knees. Emerson noticed she hadn't said a word since he got there and decided he should check for a possible head wound and other injuries. He pulled off his coat and rolled it into a ball, carefully lifting her head, he placed it under.

Baylee kept her eyes closed and listened to the sound of concern in his voice. The plan had worked perfectly, too perfectly, she thought. What was she supposed to do now? She hadn't taken the time to think her plan through, past getting him there.

Gently he slid his fingers across her scalp but didn't feel any bumps or abrasions. He thought of trying to shake her awake but restrained himself, not wanting to hurt her further. He had hoped she'd get in her car and drive away. In fact, when he'd looked out front, and she was no longer there, he'd thought his plan had worked. How was he supposed to know this crazy girl was going to run to the back of his building? Luckily for her, he'd heard her scream at the exact time he'd been locking up out front.

Emerson tried to decide if he should move her, it really was freezing out here. He was pretty sure she didn't have any broken bones but thought he'd better check her out to be on the safe side.

Emerson rubbed his hands together in an attempt to warm them up, then placed them high on her head. Feeling the occipital bone, he carefully and gently evaluated, as he slowly worked his way down toward her collarbone. Nothing felt broken or out of place, but he was out of practice. It had been a few years since he'd been in the Army.

Out in the field, a little medical training went a long way. He couldn't remember how many times he'd used what little skills he'd had when stuck in a foxhole with his men.

As Baylee lay on the ground, she knew she should open her eyes and explain what had really happened. But thought, why not see where this went. When the idea had first come to her, she'd been mad, her temperature had been soaring, but now things were different. She'd been on the ground for a while and was getting cold.

But when he placed his warm, soft hands on her neck, she almost melted. He was so gentle; it made her think back to the first time she'd seen him. But gentle wasn't what had come to mind then. A strong, powerful man, someone who liked to be in control, that's what she'd thought when she first laid eyes on him. This was a different side, a gentle side. It was a side she thought she could grow to like.

Emerson checked her right arm, then her left. Still not finding anything amiss, he continued on. Positioning his hands on her sides, he worked his way across her ribs, checking each one carefully. But with her bulky sweatshirt, he couldn't tell for sure. He asked himself, what was more important modesty or health? He slid his hands under her shirt, knowing she had a tank top on underneath. He'd seen it earlier while inside, he could even remember what it looked like. It was purple, with the word pink across it, which made no sense to him. He kept telling himself it had been the contradiction of word vs. color that had been the only reason he'd even noticed what she'd been wearing, but he knew it was much more than that.

Now, having direct access, he could feel each rib precisely. Taking his time, he couldn't help but notice how soft Baylee's skin was. He moved slowly towards her abdomen, she shivered, and once he'd reached her hips, she let out a soft moan.

Unable to take it any longer, Baylee accidentally had let a sound escape. Realizing she'd have to respond now, she opened her eyes and looked up at the man she'd been furious with earlier, but aroused by only moments ago.

Emerson's hands still rested on Baylee's hips when she slowly opened her eyes. Beautiful was the first thought that entered his mind. Shaking his head to clear it, he quietly asked, "How do you feel? I heard you scream, and once I ran back here, I found you on the ground."

Playing coy, she said in a confused, soft tone, "What happened, why am I so cold?" Taking her time, she made a slight attempt to sit up.

"Here, let me help you." Carefully he picked her up and carried her to the front of the building. "Let's get you inside where it's warm." Cradling her with one arm, Emerson unlocked the door and carried her straight to the back, pushing through the wide swinging doors.

She'd never been back there, so she wasn't sure what he had in mind when he stopped in front of a pair of tall frosted glass doors.

Gently, he laid her on a padded bench, "Hold on, a second. I'll be right back. Do you think you'll be okay by yourself?" he asked.

"Um, sure? What are you doing?" Baylee questioned.

He turned the corner and was back in less than a second.

"Can you walk?" he asked. At Baylee's nod, he took her hand and led her to the door. As he opened it, she realized it hadn't been frosted glass after all.

It was a steam room, and she couldn't think of a better way to warm up. Well, she could, but thought that was best left for now.

He guided her to a seat, handed her a towel, and found a place for himself to relax. "Are you feeling better yet? It shouldn't take long to warm you up."

What she felt was guilty. Emerson was being so kind, and she was taking full advantage of it. Well, he deserved it, she thought. After all, he'd started all of this. Baylee closed her eyes, leaned back against the wall, and told herself she had no reason to feel bad before she answered him.

"I'd love to have one of these in my apartment. I'm always cold, so it would really come in handy." She took a deep breath, closed her eyes, and relaxed a little further. A few minutes passed with total silence, then something poked her. Opening her left eye, she looked over at Emerson. "What? I was relaxing."

Emerson shook his head and said, "I don't think that's a good idea, what if you fall asleep. You might have a concussion."

"I'm fine, really. A girl needs her beauty rest sometime." Closing her eyes again, Baylee smiled.

"So, do you play the tough role with everyone, or am I the unlucky guy you picked to take down for today?" he asked.

"What you see is pretty much what you get!" Baylee admitted. "You see, I learned a long time ago to be myself, and to stop trying to be what other people think I should be. Except, of course, when it concerns my father."

"I get that, and I'm sorry I upset you, but you can be a bit rough on a guy." Emerson stood and walked to the opposite bench. Removing his shirt, he laid down and stretched out.

"I'm not usually that bad, but I had a good reason to get upset tonight, or don't you agree?" Opening her eyes, she unashamedly checked out his physique. It was much better than most of the guys she'd dated. Then she noticed a scar on his right side. She couldn't help but wonder how he'd gotten it but made no comment.

"I completely agree, you had every reason to be upset, although I think you could have at least tried to listen to my side. I didn't intend to scare your friend, and I was about to let her go when you decided to take control of the situation. Wouldn't you agree, maybe you could have handled it a little differently?"

"Perhaps, but you have no idea what Pen's been through or why she wanted to learn self-defense," Baylee said.

"You're right, I don't know, so how about you explain it to me. Earlier, you said you would answer my questions. But then, well, you know what happened."

Standing up, Baylee removed her sweatshirt, grabbed another towel for a pillow, laid down, and began telling him about Penelope's situation.

The conversation seemed to go on for hours, but when they finally walked out, Emerson looked at the clock and realized it had only been a little over an hour. He couldn't remember the last time he'd sat and had an actual real conversation with a woman. Actually, he could, but it still hurt to think about it even now, years later.

"Thanks for the steam, it really did warm me up, and I'm glad our conversation helped us both understand what happened." Baylee wiped herself off with a towel and threw it into the hamper sitting outside the room. "Now I need to find the bag that I went outside for. Then I really should be going," she said, picking up her sweatshirt.

Sidestepping her, he walked into the main gym area to the pile she'd thrown on the floor earlier. "I dropped it here when I carried you to the back."

"Thanks."

He stood and watched her toss everything in and zip it up. When she threw it over her shoulder, he noticed it also had the word "pink" across it.

"What's that look for?" Baylee asked.

Unaware he was making a face; he was a little surprised by the question. "Sorry, I just noticed you must have a thing for the color pink."

Tilting her head, wondering where that statement had come from, she said "No, actually I hate the color pink. Why would you assume that?"

He pointed to her bag and then to her tank top.

Baylee turned the bag around and instantly understood his confusion. Trying not to laugh, she shook her head. "Pink is the name of a company." Pulling her sweatshirt over her head, she slipped into her coat and walked toward the exit. She placed her hand on the door, pushed it open, turned back, and said, "Pink is the sister company of the lingerie store, Victoria's Secret. Maybe you've heard of it?"

Letting the door close behind her, she was still smiling when she pulled out of the parking lot to head home.

Chapter 14

Baylee unlocked Penelope's apartment and went inside, dropping the Pink bag along with her coat by the door. She wondered if Grace would still be there. But once Baylee turned the corner, she saw a note on the table. It said she'd given Penelope another sedative, and she should sleep peacefully through the night, but she'd be fine by morning. She asked Baylee to remind Penelope to call in and set up a private session.

Baylee put the note back on the table, then headed for the bedroom. The strong scent of cigarette smoke stopped her short of the partially closed door. She sniffed the air and tried to locate its source and wondered if perhaps there was a window open; maybe the smoke was drifting in.

She walked the apartment and checked the windows, but nothing seemed out of place, and all the windows were locked uptight. Still puzzled, she went back to check on Penelope. Pushing the bedroom door open a little further, she noticed the smell intensified.

Why does the place smell like smoke, she thought? Even when Derrick lived here, he smoked outside. Stepping over the threshold, she realized the smell was stronger in the bedroom than in any other part of the apartment. Was it possible Grace was a smoker? Baylee hadn't smelled it on her earlier. It was the only thing she could think of that made any sense.

Baylee didn't want to leave Penelope alone all night, so she decided to stay there. Slipping out of her shoes and sweatshirt, Baylee pulled the blankets back, climbed in beside Penelope, and laid her head down. Before she had a chance to close her eyes, she noticed a light on under the bathroom door.

She climbed out of bed and went to turn the light off. When she opened the door, a large cloud of smoke poured out. She immediately turned on the exhaust fan and watched it disappear. Then she noticed a cigarette floating in the toilet. Again, assuming it had been left by Grace, she flushed it and turned to go back to bed.

She located the TV remote along the way, and knowing Grace had given Penelope something to help her sleep, Baylee didn't think it would wake her if she kept the volume low.

It wasn't one of Baylee's best idea because hours later, she was still flipping through the channels and watching old reruns. Still wide awake and needing to get some sleep, she decided to try something else.

So, getting out of bed once again, she went to find the bag she'd left by the front door. Pulling things out, she grabbed her earbuds, sleep-mask, and her phone. With everything in hand, she stopped by the kitchen, took a drink of milk, and headed back to bed. She climbed back under the blankets, turned on her favorite playlist, put her earbuds in, and in moments drifted off to sleep.

Hours later, Penelope heard the buzz of her alarm and reached over to hit the snooze button. She snuggled back into her pillow, then noticed the sound of someone breathing. Sitting up, she turned and was shocked to see Baylee lying next to her.

Baylee had her eye mask on and earbuds in, so apparently, she hadn't been bothered by the alarm. Slowly remembering parts of what had happened the night before, Penelope couldn't recall how she'd gotten home and in bed. She assumed it had been Baylee who'd brought her, and thankful for the thoughtfulness, she decided she'd make coffee before waking her up.

Gently climbing out of bed, Penelope headed to the kitchen to start the coffee. Then, she grabbed her clothes for the day and went to the bathroom and took a quick shower. While she re-bandaged her wounds, she could smell the coffee was ready; so, she went to grab them both a cup.

Walking through the apartment in the early morning hours lately made her uneasy, but this morning the only thing on her mind was trying to remember exactly what had happened the night before.

Penelope poured two cups of coffee and went to wake Baylee. She wanted to let her know she had to be leaving for work as soon as she got dressed, and they needed to talk about what had happened the night before. Gently Pen pulled out one of Baylee's earbuds, then the other, she waited a split second to see if it would have any effect. When it didn't, she gave her a gentle nudge.

Getting no response, Penelope held the coffee close to Baylee's nose and nudged her a little harder than before. She finally heard a slight groan. Only one thing left to do, Penelope thought. She pinched the corner of Baylee's eye mask, pulled it up, then let it go, and it snapped back into place over Baylee's eye.

"Okay, I'm awake!" Baylee sat up quickly, not quite realizing where she was. Pulling off her eye mask, she mumbled, "Geez, I thought I was at the station. Is that coffee I smell?"

"Yes, it is, and you can have some if you get up and talk to me about last night, while I'm getting ready for work," Penelope said.

Peeling herself out of bed, Baylee walked to the bathroom while taking her first sip. "So, talk, I'm listening. I didn't get much sleep last night, so I'm going to be needing more of this," she said, pointing to her half-empty mug.

"I wanted to thank you for bringing me home last night," Penelope said while pulling on a thermal shirt.

"It wasn't me," Baylee told her. "I don't know how much you remember, but after you went comatose or whatever, and I couldn't get you to answer me; I called that lady, Grace. You said she was like your emotional 911, right? Well, she came right away, and she brought you home and put you to bed. Which reminds me, she left a note on the table. It said something about you calling and setting up a time for a private session. She must have finally seen what I've known for years; you need a lot of professional help."

"Grace was here and left a note? Oh my God, what happened last night? I'm a little fuzzy on the details." said Penelope.

"What's the last thing you remember," asked Baylee as she went to the kitchen, grabbed the pot of coffee, and brought it into the bedroom.

"I remember going to Inner Strength, and we started by doing stretches." Rubbing at her temples, she couldn't understand how she could lose a chunk of time, because as far as she knew, it had never happened before. "After that is where I'm having trouble remembering."

"At least you remember being there, right?" said Baylee. "You've been through a lot lately, so it's understandable if you have triggers."

"What do you mean by triggers? Baylee, what are you talking about? Exactly what happened last night?"

Baylee explained most of what happened but left out her own personal actions. No need for Penelope to know she'd also made a complete fool of herself, she thought.

Penelope pulled her beanie down over her head and said, "I'm so embarrassed. I can't believe I did that. Mr. Burns probably thinks I'm a crazy person. How am I ever going to go back there?"

"Don't worry about it. Emerson was actually pretty cool once I explained the situation, in my not so subtle way." Baylee took another sip of her coffee, walked over, and gave Penelope a hug. "It's okay, who's going to know? It is what it is; you can't change it now. So, you call Grace today; let her know how you're doing, and make that appointment. Then how about we do something proactive? Let's go gun shopping this weekend," Baylee said.

"Yeah, because giving a crazy person, a gun has always been a great idea," Penelope replied.

"Pen, you're not crazy. But even if you were, I'd understand, with everything you've been through. Now finish getting ready for work. We can talk later."

Baylee walked into the dining room, dumped all of Penelope's stuff out of her bag from the night before, and turned to go. "And, if you're lucky, maybe while we're out this weekend, I'll tell you what happened in the steam room with the yummy Emerson Burns. Now come relock the door, and I'll see you later," she chuckled, then walked out the door before Penelope could say a word.

Penelope locked the door and shook her head. She knew Baylee would fill her in later with all the juicy details. She returned the coffee pot to the kitchen, shoved all her stuff back into her purse Baylee had dumped, and walked to her room, with her third cup of coffee.

Suddenly, a knock sounded on the door. She assumed it was Baylee, and she'd forgotten something, so she rushed back to open it. Not bothering to check the peephole, she opened the door and was surprised to find Detective Black standing on the other side.

"Oh, hi. I thought you were Baylee forgetting something. She just ran upstairs," Penelope told him.

"Sorry to disappoint, but if you have a few minutes, I'd like to talk to you about a couple things. I got the voicemail you left me, and it sounded like you might have something you'd like to talk about, too," Detective Black said.

"Do you have new information about Derrick?" Opening the door wide, she said, "Please come in, would you like a cup of coffee?"

"Coffee sounds good, thanks." Following her into the kitchen, he laid her MP3 player on the counter. "I thought you might like this back since my tech guy is done with it."

"Please, tell me he found something," Penelope asked.

"Not much, unfortunately. My guy found Derrick's prints on it, but we both knew he would. We'd probably find his prints on everything in here. He did discover when the song was downloaded, and which site Derrick had used. But other than that, we don't have much to go on. I'm sorry, I know this isn't what you wanted to hear."

Penelope handed him a cup of coffee and refilled her own, knowing she really should slow down. Her nerves were already frazzled, and adding more caffeine probably wasn't a great idea.

"Did you find anything you could use from the lock of my hair we found?"

"Maybe, the lab told me the ribbon wasn't new. It had your DNA on it, along with his. But here's the interesting part; there was also an unknown substance on it," Black said.

"What does that mean?" Penelope asked.

"I'm not really sure. I have a few theories, but nothing concrete just yet."

"If you have a theory, I'd like to know what it is." Looking him straight in the eye, she leaned back against the counter.

"I'll be sure to tell you once I have a little more to go on," he said, giving her a look that said it wasn't going to be today. "What did you want to talk to me about? Your message was pretty vague."

Penelope pulled her phone from her pocket and signaled to him she needed just a second, "I saved a voicemail I want you to hear." She put the phone on speaker and pressed play. Once the message ended, Penelope waited for his response.

"We have a couple options. I can take your phone to my tech and see what he can find. But Derrick probably used a burner phone, so it won't help us. Option two isn't much better, but save the message and any other messages you get, and we can use it in court."

"Those are my options? Derrick is stalking me, and you can't do anything about it?" Penelope asked.

"You have your restraining order, and we are keeping a close eye on you. But unfortunately, the law as it stands, doesn't do much. It protects the stalker as much as the victim, and my hands are tied until the laws are changed." He walked over to the sink, rinsed his cup, and placed it in the dishwasher.

"If those are my options, then I guess I'll save the message and hope I live to see the day in court," Penelope said and stuffed the phone back into her pocket.

"Keep your chin up, and call me with anything new okay?" he said and turned to leave. "I'll be on my way. Thanks for the coffee,"

"I'll walk you out," she said.

He stopped, looked at her, and realized something had happened in the last couple of seconds. She seemed more guarded all of a sudden. "I'm sorry, did I miss something or offend you in some way?"

"You're very perceptive, and no, you didn't offend me. I was taken a little off guard when I saw you rinse out your cup. It seemed strange how you were comfortable enough to do that."

"Sorry, it's a habit. If I don't keep my place clean, who will? It didn't take me long to learn, little things make a big difference. After I got my first place, I had a huge pile of dirty dishes in the sink. The more I avoided it, the bigger it got. I ended up throwing all my dishes out and starting over," he laughed. "So now, when I'm done with something, it goes directly into the dishwasher. It seems to make my life much easier."

"I understand exactly what you're saying," said Penelope.

"Well, it looks like you're getting ready for work, so I'll be on my way."

"Yes, I need to hurry, or I'll be late," Penelope said. Picking up her coat and purse, she followed him out. After locking up, she put on her coat and headed to her Jeep. Knowing the Detective was watching her, she felt safe when she pulled out of her parking spot and headed to work.

The next couple of days were what Penelope thought now passed as normal. However, the fear of what Derrick might be planning was always in the back of her mind.

Chapter 15

Finally, on Saturday morning...

Baylee drove with Penelope the ten minutes it took to get to the city. They pulled into a parking garage, hailed a cab, and took off for the gun store.

"I love our big city, don't you, Pen? Shopping on the Magnificent Mile can't be beat," Baylee told her.

"I agree, but in all the blockbuster movies, it's Rodeo Drive that gets all the raves. As far as I'm concerned, California might as well be on the other side of the planet," Penelope stated.

"Believe me, I've been there, done that, and it's not as glamorous as the movies make it," Baylee said, tapping the glass separating them from the cab driver.

"We're locals," pointing to Penelope and herself. "So, how about you quit taking the scenic route, and take us where we need to go."

"Hey, lady, I'm just trying to make a living here," the driver answered.

"Well, make it on someone else's dime."

Moments later, the cabby jerked the car to the curb and stopped in front of the store. A red revolver with smoke snaking out the end hung above the door. Underneath it read, Midwest Gun: How the West was Won. "Really, Bay? How the West was Won? Are you sure this is the right place?" Penelope asked her.

"I'm sure, and who doesn't love a cowboy? Now let's go in." Grabbing Penelope's arm, she pulled her toward the door.

"That comment doesn't even make sense. What's a cowboy have to do with anything?" Penelope asked.

"I don't know, whenever I hear West, my brain goes straight to 'hot cowboy,' doesn't yours? It can't just be me?"

"I'm pretty sure it's you, but it's okay. I already know you're a little off, and I love you anyway."

Walking through the door, Penelope couldn't believe her eyes, so many weapons and ammo in one place. It didn't feel like a good idea. She followed Baylee and watched as people made their selections and asked what she assumed were perfectly appropriate questions to the salespeople.

Finally, they stopped at a counter, and Baylee spoke to a guy who looked too young to even be in the store, let alone be working there.

"Hi, my friend here needs a weapon for protection. What would you recommend?" Baylee asked him.

"Welcome to Midwest, Miss. To answer your question, I first need to ask a few of my own. Have you ever fired a gun before or had any kind of safety training?" The employee asked.

"Yes, I've fired a gun before, but I've had no training," Penelope told him.

"Then I highly recommend you take a safety class. It's not required by law, but it should be," said the employee. "Let's get all the details out of the way first, and then I can take you over to our range and let you try a few different models. That way, you can find which weapon you're more comfortable with. How's that sound? Here are the forms I'll need you to fill out." Sliding a stack of paperwork and a pen across the counter, he pointed her to a lounge area to go get started.

A little while later, with completed paperwork in hand, Penelope and Baylee walked back to the counter and handed it in.

"Great, now if you could give me a few minutes, I'll turn this in, and get your background check complete. Then we can get started on finding you the right choice for your needs," the employee told them.

After he'd gone to a back room, Baylee explained to Penelope a few of the rules on gun store etiquette. "Since this is your first time in a gun store, I'll tell you what I wished my dad would have told me. It sure would have saved me some embarrassment."

"Okay, shoot," Penelope said with a smile.

"Okay, here it goes. Never, ever under any circumstance, point a gun at anyone in the store that includes the employees."

"Duh," Penelope said.

Baylee shook her head and went on. "When he comes back, he's going to point out a few different models he thinks might fit your needs. He will check the weapon and show us it's not loaded before he hands it to you. But that still doesn't mean it's okay to point it at him."

"Again, duh… moving along," Penelope said.

"Fine, moving along. Never hold a gun with your finger on the trigger. It's a bad habit to start. Some guns are more sensitive than others. It could go off accidentally if your finger is left on the trigger. Plus, always remember better safe than sorry," Baylee said.

"But you just said he was going to check and show us it's empty."

"He will, but it still doesn't make it okay to point it at anyone. I don't recommend it, especially with all the people in here who might freak out. And most importantly…"

"Great news, Mrs. Williams, you've been given the all-clear. Now, let's start looking for the protection that fits all your needs." He picked up a revolver, opened the chamber to show it wasn't loaded and handed it to her. Then he explained what she assumed were its essential features.

But all Penelope could think of was how heavy it was. Not knowing where to point it, she angled it at the floor.

"How's that feel?" he asked.

"Heavy. I don't remember a gun being so heavy. Do you have anything lighter?" Penelope asked.

"Of course, we do." He smiled and pulled out a completely different style of gun. "Are you planning on carrying it in a purse? Or would you prefer a holster?"

"I don't know what I plan to do. I'd never planned on owning a gun," Penelope told him.

"Perhaps a different model then?" he questioned.

Baylee, who'd been remarkably quiet, spoke up. "It's okay, Pen. You can get a gun that fits in your purse, and also wear it in a holster."

"So, problem solved. Now let's find that perfect accessory," Baylee went on, trying to distract Penelope, who she thought was on the verge of chickening out. Baylee pulled Penelope to another counter, where she pointed out a pair of guns she thought would be perfect. "Look, we could get matching ones; how cute would that be? The blue for you, and of course the purple one for myself," Baylee said.

Now more at ease, Penelope responded in a preppy voice, "Oh my God, so cool."

Relieved she had managed to distract Penelope and lighten the mood, Baylee smiled. "Remember, this is supposed to be fun. So, do you see anything you like?" Baylee asked.

"I'm not sure I know enough about what I need to be able to make a decision," Penelope said.

"That's where I come in," said the employee who'd followed them to the other counter, "Point to one and just ask me. I'm here to make sure you get the one that's right for you."

Pointing to what she thought was a reasonable size gun, Penelope asked a straightforward question. "Would this stop someone with one bullet?" Thinking of Derrick's size and strength, she was pretty sure if the first shot didn't stop him, a second one wasn't going to be an option.

"Absolutely, if that's your goal, how about we start with a .380 and work our way up," the employee replied.

"Sure, you're the expert," Penelope said, nodding her head.

"Great," he responded. "Let me grab a few different styles, and we'll go back to the gun range and have you test them out. Once you pick the one you're most comfortable with, then we'll move on to finding you a holster."

Walking a few paces behind him, Penelope leaned into Baylee and asked, "Earlier, you were going to tell me, the most important thing to remember? So, what is it?"

"Oh, right. Be honest, if you're not comfortable say so, if it's too heavy or too light, mention it. You want to be comfortable, that's the most important thing. Because if you're not comfortable, you won't have the guts to pull the trigger when the time comes," Baylee whispered.

As they walked to the back of the building toward the range, the employee went over the rules of the area. After he handed them each a pair of safety glasses, along with earplugs, they all headed into the range.

"I'll go first and show you how it's done," said Baylee, after they'd put on their safety glasses and earplugs. Placing both hands on the firearm, she lined up her sights and took aim at the target. Which was at the end of their lane, maybe fifty feet away. Baylee pulled the trigger and emptied her clip, then she removed her earplugs and pushed the button to bring the target forward.

"Not bad, if I do say so myself. It's been a while since I've had the pleasure of releasing some frustration at the shooting range." Holding the target out to show Penelope, Baylee said, "You're up."

Penelope wore all her safety gear and was ready to begin. She stood in the shooters' box as she'd been told and placed her finger on the trigger. Then hesitated. Looking back at Baylee, who was giving her a thumbs up, she yelled, "I don't think I can do this," and taking her finger off the trigger, she gently laid the gun back down on the stand.

Baylee walked over to Penelope, put her arm around her, and whispered in her ear, "Are you going to let Derrick win? Because you know if he gets a hold of you again, he will kill you. Is that what you want to happen?"

"Of course not, but could you shoot your ex-boyfriend? Could you really shoot Adam? You haven't mentioned him lately. Is he really out of the picture?"

"We aren't talking about my ex; we're talking about yours. Now focus, and stop trying to change the subject. Pen, I love you and believe me, you need this. You need to feel empowered, and in control, just in case Derrick shows up again." Baylee turned Penelope back around, handed her the gun, and said, "You got this!" Stepping back into the safety zone, Baylee waited to see what Penelope would do.

Penelope stood and stared at it for a few minutes, then said, "You're right. I got this." Placing her finger back on the trigger, she lined up the sights and pulled back. She hit the target wide left of center, but she was proud of herself for hitting the target at all.

She hadn't known what to expect. She'd been worried all the memories of when she was young would come pouring back, but they didn't. All she felt was her adrenaline pumping through her veins and the power that came with firing a weapon.

After over an hour of practice time, she chose the blue Sig Sauer 9mm with a holster. Since she was already there, she decided to go ahead and fill out the extra paperwork for a lifetime carry permit, since it would take months to get approved. While she stood there and tried to remember when she'd gotten her last speeding ticket, Baylee walked up.

"So, how do you feel?" Baylee asked.

"Okay, I'll admit it, this was one of your better ideas. I'm almost finished filling this out for a lifetime permit, I didn't realize there would be this much paperwork involved," Penelope said.

"Yeah, most people don't until they start the process. So, what do you think about this purple Ruger .380? I know I don't need it, but it's purple, so it's meant for me, right?"

Knowing what her friend wanted to hear, Penelope smiled and agreed, it must be fate.

After their purchases were complete, and the paperwork was handed in, they stepped back outside, with their packages.

"Now what Bay? I don't have my carry permit, and we have a bunch of shopping left to do," Penelope said.

"No problem, we'll go lock them up in the car while we shop. It's not that big of a deal," Baylee told her.

"It's a huge deal. I'm not sure how I feel about leaving it in a car."

"Okay, here's what we'll do since you're so worried about it. Let's run by my mom's restaurant so she can put them in her safe until we're finished shopping. Then when we come back to get them, she'll beg us to stay for dinner."

"I don't want to inconvenience your mom," Penelope said.

"It will be fine, wait, and see. My mom will love it. She'll get to see us, and you will be able to relax since the guns will be locked up. Plus, we will probably get a free meal. I say it's a win, win."

"Right? It does sound pretty perfect. Okay, I'm in," Penelope said.

Hailing a cab, Baylee directed him to her mom's restaurant, Bayl's. Once arriving, Penelope waited while Baylee quickly ran inside and dropped their new "accessories" off to her mom, who agreed to lock them in the safe. After promising they would return for a quick bite to eat once they were finished shopping, Baylee gave her mom a kiss on each cheek and headed out.

Hopping back in the cab, Baylee said, "What did I tell you? Mom made me promise we'd stay for dinner when we come back." Holding her hand to her heart, she continued, "How could I possibly say no?"

"You're so sneaky," Penelope told her.

"No, I'm not. I'm the perfect little princess, just ask my father."

"Sure, you are."

They laughed as they continued on to the rest of the stores. Baylee finished almost all her Christmas shopping, except something for Penelope, but kept her ear alert for anything she made a comment about along the way.

Penelope only bought a few small things for her coworkers. By the end of the day, she was starving and ready to relax with a nice meal. Hailing another cab, they made a quick stop at the parking garage and transferred all the bags to their car. Then they set off for Bayl's, but upon arriving, they discovered a line had formed outside the door.

"Maybe you should just run in and grab our stuff. I don't think we are going to be able to get in," Penelope said.

"Don't be silly." Grabbing her arm, Baylee pulled Penelope out of the cab and onto the sidewalk.

Raising her hand above her head, Baylee shouted over the crowd to the girl standing at the door. "Zoe!"

Zoe spotted her right away and said, "Baylee, please come right this way. We've been expecting you. Your table is ready and waiting."

Upon hearing Baylee's name, the crowd parted, and curious onlookers tried to get a glimpse of her. Not only was she the daughter of the head chef here at Bayl's, but also of the world-renowned millionaire, William Reed of Reed Enterprises. Sliding through the crowd, Baylee and Penelope followed Zoe to their table.

As they took their seat, Zoe said, "Let me run to the kitchen and let your mom know you're here."

"Thanks so much, Zoe. I appreciate you helping us out back there. Tell my mom we don't have to stay; I can see the place is packed."

"Yes, it is, and lucky for us, your mom is the best chef in town. I'm sure she'll take a break and have dinner with you since she hasn't stopped talking about you two coming by for dinner since I got here," Zoe said and handed them each a menu.

"We'd better order before my mom comes out, or she'll want us to try all the specials," Baylee told Penelope.

After they had both ordered their meals and were halfway through their first glass of wine, Ella Reed walked up to their table. Bending over, she placed a small kiss on top of Baylee's head.

"Hello, darling. I'm so pleased both of you were able to stay for dinner," Ella said as she took a seat across from Baylee.

"Of course, Mother. You know there's nowhere else I'd rather be. Plus, how could I pass up a meal from the best chef in town," Baylee said, smiling at her from across the table, and taking another sip of wine.

A waiter stopped at the table and set a basket of bread down along with the appetizer they'd ordered. He quietly checked with Ella to see if everything was to her liking. Once getting the head nod of approval, he did a slight bow, turned, and disappeared through the kitchen doors.

"Penelope, it's so nice to see you again. You're looking more and more like your mother every time I see you," Ella said.

"Thanks, it's good to see you too, Mrs. Reed," Penelope said, taking another bite of her bruschetta.

It wasn't until they had started on the main course that Ella surprisingly brought up the subject of the pending investigation.

Penelope immediately looked at Baylee with a look that said, you told her?

Holding up her hands, Baylee insisted, "I didn't say a word, I swear."

"Don't blame Baylee, she isn't how I found out," Ella said. "A mother has her ways of keeping tabs on her child. I don't want to overstep, but I would like to know. How are you doing, Penelope, darling?"

"I'm fine, and thank you for being concerned," Penelope said. Tilting her head down, she tried to take the focus off of herself.

But reaching across the table, Ella patted Penelope's hand. "How are you really, darling? We're practically family, and your mother would want me to look out for you."

Penelope knew Ella would keep asking questions, so she decided the best course of action was to simply tell her the truth. "I was pretty shaken up, but I'm doing better now. I've started going to counseling." She pointed to Baylee and continued, "We're even taking self-defense classes, and thanks to your daughter, I just bought my first gun."

"I'm happy to hear you're doing better, darling, and I believe counseling is beneficial to those who really listen and try to grow. May I ask, have they caught him yet?" Ella asked.

"No, unfortunately, they haven't, but Baylee and I have each other's backs so I'm okay," Penelope told her.

"That's good to hear darling, but I'd feel better if I knew you were both safe," said Ella.

Baylee spoke up, "It will be okay, Mom; no need for you to worry, I promise." Baylee reached over and squeezed her hand for reassurance.

"It's my right as a mother to worry, darling; nothing can be done about that. But I do have a fabulous idea, and it might help ease my mind. The apartment on East Chestnut we bought for you, Baylee, is still empty. You two could stay there until all of this awfulness is sorted out," Ella said.

"Thanks for the offer Mrs. Reed, but…"

Cutting Penelope off, Baylee spoke in a soothing tone, "Mom, I understand you're worried, but we can't just pack up and hide."

"Yes, you can; people do it all the time," her mother said.

"No, we can't, or more to the point, we won't. I love you, Mom, you know that? But you raised me to stand up for what's right. I'm not a coward, and I refuse to run and hide. Derrick needs to pay for what he's done."

"Baylee, darling, I understand what you're saying. I agree he needs to pay for his crimes, but you need to let the police handle this and stay out of the way."

"We will let them handle it, Mom, but we're staying put until they do."

"Okay, darling, just remember we love you. The offer still stands if either of you changes your mind. Now I really need to get back in the kitchen before the next rush." Standing up, she leaned over and once again kissed the top of Baylee's head. Then surprising Penelope, she walked over and did the same to her.

Penelope watched as Ella turned to go back into the kitchen and thought to herself, watching Baylee interact with her mom; it always left a little pang deep inside her. It made her wonder what her own life would be like if her mother were still alive. Would her mom worry about her like Ella did for Baylee?

She'd never know, so she knew it was best to not dwell on it. Placing her napkin on the table, she looked over at Baylee and said, "I'm full, how about you?"

"Me too, I'm ready to go home and relax."

After retrieving their items from the safe, they flagged down a cab and headed to the parking garage. They thanked the friendlier cabby for the ride, paid the fee, and got into Baylee's car to drive home.

Penelope decided to make a few calls since Baylee was driving. The first call was to Grace at the Center, who she talked to briefly, then she called her boss at the gas station to thank him for his support. Finally, she decided to touch base with the owner of Inner Strength and apologize for how it all went down the other day.

Once she was finished with the calls, she turned to Baylee, who she knew had at least heard her end of the conversation and said, "I think I made peace with Emerson."

"Really? What did he have to say?"

Penelope turned to Baylee and smiled. "He recommended that he work with me one-on-one, and we take it slow. He said before I know it, I will be kicking your butt all over town."

"Did he now? Well, maybe in your dreams," Baylee said and laughed.

"Hey, you never did tell me about the steam room. What happened between you two?" Penelope asked.

"Long story short? I made a fool of myself, but that's nothing new, is it? Though I did get to see him half-naked, and I must say WOW, I was impressed."

"Yummy, Huh?"

"At one point, sweat was dripping down his chest, and it took everything I had to stop myself from reaching over and licking it off," Baylee finished with a sigh.

Penelope laughed at Baylee's own unique way of describing the scene. "It definitely sounds like it was an eventful evening. Sorry, I missed it," Penelope said.

"I don't know if I'd call it eventful, but it was interesting. Emerson doesn't seem to be too bright, though, which is kind of disappointing."

"Wait, I must have misheard you? I thought you didn't mind if a guy wasn't smart, as long as he was nice to look at." Penelope couldn't keep herself from laughing.

"Ha-ha, I'm being serious here. He actually thought my favorite color was pink."

"How? The purple streaks in your hair are pretty hard to miss."

"I know, right? But I guess I can kind of understand where he got confused. It's not like the poor guy probably buys a lot of women's underwear."

"Okay, now I'm the dumb one here," Penelope said, "What does underwear have to do with any of this?"

"The tank top I was wearing said Pink, then the bag I grabbed to throw everything in also said Pink. He was clueless and had no idea Pink was a brand name. He thought I was some crazy chick who apparently put the word pink on everything."

"Who does that?" asked Penelope.

"No idea, but I gave him a hint. I said that it's the name of a lingerie store as I turned and walked away. The look on his face was truly priceless."

"Nice, I bet you stayed on his mind for a while after you left."

"That was the idea," Baylee said and winked. "Now, on to more important subjects. I know you called Grace, did you set up an appointment, or are you planning to stay with the group therapy?"

"I'm not sure yet. I'm going to see her in a day or two to discuss the options," Penelope said, going silent for a moment she thought about how Grace had seen her at her worst and was still willing to help. She must really believe she could help her get past all of it.

"Grace mentioned that she'd help me file for a divorce, and since we never had kids, it should be pretty easy," Penelope went on. "Plus, get this. Grace said, for no extra charge, I could change my last name at the same time. She said most people go back to their maiden names, and it helps them make a fresh start.

"Is that what you want to do," asked Baylee. "Do you think it would help you start over?"

"I don't think taking my maiden name back would make a difference, but what would you think about me taking my mom's maiden name?"

"I don't remember what it was, so let's hear it," Baylee said.

"Penelope Fitch. What do you think?" Penelope asked, turning in her seat so she could see Baylee's face when she answered.

"Honestly?"

"Yes, honestly. You hate it, don't you?" Penelope waited a few seconds, and then shrugged her shoulders.

Baylee knew they were almost back to the apartments, so she hadn't said another word. Pulling into the parking lot in front of their apartment, Baylee shut off the car, leaned over in the seat, and pulled Penelope into a hug.

"I really love it! It's a name that makes you think of your mom, which puts a smile on your face before you even opened your mouth. It's a name you'll take pride in, and it will push you to be a better person. Yup, Penelope Fitch has a nice ring to it, don't you think?" Baylee said with a big grin.

"I really do, but I wanted to run it by you first. I know it will take a few months for the paperwork to go through once I file, but just knowing it will happen makes me feel better."

"In the meantime, how about helping me carry some of this stuff inside," Baylee said and handed her a few bags.

"Sure thing," Penelope said.

With their arms overloaded, they made their way to Penelope's apartment. Walking in, Penelope said, "Let's watch a movie. I really just want to veg out for a while and forget about everything going on, you know?"

"Yeah, I get it," Baylee agreed.

They threw all the bags in a pile on the floor and went over to relax on the couch. Baylee started a movie and a few minutes later, turned to make a comment about a scene, and noticed Penelope had already fallen asleep. Reaching over, she pulled a blanket from the back of the couch and tucked it over her friend.

"Sleep well, dear Pen," she whispered, and soon was asleep herself.

Hours later, Penelope woke to a room filled with hazy blue light from the television, she noticed both lamps were off, and something was making an odd shadow on the wall.

The curtain on the sliding glass door, swayed slightly from the furnace running, and the sound of the clock in the kitchen could be heard by its constant ticking. Penelope stood and stretched all the muscles in her back, which had become stiff from falling asleep in an awkward position. Reaching across the couch, she shook Baylee's shoulder to wake her.

Rubbing her eyes, Baylee looked up and said, "What's up? Is something wrong?"

"No, I heard a noise, and it woke me up. But now I don't hear it, so I have no idea what it was. I'm going to bed, and I thought I should wake you so you could at least lay down."

"Thanks, I think I will," Baylee said, taking the blanket Penelope offered. Laying down, she pulled it over herself and shut her eyes.

Penelope walked into her bedroom, pulled back the covers, and got into bed. Closing her eyes, she lay there and thought about her mother. She hoped her mom would like the idea of her taking her last name.

Her breathing became even, and she was pulled back to when she was 12 years old. "Mom!" Penelope screamed.

"It will be okay, Penny, I promise. You go get little Philly and take him to your room and lock the door," her mom whispered.

"I don't want to go to my room! I want to stay with you," Penelope cried, looking up into her mom's eyes.

Mary leaned down, and using her finger, she tapped Penelope's nose. "My brave little Penny, always wanting to help. But some things are not for children to see. Now you go do as I told you, and stay there until I come. Promise me."

Before Penelope could promise, she was pulled from her mother's arms. "What is your no-good mother making you promises about now," her father screamed.

"Nothing, Daddy, I swear," Penelope said.

Shoving her out of the way, he walked over to her mom and backhanded her. Then punched her, she tried to block the blows by using her hands to cover her face, but it only enraged him further. He suddenly grabbed her by the hair and threw her into the front of the refrigerator. Mary tried to use it for support, and hold herself up, but after what seemed like never-ending blows her knees finally gave out, and she fell to the floor.

"Oh, no you don't! You're not getting out of it that easy. Stand up!" Her husband screamed, "Tell me what you promised Penny, and why did you tell her to go to her room and lock the door?"

Mary tried to answer, but he screamed over her, and she was too weak to fight back. Making an attempt to stand, she looked over to Penelope and whispered in a hoarse voice, "GO!"

Mary's husband, Luke, must have seen her try to talk because he leaned over and laughed in Mary's face. Pulling his leg back, he turned his head and smiled at Penelope, then kicked her Mom in the ribs with all the power he had.

Fear instantly ripped through Penelope, and she knew she had to do something. "Daddy, please don't hurt her! Daddy, stop!"

Turning his head, Luke looked at her with his face bright red and a vein protruding from his temple. "Shut up, Penelope! Or you'll be next."

"But you're killing her!" Penelope cried, running toward her Mom lying on the kitchen floor. She reached out, only wanting to help her, but was stopped mere inches away.

"Penelope, wake up!" Baylee said while trying to shake her awake. "It's only a nightmare, wake up, wake up!"

Finally, realizing where she was, and that she was no longer 12 years old, Penelope opened her eyes and looked at her best friend and whispered, "If only that were true."

Chapter 16

Baylee woke to the smell of coffee and soft music playing in the background. When she walked out of the bedroom and straight for a cup of joe, she saw Penelope sitting on the couch with her laptop open, watching what appeared to be White Christmas on TV.

Pouring herself a cup, Baylee said, "Morning Pen, how long have you been up?"

"Long enough that you're pouring from the second pot." Penelope held up her cup to signal she needed a refill. "Could you please bring it in with you?"

"I sure can. I see you're watching White Christmas again this year," Baylee said while carrying in the coffee from the kitchen.

"It's the one thing we always did at Christmas; Mom, Philly, and I would pile up on the loveseat and watch it together. I've always loved this movie. I can still hear my Mom singing along."

"Sounds like a great memory," Baylee said and refilled Penelope's cup. "So, what are you doing online? Let me guess you're looking for my perfect gift this year?"

"Oh no, you caught me," Penelope laughed. "Actually, I'm looking at my schedule for the week, and trying to figure out how I'm going to fit it all in."

Baylee took a sip, "Maybe I can help. Tell me everything you have to do, and I'll help you come up with a game plan."

Penelope told her about everything on her schedule, from working both jobs, to training at the Inner Strength. Plus, there was the gun safety class she'd signed up for along with the target practice, and she couldn't forget the meetings at CMC with Grace.

"Wow, it does sound pretty jam-packed, but look at it this way. Everything you're doing is pointing you in a positive direction."

"Right! It's busy in a good way," Penelope said.

"Oh, at your next meeting, can you ask Grace if she's a smoker?"

"Sure, but why? I don't want to offend her by asking, you know how some people are," Penelope said.

"Right, but tell her, there's no judgment here. The night she brought you home from Inner Strength, the house smelled like smoke, and then later, I found a cigarette floating in the toilet. It just caught me off guard, because I can usually tell when I'm around someone who smokes, but I couldn't tell with her."

"Okay, I can ask," Penelope said, trying to focus on her future instead of looking back. "Maybe I could talk to Marty. He's been so supportive, so he might let me cut my hours back until I get done with some of my classes."

"Sure, couldn't hurt to try," Baylee responded.

The rest of the day flew by, and after Penelope helped Baylee carry all the packages upstairs from the night before, she realized it was already past her bedtime.

Her Monday morning alarm went off before she knew it, and hitting the snooze button several times hadn't helped to keep her on schedule. She'd almost forgotten that Baylee had passed out on her couch the night before.

With only minutes to spare, she wrote a quick note and put it on the coffee table where she knew Baylee wouldn't miss it.

It read:

Love you Lots!

Don't forget to lock up

See you sometime tonight xoxo P

Penelope grabbed the bag she'd need later for her appointments and took one last look around. She grabbed her keys, pulled the door closed, and locked it behind her, then headed to her job at the factory.

As the day dragged on, Penelope wanted nothing more than to finish up her last few units and be done for the day. She stopped what she was doing when she heard her name being called, looked down over the edge of the roof, and spotted her boss, Mr. Smithern standing outside the unit.

"Penelope, could you please come down here for a few minutes. I have some things I'd like to discuss with you."

"Sure thing, Sir," Penelope said. She climbed down the ladder and made her way over to the boss.

"Penelope, I'm glad to see you're back; you should've seen this place without you. It was a madhouse. I have a few ideas on how we can make sure it doesn't happen again."

"I'm sorry to hear that, Mr. Smithern; what do you have in mind?" Penelope following him into his office.

"I analyzed your department operations while you were away, and noticed all the people in your group look to Brent for answers when you're not available."

"Brent's a great worker, and I'm not sure we'd be able to do the same amount of work without him," Penelope said.

"Here's what I have in mind. I want to offer you an opportunity." He paused for a minute. "I know you have a great work ethic, and the other employees really look up to you. I think now's a great time to bring you into upper management. We'll train Brent to take over as the group leader for the electrical department."

"Mr. Smithern, I'm not sure what to say. I'm grateful for this opportunity, of course, but could I have a couple days to think about it? This is a big decision, and I want to make sure I'm making the right one."

"Oh, yes, of course! Here's some information on the benefits package that comes with the new position," he said, sliding a large envelope across his desk. "How about I give you until the end of the week, then we can meet again to discuss your decision?"

"Sounds great, and thank you again." Shaking his hand firmly, Penelope turned and headed back to her department.

Excited about the possibilities ahead, she tried to weigh the good and bad of the offer. Before she knew it, she looked at the clock and realized it was time to leave for the day. In a better mood than she'd been in a while, she clocked out and walked to her Jeep.

Penelope turned up the stereo as she pulled out of the parking lot and sang along with "Bullet for my Valentine," one of her favorite bands. She must have been driving on autopilot because the next thing she knew, she was sitting in the parking lot at Steams. Checking her watch, she saw she had enough time, so she hopped out of her Jeep and went inside.

Moments later, she was back in her Jeep and on her way to surprise someone. Once she arrived, she grabbed the box from Steams and made her way towards the purple door. She hoped Grace loved chocolate as much as she did.

With her mind still on the promotion, Penelope walked into the office without thinking. She pushed through the door and stepped right into the middle of a private session.

"I'm so sorry, I didn't think." She raised her hand and backed out of the room. Her cheeks started to warm, and she assumed they were bright red from embarrassment. Why hadn't I knocked? Why did I just barge in? She decided she'd leave the brownies in the tiny waiting room and write a little note.

"It's okay, Penelope," Grace called out, as she stood and made her way to the door. Turning back, she said, "I apologize for the interruption, Molly, if you give me just a moment, I'll take care of this and be right back."

"Yeah, that's fine," the girl responded.

Gently, Grace pulled the door closed and turned to Penelope.

"Is something wrong?" Grace asked. "It isn't like you to just stop by like this. I'm conducting a private session right now, but if you'd like to wait or schedule something for later today?"

"No, it's okay. I'm so sorry for interrupting. I wanted to stop and thank you for everything you did the other night, and give you this from Steams." Handing over the box, Penelope continued, "I need to get going, I have a shift starting soon at Marty's Gas."

Opening the box and peeking in, Grace inhaled the marvelous scent of chocolate and caramel. "Oh, turtle brownies! They're my favorite; how did you know?"

With her hand on the door, Penelope turned and said, "I didn't, but enjoy." She hurried away, still embarrassed from barging in on Grace's appointment. But she was thankful Grace hadn't seemed to be upset after she'd opened the box and discovered the brownies.

When Penelope finally arrived at Marty's Gas, she clocked in with only a minute to spare. Glad she'd made it on time, she pulled on her blue smock and walked back up front. Pleased to be working with Erma-Lee again, they chatted about things that had happened since they'd last seen each other.

"Well, bless your heart, you're looking perdy good for a girl who's been through all that now. I can barely even see them bruises on your face. Here I made you something," Erma-Lee said, as she threw something to Penelope.

Catching it in midair, Penelope opened her palm and discovered a pretty yellow daisy bracelet. She looked at her friend and smiled. "It's beautiful, thank you. Now, every time I look at it, I'll think of you. Where did you find something like this?"

"I make em from glass, and such," Erma-Lee told her. "I make all kinds of jewelry and sell it at festivals I go to. Back home in West Virginia, one of my aunts taught me all she knows about jewelry making. So, it helps in a pinch to bring in some extra money. Plus, I like doing it."

"Wow, you make these? Why didn't I know this about you?"

"I'm a jack of all trades, I hear. I can do pretty much whatever I stick my mind too," Erma-Lee said proudly.

"I love it, thank you! I'll put it on right now," Penelope said, pulling the hemp strands tightly on her wrist, making sure it couldn't fall off, before getting back to work.

"You're welcome. I made a bracelet 'cause I saw ya always wear a watch, and this won't be a bother if you wear them together."

"When my friend Baylee sees it, she's going to want one of her own. You wait and see."

"You tell her to come to see me, and I reckon we could find her something."

"Will do. So, what do you think about me starting the closing list a little early? Would you be okay at the register?" Penelope asked.

"Shoot girl, did you really ask me that? I'll be fine; you go on and start on your list."

Walking the aisles, Penelope started pulling items forward on the shelves but still managed to keep an eye on the front in case Erma-Lee needed any help.

As she rounded the endcap on the first aisle, something caught the corner of her eye. Looking out the front window, she was drawn to a pink panther license plate on the front of a vehicle. As it pulled away from the pump, she instantly knew where she'd seen it before.

Running towards the door, she opened it just in time to see it was a black Ford Explorer. Damn, she knew it was the same vehicle, but she was seconds too late. Penelope turned and walked back into the store.

"Lordy be, girl, what was that all about?"

"Doesn't matter, I didn't catch them."

"Did we have a drive-off again?"

Not registering the question Erma-Lee had asked, she asked one of her own.

"Hey, would you happen to know who drives the Explorer that just pulled away?"

"Yeah, that was Molly, she's an animal doctor. Sweet girl, bless her heart, but better with books and pets, than with people. Why do you ask?"

"No reason," Penelope answered, without realizing she'd said a word.

Finishing the rest of the closing list in a daze, she went to the front and started counting down one of the registers.

"Penelope, you alright? You ain't said a word lately. I'm starting to worry."

Penelope looked up with a blank stare on her face, then tried to smile for her friend. Her mind was filled with the knowledge, she was right. All this time and now she finally had evidence Derrick had cheated. She just wasn't sure it mattered to her anymore.

For so long, she'd worried Derrick had been cheating. But he would always make her feel like she was imagining things or was crazy. She couldn't figure out how he did it, but somehow, she always walked away feeling like she was the person in the wrong. Now she finally had the proof, but she didn't care? For the first time, she could honestly say she didn't want Derrick back.

The widest smile slid across her lips, she looked up at Erma-Lee and said, "I'm okay, no need for you to worry about me. I really think good things are going to start coming my way. I think I deserve a little good in my life, don't you?" Penelope said and winked.

"Sure do," Erma-Lee said while wiping the register counter down. "If anybody deserves it, you do, honey."

"In fact, I'm in such a good mood, how about you go ahead and go home. I'll close up," Penelope told her.

"Well, bless your heart. I know you gotta be tired from workin' two jobs. I don't mind staying."

"I know you don't," Penelope said and handed Erma-Lee her time card to punch out.

"Okay, I'll go, but you be careful, ya hear?"

"I promise," Penelope said, watching Erma-Lee climb into her beat-up old pickup and start it up. Waving goodbye, Penelope turned from the window and finished up her paperwork for the night.

With no customers for the last hour, they were open, watching the clock seemed to make the second hand go even slower. She even noticed it would take a tiny pause between each second. It was strange the things you notice when you're trying to occupy your time. Finally, it was time to close up.

Doing one last walkthrough to make sure everything was secure, she clocked out and turned all the lights off, including the overhead gas pump lights. Penelope drew her keys out of her pocket before walking out, then pulled the door tightly behind her; she turned the key to engage the deadbolt.

She felt a chill run down her spine and suddenly sensed she was being watched. As soon as the deadbolt caught, she spun and pressed her back against the door. Looking left, then right, she didn't see anything out of the ordinary, but the feeling still remained. Penelope told herself to go slow and be cautious, but every muscle in her body was screaming at her to run.

Once she was halfway to her Jeep, she couldn't stop herself and took off in a sprint. Getting safely inside, she slammed her hand down on the lock button, and it had never felt so good.

She told herself she'd probably blown the whole thing out of proportion, but now in the safety of her Jeep, it was easy to laugh at herself. Pulling out of the parking lot, she headed home but checked her mirrors frequently to make sure she wasn't being followed. When she caught a red light, she sent a quick text to Baylee to let her know she was on her way home.

As she pulled into her parking spot in front of her apartment, Penelope turned off the engine and carefully looked around. With the clouds blocking the moonlight, she only had the exterior lights from the apartment building to assist her. She wanted to make sure nothing seemed out of place before going inside. Once she found nothing amiss, she opened her door but jumped when her phone chirped an incoming message. Laughing at herself, she checked her phone and found out that Baylee was still working, and she probably wouldn't see her tonight. So, she quickly made her way from her Jeep to her apartment.

Later that evening, lying in bed, Penelope slowly opened her eyes after a strange sound had awoken her. Listening closely, she tried to figure out where the noise had come from. She'd heard the sound of metal scraping together and then a click.

Quietly, she reached across the bed for the gun she'd just purchased and hoped she'd be able to make herself use it if someone was in the apartment. She held it close to her chest as she slid out of bed and tiptoed out into the living room.

Keeping the lights off, she walked through the apartment and checked every hiding spot she could think of. After a few minutes, she realized she was going to come up empty. With still no idea of where the noise had come from, she knew she'd never be able to fall back to sleep.

With the new job opportunity still on her mind, she decided to open the envelope Mr. Smithern had given her, to see what it was all about. Carrying it into the kitchen, she turned on the light, started a pot of coffee, and sorted out all the papers. Not only was she being offered a higher salary, but also a percentage of profit sharing and a small stake in the company. Upon further inspection, she also discovered a continuing education bonus. As she took her first sip of coffee, she couldn't believe she was being offered this wonderful opportunity.

After she'd finished going through all the information, she smiled and knew she'd already made her decision. She refilled her cup and carried it along with her Beretta into the bathroom, ready to take a shower and start her day. Not forgetting what had awoken her earlier, she locked the bathroom door and laid the 9mm on the back of the toilet, just in case she needed to reach it quickly.

Arriving to work at the factory a little early, Penelope clocked in and went in search of Mr. Smithern. He'd given her a week to make her decision, but she realized she hadn't needed that long. She'd worked hard, and she'd earned this promotion. There was no way she was passing it up!

Penelope tapped on his office door and waited for a response. Moments later, his door opened, and he greeted her.

"Penelope, it's so good to see you, can I assume you've reached a decision? Please, take a seat, and we'll discuss all the details." He left the door slightly ajar and took a seat once again behind his desk.

After the meeting was finished, Penelope left his office, feeling good about the new position. It came with an excellent salary raise, which would definitely help out, but it was the continuing education aspect that had her the most excited.

Walking back to her area, she called a meeting for the whole electrical department. She explained the situation and was thrilled to tell Brent he would be taking over her position as the group leader. Most of the guys complained a little. But she was sure it was more for show than actually caring; she wasn't going to be their group leader anymore. All of them congratulated Brent on scoring a raise and the new position. Then it was over, and everyone went back to work.

The rest of the day flew by, and before she knew it, they had met the quota for the day, and it was time to clock out. The best thing about a piece rate job was the employees all knew, the faster they worked, the sooner they could leave, and the more money they made.

Penelope pulled out of the parking lot and headed straight to Inner Strength. She walked in, carrying her gear, and Emerson was there to greet her. "Are you ready, Penelope? I thought we could start with the weights before we get to the hand to hand."

"Sure, just give me a minute to change," she said, walking straight past him on the way to the locker room.

Changing quickly, she walked back out, ready to get down to business. She stood in front of Emerson, prepared for whatever he was going to dish out. She was no longer a victim, and it was about time she stopped acting like one.

Emerson pushed her with the weights, then a little further during the hand-to-hand combat. Not one time did she complain. Not one time did she want to give up. She'd decided she wanted Emerson, and everyone else to see a different side of her. To see a woman who would do whatever it took to make herself into what she wanted to be.

At the end of the session, Emerson told her to shower and meet him back on the mats.

Penelope came back out, her hair still dripping in her eyes. She wrapped the towel around her head and walked over to where Emerson was sitting. Plopping down not so gracefully, Penelope said, "My muscles hurt, ones I didn't even know I had."

"You worked hard today. I pushed you, and you're finally starting to push back. I consider it a very positive sign. The hand-to-hand technique is still a little rough, but it will get easier once we put a little weight on those arms of yours," Emerson said.

"Thanks, I'm trying, but you're still kicking my butt."

"Well, I would hope so. I do have how many years' experience on you? Plus, the army helped me out a lot in this area too." Standing up, he held out his hand and pulled Penelope to her feet. "I have you on the schedule for the day after tomorrow, so I'll see you then. Have a great evening, Penelope." He turned to go hit the showers himself.

"Thanks, you too." She waved goodbye, walked outside to her Jeep, and climbed in. Wondering what Baylee was up to, she pulled her phone out of her bag, hit speed dial, and waited for her friend to answer.

"Hello."

"Hey girl, what are you up to? I'm on my way to the shooting range, and I thought if you weren't busy, you might like to meet me there."

Baylee was painting her toenails while she held the phone by her shoulder to answer, "Absolutely! I'll see you there, just go on in and get started. I was painting my toes, so it's going to take me a few extra minutes."

"Okay, no problem. See you in a few," Penelope said and ended the call.

Baylee sat on the bed and stared at her toes while she tried to figure out what to do. She knew it would take forever for them to dry. Then she remembered her mom telling her ice water would help them dry faster. Hobbling out to the kitchen, she grabbed the needed supplies and sat on the floor. She couldn't remember the exact amount of time required, so she set the timer for four minutes and hoped it would work.

Not being able to stand the freezing water any longer, she pulled her toes out in only three minutes. She couldn't tell if the polish was dry because her toes were frozen, but she thought it would have to be good enough. Baylee didn't want to waste any more time, so she stood up and walked into her room. She pulled on a pair of wool socks and her warm Sorel boots. Grabbing her new favorite sweatshirt and gear, she headed out the door.

Once she arrived at the gun range, Baylee grabbed her bag and climbed out of her Porsche to the unmistakable sounds of muffled gunfire. The wind caught her hoodie and pulled it off her head as she sprinted towards the door, making her wish she'd taken the time to also grab a coat.

Baylee walked in and went straight to the counter. She signed in, paid the fee, and bought a couple boxes of ammo. After she tossed everything in her bag, she went in search of Penelope. When she entered the range area, she watched as her friend took aim and let loose. Baylee couldn't believe how relaxed and natural Penelope looked with a weapon in her hand. It sure was a far cry from the way she'd been the day she'd purchased it.

Emptying her clip into the target, Penelope watched as the bullets went dead center time after time. It was easy to hit a target when you pictured a certain someone on the other end. She removed the clip and started to reload when Baylee walked up beside her into the safe zone.

"You look so natural like you could've been born with a gun in your hand. Dare I say, you could actually become better than me?" Baylee teased.

"I wouldn't go that far," Penelope said with a wink. "But it's a lot easier when you know your life might depend on it. The self-defense moves I'm learning are only going to help so much, and it's always a good idea to have a backup plan."

"So, tell me, how are the self-defense classes going? Are you kicking butt yet?" Baylee asked.

"I think the classes are going really well. In fact, I even received a compliment today from Emerson, if you can believe that?"

Trying to sound nonchalant, Baylee said, "That is impressive, I didn't realize he was capable of a kind word." She peeked back over her shoulder and tried to gauge Penelope's mood about her comment.

"Well, if I didn't know better, I'd say you have a thing for my instructor," Penelope teased.

Baylee walked into her shooters' box, took aim, pulled back the trigger, and let the bullet fly. "What? No, don't be ridiculous." Unfortunately, the bullet went wide and hit the corner of the paper target. She felt her cheeks flush and didn't bother to look at Penelope for her reaction. She already knew what it would be.

Unloading the rest of her chamber, she thought, it was no wonder she couldn't hit the target. Because if she were honest with herself, she'd admit she hadn't been able to get Emerson off her mind for some time now.

Baylee holstered her weapon, pulled off her safety glasses, and let Penelope take her place while she took a seat in the safe zone. "Let's say I am interested. I'm not saying I am, but if I were, I might be curious to know if he had asked about me?"

Penelope smiled to herself, lined up her next shot, and flippantly said, "He might have mentioned something, but my memory is foggy."

"Sure, it is," replied Baylee. "So, what's it going to take to clear your mind?"

"I don't know, maybe a little wager?" Penelope asked, wanting Baylee to see how much better her aim was getting. And what better way, she thought, than to beat her in a target contest.

Baylee stood, raised her left eyebrow, and said, "Okay, what do you have in mind?"

Penelope pulled two new targets from her bag and wrote their names on them. "I say, whoever gets the most bullets through the center wins. That's 15 bullets, one try, no do-overs. What do you say? You in?"

"Absolutely, have you ever known me to back down from a bet? So, what are we wagering?" Baylee asked.

Penelope started reloading her clip, "When I win, you have to go ask Emerson out to dinner."

"Pretty sure of yourself, but what do I get if I win," Baylee asked.

"I'll let you know what, if anything, was said about you."

"Okay, sounds like a win, win to me," Baylee agreed, smiling because she knew the chances were slim Penelope would be able to pull this off.

Penelope let Baylee go first, and she did pretty well, which didn't really surprise her. "10 out of 15 isn't bad. Now it's my turn. Let me show you how it's done."

Penelope steadied her nerves and took aim. Once the last bullet had left the chamber, and the slide locked open, signaling to her, the magazine was empty. She released the trigger and holstered her weapon. She reached over and pressed the button to bring the target back as she said, "I've gotten a lot better."

"Wow, I can see that." Baylee leaned around Penelope and yanked the target down. "We should frame this. I bet you couldn't hit that many perfect shots again if you tried."

"Really? You don't think so?" Penelope said as she reached into her bag and pulled out target after target from that day, with all perfect shots.

"You, my friend, are a cheater! I can't believe you did that to me. What a dirty trick; you knew I couldn't beat you. I want a rematch," Baylee said, as she started to stuff everything in her bag.

"I wouldn't call it cheating per se. Maybe a little on the shady side, but are you really going to hold it against me?" Penelope asked.

"Of course, I am. I'm a great grudge holder."

"Come on," Penelope pleaded. "I've been practicing every chance I get, and I think it's finally paying off, don't you?" Not being able to take the smile off her face was evidence enough of how proud she was of herself.

"I'll think about it. Do you know what the best part of all of this is? If Derrick shows up, I have no doubt you'll be able to handle it. He, on the other hand, won't see it coming."

They walked out arm in arm, laughing about what Derrick would think if he could see her now. Penelope was no longer the shy little mouse who always let him have his way. She was finally becoming the woman she'd always wanted to be.

"I'll meet you back at the apartments." Penelope said and hugged her, "I want to run some things by Grace, then I'll head that way."

"Sounds good, but I'm beat from working all these extra shifts. I'll probably just crash for the night. How about we touch base tomorrow?"

"Okay, get some rest," Penelope said, giving Baylee another hug before she climbed into her Jeep. She made a quick call to Grace, asking if it would be okay to stop by and discuss something. Then she pulled out of the parking lot and headed toward Choices Make Changes. Once she arrived, she walked in and went straight to Grace's office. This time the door was wide open, but she knocked anyway.

Looking up from her desk, Grace said, "Please come in. I was surprised when you called. I assumed I wouldn't see you until tomorrow's meeting."

"Oh, I'm sorry. I know it's late. It can wait."

"Don't be silly, dear, please take a seat. I have another hour of paperwork to complete before I leave anyway. So, tell me what's on your mind."

"I've been thinking about something you mentioned to me the other day. About helping me get a divorce. I'm ready to get started, but I'm not sure if it's possible since he's technically a missing person."

"Missing, found, none of that matters, dear." Grace stood and opened a filing cabinet. Pulling out several papers, she clipped them together and handed them to Penelope. "Fill out these forms, pay the fee at the courthouse, and place an ad in the newspaper. Have you decided if you want to go back to your maiden name, yet?"

"I need to place an ad in the newspaper?" Penelope asked, flipping through the pages.

"The ad is to notify all interested parties. Let's hope he's not much of a reader. If he doesn't see the article and protest, before you know it, you, my dear, will be a free woman."

"Thanks, Grace. I'll go home, fill all these out, and take them to the courthouse when I get a chance. I do have a question, though."

"What's your question, dear?" Grace asked.

"You said I could switch back to my maiden name, but could I switch to my mom's maiden name instead?"

"That will be up to the judge's discretion, but I recommend you write a letter to explain the reasoning behind wanting to take her maiden name instead of your own. If your reason is sufficient, I don't see why the judge would refuse."

Penelope never imagined it could be so easy to get a divorce. Holding the papers in her hand, she turned to go then stopped. Looking back, she said, "Thanks again for all your help, and I'll see you at tomorrow evening's meeting."

Penelope exited through the purple door and wrapped her scarf around her neck a second time. Pulling it up to cover her nose, she hoped it would help with the frigid temperatures. Only a few feet from her Jeep, she stopped.

Penelope stood frozen as she watched her headlights flash and her horn sound. How's that possible, she thought? A car doesn't unlock and lock itself on its own. Slowly she pulled her keys from her coat pocket. Staring at the key-fob, she realized it must be Derrick. He was there, somewhere hiding, watching her while he held her extra fob in his hand.

Chapter 17

The following day, Penelope hustled at work so she could leave a little earlier than usual. She drove straight to the courthouse and was thankful a nice lady helped her file everything she needed. She even attached Penelope's letter to the judge for his consideration of her name change. After she paid the filing fee, she was given a copy of her records. It was hard to imagine in only sixty days, she could be a single woman again, with a brand-new name.

Glancing at her watch, Penelope realized it had taken longer in the courthouse than she'd thought. She needed to hurry, or she'd never make it on time for group at CMC. It was scheduled to start in less than ten minutes.

Penelope finally arrived almost twenty minutes later, and everything looked to be well underway. Walking in quietly, she was shocked to see Grace standing in the middle of the room, crying. She seemed to be talking about someone in the hospital and the condition they were in.

Looking around to see who might be missing tonight, Penelope slowly took her seat next to Abby. Not wanting to disturb the meeting, she leaned over and whispered.

"Who's Grace talking about?"

"Oh, I don't think you know her," Abby said. "She quit coming before you started. She was a nice girl and loved animals. If I'm not mistaken, I want to say she's a

Veterinarian. Grace always told her to be careful because picking up a stray dog wasn't the same as picking up a stray man. I think you would have liked her, though. Her name is Molly."

"Molly?" Eyes wide, Penelope thought the chances were slim that it could be the same girl. "She didn't happen to drive a black Ford Explorer, did she?"

"She sure did, with a pink panther license plate on the front. You couldn't miss it. Do you know her?" Abby asked.

Shocked by what she was hearing, Penelope said, "I think I just might. Do you know what happened to her?"

"Grace just told us that the current boyfriend beat her so badly it put her in the hospital. It sounds like she's in pretty bad shape, I guess. They think she may never walk again. Can you believe he broke her spine in three places?"

Penelope was stunned by what she'd heard, she sat in a haze for the rest of the meeting. A single thought repeated itself in her mind. Molly's beating had been meant for her.

She hadn't noticed when Grace walked up and laid a hand on her shoulder. "Are you okay? You were very distant tonight; has something happened?" Grace asked.

Blinking her eyes, Penelope looked straight up into Grace's face. Then she suddenly noticed the room was empty, and only Grace and herself remained. She stood abruptly, accidentally knocking over her chair.

"I'm so sorry, I need to go," Penelope said, quickly grabbing her bag as she turned to leave. She didn't have time to give an explanation for her behavior. All she knew was she needed to get out of there as fast as she could.

Her thoughts were racing, and the only thing she could think of was talking it out with Baylee. There was no way this could be a coincidence. She was almost certain Derrick was the boyfriend Grace had been referring to.

Before she pulled out of the parking lot to go home, Penelope sent Baylee a quick text letting her know she needed to talk.

Once she arrived home, she still hadn't heard from Baylee, so she decided she'd try to take her mind off things by soaking in a hot bath. With music softly playing in the background, and holding a book she'd been reading, Penelope was startled when Baylee came running through the bathroom door.

"Oh my God, Baylee! You almost scared me to death," Penelope screamed.

"I'm so sorry, I didn't mean to scare you. Didn't you get my text?" Baylee asked.

"No, sure didn't," Penelope said, stepping out of the tub and reaching for her towel.

"Well, you're not going to believe the awful day I've had, and I couldn't wait to get home to talk to you about it."

"You first. Tell me what's happened that I'll never believe, while I get my pajamas on. Then I'll tell you something I found out about at group," Penelope said.

"Well, the reason I couldn't text you back right away was, because I was in my boss's office," Baylee said as she followed Penelope into her room while she looked for her favorite pj's.

"Why? What happened?"

"Mr. Karp pulled my partner and me off our shift and demanded we go see him immediately. Apparently, someone made an anonymous call to his office. They claimed they had information about some of the drugs we carry on our ambulances."

"Okay, what kind of information," Penelope asked, as she pulled her top over her head, and took a seat on the bed.

"The kind that points the finger at me, personally," Baylee said. "They claim I have been stealing medical supplies and drugs from our department. How absurd is that?"

"Right, like you couldn't afford to buy whatever you'd need," Penelope spoke up.

"I've been sitting in my boss's office for hours, while someone went through our ambulance and counted everything."

"Well, I guess the bright side is, they didn't find anything missing or not accounted for. Right?" Penelope asked, patting the bed, so Baylee would sit down and quit pacing.

Baylee shook her head and said, "I can't sit down, I'm too edgy. There is no bright side here, Pen!"

"What do you mean? There has to be. I know you, and you'd never do something like that."

"True, I wouldn't, but I can't prove it wasn't me either," Baylee said, and finally sat down on the corner of Penelope's bed. Dropping her head in her hands, she said, "What am I going to do, Pen?"

Leaning over, she gave Baylee a hug and said, "I don't know, but there has to be something. Don't you keep your ambulance locked? How could someone get anything out of it without being seen?"

"I don't know, I've asked myself all these same questions. Of course, we keep it locked unless it's at the station. Plus, we keep the interior cabinets locked, at least the ones with the medication in them. There are some pretty strong ones we keep in there. Someone could easily kill themselves or someone else if they didn't know what they were doing."

"What did your boss say? Did he believe you?"

"He said he wanted too, but for now, he had no other choice than to suspend me until the investigation is complete.

He promised if they can prove I did nothing wrong, he will expunge it from my record."

"That's a good thing, I guess," Penelope said. "So, what are you going to do?"

"I don't know exactly, but I'm not going to sit around and wait for whoever's doing this to come up with more accusations against me. I need time to think, and I guess I have plenty of that now. So, I can come up with a plan."

"Okay, let me know if I can help," Penelope said. "While you're thinking about that, let me tell you what freaked me out today."

"Okay, what happened?"

After repeating everything she'd learned today, Penelope sat and waited for Baylee's response.

"Wow, small world. But you can't know for sure if it's the same girl."

"Don't pull that with me, you know as well as I do, that I'm probably right. Which means, Derrick did this to her, because he couldn't do it to me. I'm responsible for this."

Baylee stood up, walked over, and grabbed Penelope's arms. Pulling her to her feet, she said, "This isn't your fault, period. It's Derrick's if he did this, then it's on him, not you."

"Logically, I know that, but knowing it and feeling it, are two very different things. You know?"

"Well, let's go eat something and try to relax for the rest of tonight. Tomorrow is a new day, and maybe we'll see things in a different light," Baylee said, pulling Penelope into the kitchen.

After they'd eaten and tried to relax, with little to no success, Baylee went back up to her apartment. Penelope went to bed, knowing her alarm would be going off before she knew it.

The following morning before leaving for work, Penelope made sure she had everything she needed for the day, including everything for her self-defense class.

Work went smoothly as she trained her replacement, Brent, on everything that was expected of him once he took over. She knew, the quicker she trained him, the better it would be for both of them. But her mind was still occupied with the new information she'd learned only the day before about Molly. She was having a hard time keeping focused on the task at hand.

Relieved when they finished their last unit for the day, Penelope hurried to clock out and get to her Jeep. She was looking forward to her next training class with Emerson. She hoped it might help her focus on what her next step should be.

Penelope pulled into the parking lot at Inner Strength, grabbed her bag, and went inside. Realizing she was early for her appointment; she went straight to the back to change into workout clothes. She decided instead of sitting around waiting for Emerson to finish up with his client, she'd go ahead and get started with the weights.

Glad she'd thought to throw her earbuds in her bag earlier, she plugged them in and turned on her favorite workout music. After 20 minutes of some heavy lifting, she hadn't realized Emerson had joined in. She pulled out her earbud and asked, "Are you ready to start? Sorry, I get lost in the music sometimes."

Smiling at her with sweat dripping down his chin, he said, "I thought we already had started. I think another couple minutes of this, and then we can switch to some hand-to-hand. How's that sound?"

"Sounds good. Whenever you're ready."

The rest of the training was strenuous, but she thought it was good to let some of her frustration out. She hated even thinking about what Derrick had done to Molly instead of her. It was enough to keep pushing her forward, even when she was nearly ready to give in.

Once the session was over, Emerson told her she was getting better every time they met. With the compliment in her head, she showered, changed, and watched him start his next session as she walked out to her Jeep.

Noticing she was almost out of gas, she thought it was a sign to stop procrastinating and go talk to Marty. She knew she'd put it off long enough.

Taking a left into the station, she pulled up to a pump and started to fill her tank. She turned her back to the wind, as she scanned the storefront to see who was working tonight's shift.

She knew Marty was still there because his car was sitting in the parking lot. And she could see Erma-Lee standing at the counter ringing up a customer. Tugging her coat a little tighter, she replaced the nozzle and went inside to pay. Before she'd even had a chance to reach the door, she could hear Erma-Lee screaming her name.

"Penelope, you're back!" She said while holding the door open for her to walk in.

"Calm down, you act like you haven't seen me in years," Penelope smiled, happy to be missed.

"Well, maybe I feel like I haven't." Holding her at arm's length, Erma-Lee continued. "Now, let me get a good look at ya." Once she was satisfied, she tugged at a piece of Penelope's hair. "The hair-do suits ya, you're just as cute as a button." Grabbing her hand, she led Penelope further into the store. "I've been having a bad feeling come over me lately, I was starting to wonder if something might be wrong with you. I tried to call a couple times, but never did reach ya."

"I've only been gone a week, but next time leave me a message, and I'll call you back."

"Oh, I don't know. I don't much like leaving a message on one of those machines."

Shrugging her shoulders, Penelope said as she paid for the gas. "Up to you. So, tell me, anything new around here since I've been gone?"

"I can't believe you ain't heard yet. You're looking at the brand-new store manager." Erma-Lee leaned over to whisper, "I was so excited, I peed a little. Ssh, don't let that get around."

"Congrats, I'm excited for you, not pee-myself-excited, but excited just the same." Penelope raised her hand to give Erma-Lee a high five but was pulled into a hug instead.

"Don't you go thinking, you can get one over on me. I know you were the reason I got this job. You told Marty to give me a chance, and I'll be forever grateful. If ya ever need anything, just holler."

"You earned it. Just keep being you, and I'm sure you'll do great. So, is Marty around? I need to talk to him."

"He's back in his office, you know where to find him." Erma-Lee pointed to the back; about the same time, a regular came in.

"Hey ladies, looking good today," he chuckled with a grin.

"Well, you know us. We do aim to please. What can I get ya?" She did a little curtsy and headed behind the counter.

Penelope loved how Erma-Lee interacted with the customers, she was going to do just fine. Smiling to herself, she turned and headed to the back office. She tapped lightly on the door jamb and waited for Marty to look up.

"What is it," he said without taking the time to stop and notice who it was.

"It's your most trusted employee; were you expecting someone else?" Not waiting any longer to be invited in, she took the seat opposite him.

Marty's head snapped up as he realized who had taken a seat. The corner of his lip turned slightly, "Tell me you've sorted all your stuff out, and you're ready to come back to work. All the employees have been driving me crazy, asking about you. Everyone's missed you being here."

"Everyone, huh?" Raising her eyebrow, she waited for a response.

"Well, you know how it is," he shrugged and quickly looked back down at his paperwork.

"I'm sorry I haven't been by sooner; I shouldn't have kept putting it off. I heard the good news about Erma-Lee taking the position at the new store."

"When I didn't hear from you, I assumed you wouldn't be coming back. So, I took your advice and started paying closer attention. Erma-Lee really is all the things you said she was. She's great with the customers, and she treats this place like her own."

"What more could you ask for, right?" she said.

"I think she'll work out just fine. Tell me about you. Have you made any decisions yet? And if so, do they include any of us here?"

"I have made a few. When we talked last, I told you I needed to find out what I was passionate about. Well, I haven't figured it all out yet, but I can tell you a few things. The factory offered me a new position, with a nice pay increase, which you know I can't pass up. This new job allows me to go to college and to start turning my life around. So, I won't be coming back to work here."

Standing up, he walked around his desk, reached out, and took her hands. "I am going to miss you; you're like the daughter I never had. If you ever need anything, day or night, just know I'll be there." Pulling her into a fatherly hug, he kissed the top of her head.

A single tear slid down her cheek as she said, "I'm going to tell your daughter, Francie, you said that," Penelope teased. Hugging him back, she really wished he had been her dad; her life could have turned out so much differently.

"I'd wish you luck, kid, but you don't need it; just remember hard work pays off. And you'll be just fine,"

"Thanks for everything and for giving me a job when I needed one. But it's not like you won't ever see me again. I still need to put gas in Dime, and you know I don't trust those other stations. You'll probably see me so much you will think I still work here."

Handing him the keys to the store, and the old ratty smock he insisted they all wear, she gave the office one last look and turned to go.

Congratulating Erma-Lee once more before she left; she finally headed home. Penelope had been dreaming of a glass of wine all day. Since she had finally gone and talked to Marty and quit procrastinating, she felt she deserved it.

The next week went by in a blur.

It was getting close to the holidays, and Penelope was pleased with the progress she'd made. More than that, she hadn't heard or seen anything from Derrick, and she was closer every day to getting her freedom.

Penelope helped Brent oversee inventory day. It was a mandatory count day, and the whole factory had to on the last Friday before any holiday shut down. After her electrical group finished everything that was required, Penelope handed out the small gifts she'd gotten for each of them. Surprised to receive a few back, she wished them all a happy, fun, and safe holiday. She pulled her phone out and sent Baylee a text to let her know she was finally done with work for two whole weeks. She also informed her she was on her way to see Emerson, and then finally to her last gun safety class. As she left the parking lot for two whole weeks, she thought about what she'd told her workers, about having a safe and wonderful holiday. She doubted Molly would be having a good one since she was probably still in the hospital.

She'd asked Abby to keep her updated, and she'd received a few texts from her. No release date had been given yet, the last she'd heard. Penelope drove to Inner Strength but wasn't sure how she was going to keep her mind on the class. Midway through, Emerson pinned her to the floor with little to no effort.

"All right, Penelope, what's going on?"

Still deep in her own thoughts, she barely heard the question and gave no response.

"Whatever it is, you need to focus. Do you think an attacker is going to take it easy on you because you have a lot on your mind? Well, think again." He reached out and pulled her to her feet in one swift move.

The second half of the class went a lot better once Penelope realized Emerson was right. Derrick wouldn't hesitate to take advantage of her if she were distracted, that was for sure. Pushing all her thoughts to the back of her mind, she focused on what was in front of her.

What was in front of her, was Emerson and she was going to make damn sure he didn't pin her again. Every move he made, she had a counterattack. The sweat on his brow proved when she stayed focused, it was no longer easy to take her down.

Penelope realized she could almost anticipate his next move, but this meant he could probably do the same with her. Not liking the idea, she decided to change things up. She watched and waited for the perfect opening, then made her move.

Emerson always told her to use her height to her advantage. He always said, "focus on what's in front of you. Don't try to punch a giant in the face, bring the face down to you."

Using that logic, she turned her back to him, and let him think she was off guard. Like a pawn, Penelope maneuvered him exactly where she wanted.

Once he was directly behind her and getting ready to make his move, she leaned back into him, taking him off guard. Using all her weight, she stomped on his foot, elbow jabbed him in the gut, and spun to face him. Precisely as she had planned, he was now bent over, giving her better access to his pretty face. Grabbing a handful of his hair, she yanked his head down while driving her knee upward.

Using her momentum, Penelope twisted his wrist as she pulled his arm behind him, using it as leverage to force him onto his belly. Jabbing her knee into his back, she leaned over and whispered in his ear. "I'm no longer distracted; do you want to try to take me down again?"

She let go of his wrist and placed both feet on the floor. She was about to turn and go hit the showers when she noticed blood on the mat.

Emerson slowly got to his feet, holding his nose he turned towards her. "I'm pretty sure you just broke my nose."

"Really? I'm sorry. I guess you shouldn't have taught me so well. Here take this." She threw him a towel. "I didn't mean to get so carried away, but once I started, it just seemed so... natural."

Grabbing the towel, he applied pressure while leaning his head back. "I'm fine. This isn't my first broken nose, and I'm sure it won't be my last. It just needs to be reset and iced down."

She knew the sound of a bone breaking, it was a sound she'd heard quite often as a kid. The noise alone, always made her inhale quickly and think, oh no, this is going to hurt.

Emerson walked over to the first aid kit hanging on the wall and pulled out a roll of white athletic tape. Knowing full well what it was going to feel like, he placed a thumb on each side of his nose. He told himself it would feel better once it was done. He took a few light breaths to keep his throat from filling up with blood, and quickly jerked his nose back into place and drew a piece of tape across it.

"Penelope, it does seem we are done here. You've proven to me you can indeed protect yourself. You've done well, better than I expected actually. I'd be proud to have you in a foxhole with me anytime."

"Thanks, Emerson I'll keep that in mind. But I think you misunderstood. Yes, I can defend myself, but that doesn't mean I'm done here."

Raising his eyebrow, he said, "Okay?"

"This place," she motioned, "gives me a really great workout, plus I enjoy it now. It helps relieve stress, and we all know I have enough of that in my life."

Turning to go hit the showers, she swung a towel over her shoulder and yelled back, "Sorry to inform you, but you're stuck with me. At least until the end of the month, because I'm paid up until then." She smiled to herself, pushed through the swinging doors, and finally stepped into the hot shower she'd been dreaming of.

Not having enough time to really enjoy the shower, she quickly changed and headed back out into the cold. One more appointment to go, she thought. Then she could relax for the rest of the evening with a large glass of wine.

Penelope arrived a couple minutes early for her last gun safety class and pulled her phone out of her bag to check for any missed calls or messages. She couldn't believe Baylee hadn't gotten back to her yet. Typing a quick text to ask if she should be worried, she heard her name being called.

Sliding her phone back into her bag, she looked up in time to see the instructor, who would also be the one testing her walk towards her. Eager to get the last session finished and the certificate of completion in hand, she met him halfway across the room. They went over everything she'd learned; she took a short-written exam and a final target test. Passing all with flying colors, she left with a smile on her face, holding the piece of paper she had worked so hard for in her hand.

She was ready to celebrate, so she stopped and picked up a few bottles of wine on her way home. Pulling into her apartment complex, Penelope took the corner a little sharp. Before her back-end could swing up around her, she turned her wheel into the slide and pulled herself out of it. Crisis averted; all she wanted was a long hot soak and a tall glass of wine.

I wonder how much wine a person could drink in a single night, she thought. Laughing out loud, she knew she wasn't being honest with herself. What she really wanted to know was how much wine she could drink in a single night, and it was about time to find out.

She made the last turn towards her apartment and noticed a reflection of red and blue lights bouncing off the snow. While looking for the source, her stomach plummeted. She knew like everyone else, red and blue lights meant something was wrong. The closer she got to her place, the brighter the lights had become.

Chapter 18

Penelope tried to pull into her parking area, but it was blocked off with police tape. An officer was directing traffic to another lot. She rolled down her window as the officer approached.

"Sorry, ma'am, this lot's been closed. No one in, no one out, those are my orders. So, you'll need to park elsewhere tonight."

"But I live here. Could you tell me what's going on? Or at least tell me which apartment?"

"No ma'am, I'm unable to give out any information during an open investigation."

"Okay, thanks anyway, officer." She rolled up her window and started to turn around. She knew the best alternative lot was the one opposite her building, so she went in that direction.

Any hope she had for finding an empty slot was dwindling by the second. She'd known her chances were slim, but she still thought she might get lucky. By the third time circling the parking lot, she was about to give up when she spotted an empty slot on her left. Swinging wide, she stopped short, discovering someone had been rude and taken up two spaces.

Slamming her hands down on the steering wheel, she understood why people had road rage. Why did people have to be so inconsiderate, she thought. Anyone who would take up more than one parking space deserved what they got in life.

Maybe the next time she heard someone say they had their car keyed, or someone let the air out of their tires, she might look at them and say, "Well, maybe you deserved it."

If it wasn't so damn cold out, she might have considered a friendly approach. Like maybe leaving a note to tell them how rude they were. But she wasn't going to freeze her rump off and play nice. Screw that.

All she wanted was to get inside her apartment, open a bottle of wine, and let the day melt away. Was that too much to ask? Apparently, since she had already wasted how much time trying to park.

She thought the best option might be to use her Jeep and move the car herself. Then again, she would freeze during the process, and it would take more time than it was worth. Plus, getting a scratch on Dime wasn't worth the risk.

With no options left, Penelope decided to make her own parking spot. After all, what good was a four-wheel-drive Jeep if you never used it, she thought.

She spotted a large pile of snow from the plows at the end of the drive. She decided it was as good as she was going to get. So, she lined herself up, leaned over, and rubbed her dashboard.

"Come on, Dime, you got this." Throwing him into four-wheel drive, she started the climb. Thinking to herself, sometimes, a girl just needs to do what works.

As she gathered up her things, she noticed she could see her apartment building from up there. The night sky was still lit with flashing lights from several police cars. She watched as a couple of the officers got out of their squad cars and walked toward her corridor.

Her first thought went to Baylee, and how she hadn't heard from her all day. Forgetting everything else, she quickly hopped out and started dialing her phone as she made a run down the snow hill for the building.

She didn't notice when the voicemail came on, as she was once again stopped by the officer from earlier.

"I'm sorry, ma'am, but I can't let you go in there."

"What do you mean? I live there!" With the phone still pressed to her ear, but long forgotten, she tried to push past him. When that didn't work, she luckily spotted a familiar face amongst the officers.

"Detective Black! Over here." She yelled, trying to get his attention, but wasn't close enough for him to hear.

"Look, see that detective over there? He's the lead investigator in a case I'm involved in, if you'd go get him, I'm sure he can clear this whole thing up."

"I'm sure he could, but you need to step behind the tape ma'am. I will not tell you again."

"Are you kidding me? Really?" She turned around and made her way under the police tape. She knew, yelling at the officer wasn't going to help her at this point. What she needed was to come up with a plan.

Maybe she could see more from a higher advantage point. Her Jeep would work, she thought, so she climbed up the snow and got back in. After a few minutes of watching the apartment and a ton of calls and texts to Baylee, she was still no closer to knowing what was going on.

Penelope had no clue how long it would be until she could get into her apartment, so she decided what the hell, and opened a bottle of wine. Baylee thought Penelope having a wine corker on her keychain was a dumb idea. Not so dumb now, was it, she thought.

With no one around to impress, she didn't have to worry about not having a glass and drank straight from the bottle. She took her first swig and watched the apartment building for any clue about what was going on. Several officers repeatedly went in and out of the corridor holding bags, with what she assumed was evidence.

Penelope thought the wine must have been keeping her calm because all she wanted to do was blaze through the stupid police tape and run in to find out for herself what was going on.

Watching from afar was driving her crazy. She knew they were in her corridor, but there were six different apartments in her building. Which one were they in? Was someone hurt? It all came back to Baylee in her mind, and why hadn't she heard from her?

Moments later, she watched as a black van was allowed to enter the secured location. Upon further inspection, she noticed it had the letters CPDCO on the door. Penelope quickly pulled out her phone to look it up and was shocked to find the letters stood for Chicago Police Department Coroner's Office. Two men exited the van and went inside.

As she sat there staring at her phone, it began to ring. Caught off guard, she fumbled to answer it.

"Hello?" Penelope answered.

"Where are you? This is Detective Black; we have a situation."

"Really? A situation, you say?"

"Now is not the time to joke around, Penelope. Tell me where you are, and I'll come to you. I don't think it's a good idea for you to come to your apartment right now."

"So, you don't think it's a good idea, huh? Well, your about two hours too late. I've been sitting out here in my Jeep freaking out and wondering what's been going on. I can't get ahold of Baylee, and it's not like her to not call or text me back."

"I'm walking outside right now, where are you?"

Looking over, she saw him standing on the sidewalk in front of her apartment. She reached over, flipped the switch on her overhead trail lights, so he would easily spot her from across the parking lots.

"Do you see me now?" she asked, realizing he'd already hung up and was walking her way.

"What made you think parking up there was a good idea?" he asked.

Shrugging her shoulders, she said, "Would you rather I hooked up my tow strap and pulled someone else's car out of my way?"

"Was that another option? Wait, never mind, don't answer that."

Before he could climb up the snowbank, get in the car and close the door, Penelope started throwing questions at him.

"Whoa, slow down," he told her, getting in the Jeep. "We'll figure all this out, I promise. So, you said you haven't heard from Baylee, and that's not her normal behavior? Does she usually always respond right away when you call or text her?"

"Yes, always. Baylee knows I'd be worried, and she wouldn't do that to me. We stay in contact throughout the day and always send a text to let the other one know what our plans are. It's our version of a buddy system. But I haven't heard from her all day."

"So, here's the deal; I'm going to give it to you straight." Turning to face her, he wanted to see her reaction to the news.

"Do you remember when you called me the morning your alarm went off? I walked around and checked everything out; well, what I didn't tell you then was...I found a cigarette butt on your balcony that night still smoldering. I bagged it and had it sent to the lab for testing."

Penelope seemed to be holding up pretty well so far to the new information, Detective Black thought. She obviously wasn't happy about being kept out of the loop, but still, under the circumstances, he was quite impressed by her calm state.

"Okay, so what did the results show?" she questioned.

"Nothing I didn't expect. I assumed it would prove to be Derrick's, which it was, but it still didn't tell us where he'd been hiding out."

"Let me get this straight. You're telling me you know nothing more now than you did then?" Penelope pulled the bottle of wine from the center console and downed half of it in a single swallow.

"Yes and no. No, I didn't learn anything new with the tests, but I did learn a lot tonight. Let me explain," Black said as he pulled the bottle out of her hands. "You do realize this is considered an open container, right?"

"Really! You're going to blow me shit about having a drink? If I could actually get into my apartment, I would be soaking in my tub, listening to music and having a glass there." She reached over and snatched the bottle back out of his hand and took another long pull.

Black figured he'd pick his battles, and knew she might need the wine before he was through telling her the rest.

"Let me ask you this. Do you know your downstairs neighbor, Mrs. Linda McCloud?"

"Not really, she never leaves her place. I went and introduced myself when we first moved in, but I think I have only seen her a couple times. Why are you asking?" Realization hit about the same time she asked the question. That must be who died, and why the coroner's van was there.

"I don't understand? She was an older lady who died. Why would you guys tape off the whole lot and not let anyone into the apartments?"

"You're right, she was an elderly woman, which makes this much more disgusting in my eyes." He shook his head and tried to erase the image stuck in his mind from earlier.

"I need to ask you a few questions, do you think you're up for it?" He knew her thinking was impaired, he'd seen her down half the bottle himself, but Black needed to try to get all the answers he could.

"Sure, fire away, I have nothing else to do tonight," she said with a slight slur. Penelope shook the bottle to make sure it wasn't quite empty. "Okay, detective, now I'm ready."

"Everything I've had tested has all come back with trace amounts of a certain substance. At the time, the information didn't really help because it can be found almost anywhere. Tonight, that all changed, I believe I've located the source," Black told her.

"Okay, don't leave me hanging, spill already. What's the source?" asked Penelope as she drank the last of her wine. Throwing the empty bottle into the backseat, she reached for another, glad she had the foresight to buy more than one, earlier in the day.

"Mrs. McCloud was the source!" He gave her a second for it to register then went on. "Well, not Mrs. McCloud exactly, but her cat. The one substance that kept showing up in all the samples was cat dander. Mrs. McCloud had a cat, which is right now getting tested to see if it's a match."

"So, you're basing your theory on a cat?" Penelope asked.

"Partly yes, but we also have a witness in the hospital. The witness told us to come here, and that's when we discovered the body. My tech tells me preliminarily it looked like she was murdered weeks ago, but then there are very recent wounds as well. It's a strange case to have premortem and postmortem wounds on the same victim. I guess we'll have to wait until after she thaws out, and for the autopsy to be finished before we'll know more."

"Who's the witness you're talking about?" She had a gut feeling she knew who it would turn out to be, but she needed to ask.

"You know I can't tell you, but here's what I think happened. I think Derrick's been hiding out in your neighbor's downstairs apartment. That way, he'd be able to keep an eye on you, and he'd see you come and go. Once you left, he could sneak out or have someone pick him up."

"Are you serious? If what you're saying is true, then why hasn't he killed me already?" Penelope was still absorbing what he'd told her. She barely knew the woman, but now she felt as responsible for her as she did for Molly. She wondered if Detective Black knew about her, but she wasn't up for discussing it right now.

"That, I'm afraid I can't answer. I just don't know."

Penelope shook her head and said, "Your theory doesn't make sense. Why would he just stalk me? It doesn't seem like it would be enough to satisfy him."

"I disagree, stalkers take great pleasure in the fear they cause. It's like a cat and mouse game. But I do agree and think things will escalate. Derrick won't be appeased for long. Maybe it already has. The morning you woke up to music, I think he must have found a way into your place and set it all up. Perhaps the writing on the mirror wasn't old like we originally thought. He could have been watching you shower and knew when you were almost finished. So, he quickly wrote it before he snuck out."

Penelope felt ill, and all the wine she'd drank was about to come back up. Clenching her stomach, she opened the door and painted the snow red. She needed to find a way to calm down and think things through. Derrick had been much closer than she'd realized. What game was he playing, and how far would it go?

"Are you going to be okay? I need to be getting back, I'm not sure how long all this is going to take, but you'll need to find someplace else to go until we find Derrick. I want you and Baylee out of eyesight."

"I have a problem with that already. Don't you listen? I don't know where Baylee is! She's upset, because of something that happened at work, I know. I could call her parents, but I don't want to worry them," Penelope said.

"I'll go see what I can find out. Stay here, and keep trying her cell. I'll be back." He opened the door and was gone.

Chapter 19

Why, is it so cold in here? Waking up shivering, Baylee instinctively reached out to pull her blankets over herself. Not being able to move her arm didn't alarm her. She just assumed it was asleep like the rest of her body should be. Not quite awake yet, she tried to turn over. That's when it hit her... she was no longer in her bed.

She told herself to stay calm and think, but it wasn't as easy as it appeared on T.V., when someone found themselves in a frightening situation. But she knew crying and freaking out wouldn't solve anything either.

Lying there in the dark, in only her nightshirt, Baylee listened for any sound. It might give her information on where she was. Was she alone, or was someone there with her? She didn't hear anyone breathing and heard only silence.

The loud buzzing in her head was interfering with any sounds that might be around her, but she couldn't give up.

Okay, one thing at a time, she told herself. Since she'd heard nothing, she decided to try to move. Baylee lifted her head and attempted to sit up, but she hit her head on something hard. Reaching out to figure out what kind of place she was in, Baylee discovered her hands were bound together in front of her. Thankful she wasn't claustrophobic; she slid her hands across the surface above her. It felt rough, gritty, and cold. Wherever she was, it was pitch black, that was for sure. She'd hoped her eyes would adjust to the darkness, but they hadn't yet. And without the help of her eyesight, she couldn't figure out where she might be.

Trying to straighten her legs revealed that they too were bound and wherever she was, it was too small for someone even her size

"Okay, so my hands and legs are useless, and I can't see a damn thing. How am I going to get out of this?" she told herself. Taking a deep breath. She switched to her professional mindset, no emotions, just assess the facts.

At some point, whoever took me has to come back, right? And when they do, I need to be ready, she decided. Baylee pulled her wrists up to her mouth and started chewing on the restraints.

As she lay there, she fought the feeling of hopelessness. She had to find a way out. Finally, she heard something, a faint scratching sound, but she couldn't tell where it was coming from. She tilted her head and listened. There it was again. It sounded so close. She wasn't sure if she should stay quiet or try to draw attention to herself. With her hands still bound, she didn't have many options, because she wasn't sure if whoever had done this was still around or not, so, for now, she decided to stay quiet.

Hours later, shivering uncontrollably, she wished she could find anything to cover herself with. She'd never been this cold in her life. Her teeth kept chattering, and she could no longer feel her toes. What she needed to do was find a way to warm herself up, but not having much room to move was going to make it a challenge.

Since running in place was out of the question, she moved her legs the best she could. Pulling her knees up to her chest as far as they could go, she then straightened them out and kicked the surface below. It seemed to move the entire space she was in. Making sure it wasn't her mind playing tricks, she tried again. Once again, the whole thing moved. It sounded hollow? Okay, that's a start. Now, what sounds hollow, she thought? As she continued to kick it over and over, she noticed whatever the structure was made of, it had a little give. So, it wasn't concrete or steel.

"That's good, I guess. Whatever I'm in, I might still have a chance of escaping," she said to herself.

She knew it wasn't concrete because concrete didn't move. But every time her bare feet hit it, it sure felt like something immovable. After what felt like hours had passed, she clenched her jaw so her teeth would stop chattering. Baylee refused to lose hope, she would make it out of this alive. One way or another, she would get free, and whoever was responsible better watch out.

None of this made any sense to her. Still, no closer to any answers, she lay there and thought of who, what, why, and where. She would think of when later. An ex-boyfriend, maybe? No, she didn't think so. The only person she knew crazy enough to do this was Derrick unless she had really screwed up and pissed off the wrong person. Wait, what about whoever was framing her at work? Who was the mysterious someone who'd called in a tip? Could Derrick also be her accuser? Or was it someone else entirely?

Okay, let's say it was Derrick, what could have set him off to take such extreme measures? Was he trying to punish Penelope through doing this to her? Did he honestly think he would get away with it or was getting away, not in his plan?

The last thing she remembered was lying in bed watching the late show. One of her favorite singers was going to be a guest. I don't know if I stayed awake long enough to see them or not, she thought. Then what? Trying to remember was making her very tired, but she was afraid to fall asleep. I need to stay awake, think it through, figure it out, she kept repeating over and over.

How did I go from sleeping in my bed to waking up here? Somehow, whoever did this must have broken into my apartment and drugged me. Because that's the only way, they would've ever gotten away with it. Oh my God, maybe the accuser is trying to cover their own tracks. Did they drug me with the stolen medication from my own ambulance? But what if it was Derrick, what if all of it was Derrick?

"Oh, No! If Derrick could break into my apartment, then he could break into Penelope's. I need to get out of here and warn her." Lying there, she started to laugh. That's funny, how am I supposed to help her? I think I'm the one who needs a little help this time.

Not sure how long she'd already been there, Baylee was sure of one thing, and that was Penelope would stop at nothing to find her. Knowing she was already showing signs of hypothermia, she only hoped her best friend would get there in time.

Suddenly there was a sound to her left, turning her head, she once again tried to figure out what it was. She held her breath, then without warning, a bright light was shining in her eyes. The light was blinding, she couldn't see anything. Then, she heard a voice.

"Hello again, Baylee."

Chapter 20

Penelope woke to the smell of coffee, and her eyes opened automatically in search of the source. Unfortunately, she also woke with a terrible headache, cramped neck, stiff back, and still no answers. With reality setting in, she turned to her right and watched Detective Black take a sip of his coffee.

"Anything yet?" Penelope asked, pulling herself out from the layer of coats she was wrapped in.

"Nothing," Black said, "I thought for sure he'd return to the scene of the crime."

"Yeah, well, tell me you have another plan and give it to me straight. We've sat in this car all night watching for Derrick, and he never showed up. How are we going to find him? I know he has something to do with Baylee's disappearance."

"I don't know exactly," he told her.

"What do you mean you don't know exactly? Are you telling me you don't know what to do from here?" She leaned across the Jeep, getting into his personal space, so he understood how vital her next statement was. "Get off your ass and do something! I don't care what, anything! We have to find her!"

"I understand your concern…"

"My concern? Really? No, you don't, or you wouldn't sit there and say that. She's my best friend, Black, I can't lose her. She's all I have left in this world. Do you understand?"

Not being able to sit still any longer, Penelope popped open her door and took off at a run for her apartment.

Fast on her heels, Detective Black yelled out, "I'm sorry." As he caught up to her, he apologized further. "I didn't mean to act like you're just another case. I'm tired. As you pointed out earlier, I've been up all night with binoculars watching and waiting for Derrick to show up. Can we please go back to the Jeep? The sun has barely come up, we could still get lucky. You never know he might show up."

Taking Penelope's arm, he led her back to the Jeep. He knew he needed to come up with another plan since this one looked to be a bust. But not being able to locate Derrick was only half the problem. Since he knew Penelope was convinced, Derrick had something to do with Baylee's disappearance.

He had no evidence of foul play, so he couldn't just walk into Baylee's apartment and take a look around. He'd put in the request for a warrant to search it the night before when Penelope had told him Baylee was missing. He wasn't going to be the one to screw this up and let Derrick get off on a technicality. Black only hoped with the evidence piling up, the judge wouldn't make him wait the 24-hour waiting period before issuing it. Hopefully, if Derrick had been the one to take her, he'd find a clue to lead him in the right direction.

As they climbed back into the Jeep, his phone rang. Pulling it out of his pocket, he quickly answered.

"Black here."

Penelope sat and watched as he spoke, hoping for some good news. She hated not being able to hear the other side of the conversation because he was just answering yes and no.

But it wasn't long before he hung up and was climbing back out of the vehicle.

"Where are you going?" Penelope asked.

Making his way around to the driver's side, he pulled open the door, "I need to drive. I'll explain on the way."

"On the way where?" Penelope questioned, climbing across the console to the passenger side. "Is it Baylee? Have they found her?"

"Sorry, it's not Baylee. It's our witness at the hospital. She just woke up from surgery and is asking for me. She says she has more information on Derrick." Shoving the Jeep into drive, he maneuvered it off the snow pile and took off for Edward Memorial Hospital.

"Hey, be careful with Dime; he's my pride and joy." She said as she stroked the door panel. "Maybe I should drive."

"Don't worry, your precious Dime will be fine. After all, I am a trained professional."

"All the training in the world won't help you if you wreck my Jeep. And that's not a threat, it's a promise."

They were both silent for the rest of the drive. It wasn't long until they were pulling into the parking garage at the hospital and went inside to ask for the room number.

"I hope she can help us. I have a bad feeling we're running out of time," Penelope stated as they made their way to the correct floor.

"It will be okay; I'll try to make it quick. I need you to stay out here, while I go in and see what she has to say," Black said, pulling a few bills from his pocket and pointing to the vending machines along the wall. "I'm sure you could use some caffeine; I know I could. How about you grab us something while I'm in there?"

"Sure, no problem," Penelope said. He must be crazy if he thinks I'm not going in there to meet this witness, she thought.

The dollars were crumpled from his pocket, but she managed to get the machine to take them. Finally, the last soda tumbled down the opening, and Penelope bent over and pulled it out.

She walked down the hall towards the room where she knew the detective had gone. She quietly cracked the door ajar and heard soft-spoken voices on the other side. Not willing to wait outside any longer, she pushed the door wide and stepped over the threshold into the room.

Everyone stopped talking mid-sentence and turned to look at her. Detective Black stared daggers from where he stood at the end of the bed, while a nurse on his left was taking what she assumed was the patient's vitals.

"What are you doing?" Detective Black whispered, "I thought we agreed you'd stay in the hall?"

"Well, here's the thing, Penelope told him. "That didn't really work for me. I need answers, and I need them now. If this girl has them, then I'm not leaving until she talks."

Turning to the patient, the detective lightly tapped the bed rail and said, "Excuse me for one second while I take care of this. I'll be right back, okay, Molly?"

Not waiting for a reply, he turned, made a grab for Penelope's arm, and tried to lead her out of the room. As he whispered under his breath, "You can't be here. You need to leave. This could jeopardize the entire case."

"I don't care; I need to speak to her." Penelope pulled free and walked to the bed.

"Hi, Molly, I'm Penelope. I was told you might be able to help me." She handed the girl one of the vending machine drinks and continued. "Do you have more information about Derrick?" She was trying to stay calm when all she wanted to do was shake the girl and make her tell her everything she knew.

Molly waited until the nurse was finished, and left the room, then spoke. "I'm so sorry; I didn't know about you. I had no idea Derrick was married. I didn't find out until the Detectives told me yesterday."

"It's fine, I'm not here about that," Penelope told her. "I don't blame you. I'm sure you didn't know. It wasn't like he was going to announce it. But right now, if you want to make it up to me, I could really use your help."

"You want my help? Don't you hate me?" Molly sat on her bed, holding the can of soda, afraid to look at Penelope. "How can you even stand to look at me? I'm so ashamed. I'd never have gotten involved with a married man if I'd have known."

"Okay, look. I think we're getting off track here. I just need to know if you have any information, if not, I'm out of here," Penelope stated.

"Take it easy. Give the girl a break; she's probably in a state of shock and needs a little time," Detective Black said.

"I can't give her a break. I don't have the luxury of time. I'm worried about my friend and what Derrick might be doing to her this very minute. And if this girl has information that could help find her, then I need it now."

Turning towards Molly, Penelope asked, "Well, what do you say? Can you help me?"

Waiting only a moment, Penelope turned to walk away. As she reached for the door, she heard her name being called.

"Penelope, please wait. I want to help you. It's the least I could do."

"Okay, what can you tell me?" Penelope said, returning to her bed.

"A colleague of mine came by to see me earlier, with some very disturbing news of his own. I believe it might be linked to Derrick," Molly said.

Detective Black stood back and listened as the two women discussed the details. While he took notes, it intrigued him to watch Penelope take over the situation and get what she needed out of it. He knew it was a bad idea for her to be anywhere near the witness. However, Molly genuinely seemed to like her and opened up very quickly about what she knew.

Chiming in, Detective Black asked, "Do you give permission for a search team to head to that location?"

"Yes, absolutely. Anything that would help," Molly said.

Once Penelope had gotten all the details she could, she turned to go. Stopping short of the doorway, she turned back to Molly.

"Thanks for all your help, I really appreciate it. You may have just saved a life today," Penelope said. Then turning to Black, she continued, "Let's go, Detective. Let's see if we can find Derrick."

"I think that's supposed to be my line," he said, following her out the door. He grabbed his phone as they walked, punched in a number, and waited.

"Hello Sergeant, I need an investigation team in-route to Hinsdale Veterinary Clinic, they need to secure the location and collect any evidence on the scene as soon as possible. I have just gotten permission to do the search. Yes, Sir, the other warrant came through, and I'm on my way to those apartments now. Thank you, Sir." Hanging up, he slid the phone back into his pocket and turned to Penelope.

"I'm not sure what we're going to be walking in on, once we get there. So, I need to go in first, is that understood?" Black asked.

Penelope sat in the passenger seat, staring out the window, afraid of what they would find once they arrived. With a nod of her head, she signaled to Black that she understood, but didn't want to talk about it.

From the outside, the apartments looked exactly like they had only hours ago, but Penelope had the feeling something had changed. As she followed Detective Black up the stairs to Baylee's, she couldn't help but worry about what they were about to walk into.

Handing over the keys to Baylee's apartment, Penelope watched as Detective Black drew his weapon moments before he entered. Turning back, he said, "Stay here, don't come in until I give you the all-clear. Okay?"

Penelope nodded her head and stood in the doorway to keep watch and waited for him to give the signal.

"All clear," Black said as he hustled towards the door to keep Penelope from entering any further. "Wait… don't come in, you don't want to see this."

Penelope stepped over the threshold and into Baylee's living room. "Too late, and you're right. I don't want to see it." She could do nothing but stare, almost every inch of wall space was covered in what looked like blood.

Detective Black tried to cover her face and lead her out, but she wouldn't allow it.

"Stop it. I'm not leaving. I've been told what to do for far too long, that time's over now. Did you find the clue?" She looked up at him with hope in her eyes and pointed to the far wall. Written in what she feared was Baylee's blood was:

FIND THE CLUE SO YOU'LL KNOW WHAT TO DO.

"No, I haven't located the clue yet. Just wait a minute, Penelope, and take a few deep breaths to calm down." Black said, grasping her arm to keep her from leaving the room. "Let me go first, you need to be ready to handle what else we might find."

"Let me go," Penelope said, pushing his hand off her arm. "What I need is to find the clue. It's the only lead we have to find Baylee."

Reluctantly, he let her help with the search, but once they had gone through the whole apartment, they still came up empty.

"Maybe Derrick wrote it to make us waste our time. Maybe there is no clue." Black said, rubbing his scruffy face in a sign of frustration.

"No. There's a clue; we just have to find it. Give me a couple minutes to think this through." Where could he put a clue that would have the most impact on me, Penelope thought. Where would Derrick leave a message to send me into a panic?

Suddenly believing she knew where; she ran to Baylee's bathroom and turned the shower on full blast. Watching the mirror as the steam rose, Penelope hoped a clue would reveal itself.

"Good idea," Black said, standing in the doorway. "You think he left a message on the mirror like at your place? How about we give the steam time to work, while we go back and take another look through her bedroom?"

"Right," Penelope agreed. "We might be able to find something he missed, or better yet, find something he didn't intend on us to find." Closing the door behind her, hoping to speed up the process, she turned her attention back to the bedroom.

"You know, I have to ask," she looked again at the blood-spattered walls and bed. "Would Baylee be able to survive this amount of blood loss?"

When he didn't answer, Penelope bent over and looked under the bed. She couldn't believe what she'd found, but there it was, just out of reach. She looked for something to assist her and spotted Baylee's favorite pair of stiletto boots within arm's reach. Grabbing one, she used it to drag the item out from under the bed.

Holding up Baylee's cell phone like a prize, she said, "Bet he didn't expect us to find this."

"Turn it on," Black said. "Maybe there's a clue on it."

Knowing it would likely be dead by now, Penelope reached for the cord Baylee always left by her bed, and plugged it in. The screen immediately came to life, and so did a glimmer of hope within herself. A picture of the two of them from a couple weeks ago shopping in town was Baylee's home screen picture.

Determined she would see the beautiful smile again, Penelope started scrolling through looking for anything that might help them. Disappointed, she laid the phone on the bed.

"Wait!" Penelope said, jumping up and running to the closet. "Her gun!" She pulled down an old shoebox and pried open the lid, only to discover it was empty.

"He must have taken her gun!" she explained to Black. "She always kept it in this box, right here in her closet. But how would Derrick know it was there?" she asked.

"I suspect he's been watching you both for some time now. He would probably wait to sneak in until he knew you left, or when you were sleeping."

Detective Black needed to call it in as a crime scene, but before he got a chance, his phone rang.

"Detective Black," he answered, holding up his finger for Penelope, to signal he needed a minute. "That's good news. It explains a lot of what I'm seeing over here at the apartment. Yes, go ahead and send the crew this way, it's going to be another long night." Hanging up, he pocketed the phone and sighed heavily.

Instantly set on edge, Penelope asked, "What's the sigh about?"

"Like I said, it's going to be another long night. The call I was on, just confirmed everything Molly told us was indeed true. Her associate let the team in, and the crew discovered a few vials of medication are missing, as in some powerful tranquilizers and sedatives. They also said several units of blood are missing. Once we test the blood on the walls, I believe it will prove to be animal blood."

"Wow, that's great news," Penelope said. "At least now, I don't have to worry that he killed her right here and spread her blood all over."

Black only nodded in reply.

"But we need to hurry and figure this out. She's been missing for too long, and I can't imagine he'll keep her around much longer," Penelope said, heading back to the bathroom.

Opening the door, the scent of Baylee's body wash hit her square in the face. It triggered an emotion she wasn't ready for and made her reach out to the wall for support. Oh, how she loved that smell, it reminded her of her best friend and all the good times they've had.

Behind her, Black tapped on her shoulder and pointed to the mirror.

Trying to focus on why she was here, she looked up, and there it was.

ALL I'VE LOST WILL COME AT A COST
TEXT 555-4464

"That's it," Penelope cried, pulling out her phone, she started to text the number.

"Stop, don't do anything," Black said as he left the bathroom at the sound of people entering the apartment.

She assumed the officers he'd asked for were walking in, and he'd be bringing them up to date. She waited but feared it would take too long, so she hurried out to ask him what her next move should be.

Silence met her once she entered the room. All the officers stopped what they were doing and stared in her direction.

"Sir?" one of them questioned the Detective, as to why a civilian was there.

"Don't worry about her, she's my responsibility. The Sergeant is aware of the situation. So, you can continue on with what you were assigned. Thank you."

He turned towards Penelope and led her back into the bathroom to see the clue again.

"A phone number? I thought he'd be smarter than that," Black told her, pulling out his phone and immediately asking someone to run the number. "I should've known better," he said a few minutes later, as he hung up. "It's another burner phone, so there's no way to trace it. Go ahead and send a text and see what he replies."

Penelope still holding the phone punched in the number and typed. "When and Where? PS. You better not hurt her."

The response was immediate. "Took you long enough. Time is not your friend."

"Stop playing games," Penelope texted.

"Come alone! No cops, remember your actions have consequences. Meet me at the old factory on South Ashland Avenue in three hours," was the reply.

Staring at her phone, Penelope realized he could be talking about several different places out on Ashland.

Looking to the Detective, she said, "There are how many abandoned buildings out on Ashland? How am I supposed to figure out which one in time?"

"Give me a few minutes. I'll find the connection," Black said while he walked out of the bathroom with his phone in his hand.

Just then, another text came through.

"Do you need another clue? The shiny new penny isn't so bright, after all."

Seconds later, Detective Black came rushing back to her. "I got it! It's the old abandoned paint factory. Baylee's parents bought it years ago and still own the title."

"Nice work, Black, now I can send him one final text," Penelope said with a dangerous look in her eye.

"No clue needed, so you can shove it. See you in three hours." She hit send and slid the phone into her back pocket, veered around the Detective, and headed straight for the door.

"Hey, where do you think you're going," Detective Black asked, knowing full well she was planning to attempt this on her own.

"I'm going to go get Baylee, where do you think I'm going? Look, Detective. I appreciate all your help, but you read the texts I have to go alone. Plus, you have rules and red tape, I have nothing holding me back," Penelope insisted.

"The hell you don't! How about making sure you see your friend alive. Your chances are better with my help than without. Now we've only got a couple hours to come up with a fool-proof plan, so we better get to it," he said as he followed her out of the apartment.

Holding up two fingers, he said, "Be right back. Stay put for once, will you?" Not waiting for a reply, he opened the door, stood and spoke with the forensic team. "Please make sure you lock this place down after you've collected all the evidence and cleaned up."

"Sure thing, boss," One of the guys yelled back.

"Oh, and one more thing, can you let me know what you guys find as soon as you have anything."

Getting a thumbs-up was good enough for him. He knew he had a great team, and they would always go the extra mile when he asked them too.

Walking back out, he was surprised to see Penelope still standing on the landing, waiting for him.

"You're learning, I see. Thank you for staying put," he told her.

"Well, don't get used to it. I'm not planning on making it a habit," Penelope said, walking around him and down the stairs.

Chapter 21

With the three hours almost up, Penelope was focused on the most important things, getting Baylee back and making sure Derrick paid for everything he'd done.

"I swear, if he hurt her, I'll kill him," Penelope said under her breath. Then she remembered, one of Detective Black's techs had attached an extra button with a hidden camera and mic in it to her coat. "Um, if you guys heard that, could you please delete it? We wouldn't want it to look pre-meditated if something were to go wrong, and Derrick ended up dead."

She knew the plan, and pulled over to the side of the road where she'd been instructed, less than a block away from the factory. She engaged the parking brake and picked up her phone to call Black and let him know she was at the agreed location.

"I'm on my mark," she said, once he answered.

"Give me a few minutes; I'll signal you when we're ready for you to proceed," Detective Black responded.

Knowing every minute counted, Penelope hoped Baylee could hold on a little longer. She knew personally how a few minutes could feel like a lifetime.

Suddenly her phone vibrated; opening it, she read, "You're good to go, do exactly as we discussed."

With her energy level up, she released the brake, threw her Jeep into drive, and rubbed her dashboard. "Come on, Dime, let's do this. Let's go get our girl back. Hang on Bay, we're coming."

With only a hint of light left in the sky, Penelope slowly drove through the rusted double gates that led to the factory. Instantly, she knew why Derrick had picked this location. The old paint storefront no longer stood where it once was, but this was where they'd met, that hot summer day years ago.

Penelope pushed the memory from her mind and focused on why she was there. With several buildings scattered throughout the lot, she wasn't sure which way she should go. Looking for any sign of where Derrick or Baylee might be, she stopped and surveyed the area.

A flickering light caught her eye, so she headed in that direction. Hoping it wasn't a trap, she started talking to herself as well as whoever was on the other end of the mic, giving some description of what she saw as she went.

"I see a light, over to my right. I'm heading that way now. There's still been no sign of Baylee or Derrick. I'm about to turn the corner of the first building; let's see where this mysterious light is taking me."

Slowly, she crept around the corner. The only sound was that of her snow-packed tires and her rapidly beating heart.

"There are buildings on both sides of me; it gives me the feeling of being in an alleyway. It looks to be mostly boarded up, except for a few broken windows on the third floor. I have the feeling I'm being watched, and more than just by you guys. I'm going to keep moving forward. I see an old faded sign ahead."

Almost fifty feet from the end of the building, there was a ramp leading to a cargo door on her left. But with the light still flickering up ahead, she decided to steer clear for now and follow the light. Able to read the sign from this distance, it stated employee parking was in the rear of the building.

Going solely on instinct, she crept to the end of the building and stopped. Finally, she discovered the source of the light. It was a fire she assumed Derrick had started in a fifty-gallon drum.

A few old cars were scattered throughout the lot; some had years of dirt on them, while others had barely enough parts left to decipher the make or model. With still no clear sign of what her next move should be, she drove a couple more feet closer to the fire and turned off her engine.

Penelope wanted to make sure Detective Black and his guys knew where she was, so once again, she spoke into the mic. "I'm in the back lot behind the buildings. I'm going to exit my Jeep now and take a walk around to see if I can locate Baylee. I hope the camera you guys installed is still up and running. Here goes nothing."

Opening the driver's door, Penelope stepped out.

"Derrick! I'm here," she shouted.

Turning in all directions so the camera could see what she was seeing, she yelled, "Let's get on with it. You know why I'm here and what I want. Where is she? Where's Baylee?"

Silence was all she heard. "I know you're here. Stop playing games!" Walking further into the open, she waited; she was sure he would make his presence known at any time.

The crackling of the fire and the snow under her boots were the only sounds she heard. Slowly making her way across the lot, she felt exposed and wished she still had the cover of her Jeep. She spotted a couple of old vehicles parked close to the fire and went in that direction. She thought at least she wouldn't be out in the open, and any cover was better than none. Penelope could sense she was being watched, but Derrick still had yet to make his move.

The strong scent of burning plastic and rotten food had Penelope pulling her scarf up to cover her nose, she hoped it would help with the smell, and kept moving.

Stopping short of the first vehicle, she knew Derrick could be hiding in any one of them. She knew she had backup, and it helped to push her forward because at this point, she had no evidence whether Baylee was even here, or if it was just another one of Derrick's sick games. Maybe this was all a ploy to get her out here.

"Derrick, come out and tell me what you want."

Penelope heard a sound and turned to her left. She wanted to make sure the camera could take in the scene, just in case they needed to move in quickly. Softly she stepped toward the sound to see if she could locate its source. Hoping to hear it again, she yelled, "Hello, is anyone there? Baylee, is that you?"

A very faint scraping noise, to her right, caught her attention. Determined to find out where the sound was coming from, she looked around and tried to narrow it down.

Only a foot away was a dirt-covered pickup, with all the windows broken out. It looked like it had been sitting there for a long time. Peeking inside, she could see the rats had taken over, there wasn't much left of the interior.

Walking around, she looked for any sign someone had been in or near it lately. Seeing nothing, she moved on to the next car in line. She wondered why someone had left them all here because, at one point, they must have been running, so why would someone just abandon them?

Then came the faint sound again, she walked past the next car, which seemed to be the oldest one there. "Baylee, if you can hear me say something or make a noise so I can find you."

Penelope stopped and listened, but heard nothing. She tilted her head and looked down, then momentarily forgot about the camera. She forgot about the cops and detectives; she even forgot about Derrick. Looking down, she noticed something much more interesting.

There were odd markings on the ground. It looked like something, or possibly someone had been dragged through this part of the lot. Taking it as a sign, Penelope quickly followed.

The marks ended at the trunk of an old Cadillac. This one didn't have years' worth of dirt covering it. Nor did it have all the windows broken out. This had to be it, she thought.

Leaning over, she pressed her ear to the trunk and tapped lightly, then waited for a response, but heard nothing. Not willing to give up, she knocked louder, but still, no sound came from it. She quickly tried to open the driver's door, hoping she might get lucky, but of course, it was locked.

Baylee has to be in there, Penelope thought. If the scraping sound had been her, she'd gone silent. Maybe she passed out and can't respond, or Derrick had taped her mouth shut. It sure wouldn't be the first time he'd done it.

Crouching down next to the bumper, she noticed a small dent on the corner of the trunk lid. If I could bend the edge a little more, I might be able to see inside.

Penelope stood up, and quickly examined the area, spotting a piece of wood under the car beside her. She grabbed it and gave it a try. She wedged it under the dent, and slowly pushed down, hoping it would do the job. She watched the corner lift a fraction as she pressed down, and it gave her a little hope. I only need a little more, she thought as she tried again, using all of her body weight. But the board wasn't strong enough to hold her and broke. Tapping lightly on the trunk lid, she said, "Don't you worry, Bay. I'm not giving up, and neither should you. I have another idea, hang on."

Penelope ran to the back of her Jeep. She opened the door, flipped up the carpet, and searched for her tire iron. Where is it? I know I had one in here. Then remembered how she hadn't put it back after using it as a makeshift weapon, on the night she thought someone was in her apartment. Penelope sadly smiled as she remembered who the someone had turned out to be. It had been Baylee, standing in her kitchen cooking, holding a beer, and singing at the top of her lungs.

Penelope made herself focus back on the present, as she looked for anything she could use. The only thing left was the jack, so she figured why not, and grabbed it. She ran back to the caddy, not taking time to explain to Baylee what she was about to do. Giving it everything she had, she lifted the jack high above her head and slammed it through the driver's side window, then she reached in and unlocked the door.

Now with the car open, she looked for a trunk release button. Not finding it beside the driver's seat, she went to the glove box next. Found it! Pushing it several times, she realized it wasn't going to work. As she climbed back out of the car, she couldn't understand why it wouldn't open. She walked around to the back and noticed it had lifted a fraction more. Now that it had a tiny open space, she hoped she'd be able to see in. Crouching down next to the trunk, she peeked in, and there was Baylee, lying motionless.

"I've got you Bay, hang on!" Penelope told her, she turned and continued to look for anything she could use. Again, finding nothing, she yelled into the hidden mic. "I found Baylee, get in here, and bring an ambulance, hurry."

While she waited for backup to arrive, Penelope knelt back down beside the car and spoke softly to her friend.

"I'm here, Bay; everything's going to be okay now." As tears ran down her face, Penelope encouraged Baylee to hold on and explained how help was on the way. Baylee still hadn't said a word, so Penelope peeked in once again and could see her lying there, with only a shirt on. Getting more worried by the second, and tired of waiting for back-up, Penelope stood and decided to look through the car again for anything that might help. She opened the back door and spotted a pair of pliers just under the front passenger's seat.

"I think I might've found something to help us," Penelope said, leaning further in to reach them. "Almost there… only a few more inches."

Suddenly an arm wrapped around her waist and jerked her back out of the vehicle.

"I knew you'd come," Derrick whispered softly in her ear. "A sucker to the end. Have you missed me?" he asked, laughing. He pulled a gun from his pocket and pressed it firmly against her temple. "I've missed you."

He forced her to walk towards the trunk of the car, and Penelope knew this was it. This was her do-or-die moment. "Why don't you let Baylee go? This is between you and me, she has nothing to do with it," she told him.

"Really? She's the reason I got you here, isn't she? So, I'd say she's already a part of this. Plus, Baylee and I had some issues to work out, but I must say I'm feeling much better about it now." Reaching over, he pulled on a cable, and the trunk flew open.

The full view of Baylee lying in the trunk shocked her. With a quick intake of breath, she tried to evaluate Baylee's condition. Her eyes were closed, and she appeared lifeless. There was dried blood around her wrists and feet from what Penelope assumed was Baylee trying to free herself. But what stood out the most was the swelling and bruising covering her head and torso. She was almost unrecognizable, even to Penelope.

"Well, your friend Baylee here isn't going to be winning any beauty pageants in the near future, but she did learn a little thing about there being consequences for her actions. Isn't that right, Baylee," he said, while he laughed.

With the gun still at her head, Penelope wasn't sure what her next move should be. What could be taking Detective Black so long, she thought. Then she remembered this was all being recorded and knew she needed to get him to confess to everything he'd done.

"So here we are, just like you wanted," Penelope said. "But there is still one thing I don't understand."

"Really? Only one? Because I bet, you don't know the half of it."

"Really? Then why don't you explain it to me?"

"Where to start? Hmmm, well, apparently you already know about Molly, so let's start there, shall we?"

Feeling his arm around her throat relax a little, she knew she was making the right move. I just need to keep him talking, she thought. Then Detective Black and his guys can run in here and take him down. But not before I let him dig his own grave.

"I met Molly at the club, and she seemed to gravitate towards me. What can I say? I'm a good-looking guy. Anyway, you saw me walk back to her car that night she dropped me off. I was giving her my burner cell number."

Keep him talking, Penelope thought. "Was that Molly in the black SUV? The one with the pink panther license plate?"

"Yeah, that was her. And here's something I bet you don't know. She called me the next day while you were out shopping with, her," he said and pointed to Baylee, lying in the trunk and went on. "She stopped by the apartment, and if you only knew the things we did while you were away, especially on your favorite blanket. So later, when you stabbed me, she had no problem picking me up."

"I'm sure you didn't tell her the truth about how or why you'd been wounded?"

"Nah, I told her I was stabbed while someone tried to rob me. Of course, she bought the whole thing. And the best part was she's a vet, so she patched me right up. She even had painkillers for me to take, among other things. And here I am."

"Lucky us," said Penelope, "I'll have to thank her."

"I really doubt you'll get the chance, but good luck trying. What fun would this be if you didn't make an effort?"

He looked so proud of himself that she'd love to knock him down a peg or two, Penelope thought, desperately.

"That can't be all. How'd you get Baylee? I know she'd never come with you willingly."

"Why can't you figure out anything on your own? Do I have to explain everything to you?"

"No, I've figured out a few things. I know you went to my work and put a lock of my hair in my jeep."

"Did you like that one? Pretty smart of me, right? Oh, and to answer your question. I waited until Baylee fell asleep and drugged her. It came in real handy, Molly being a vet and all. I had complete access to all the drugs in her office. One little shot and Baylee was down for the count."

One more thing, Penelope thought. That's all I need him to admit too.

"So, if everything was so great with Molly, why did you come back to the apartments?"

"For you, of course. I came back for you. What better way to keep an eye on everything than to be right downstairs? And the best part was, you never even knew. I could come and go from our apartment anytime I wanted, Baylee's too."

"But how? I had all the locks changed."

"Did I forget to tell you? A couple months ago, my buddy, Matt, was hired as a maintenance guy for the apartment complex. So, I had no problem getting my hands on a master key."

Now it all made sense, she thought. How he'd been able to write on her mirror, set up her alarm clock, and everything else she hadn't been able to figure out. Hoping he would relax his grip a little further, Penelope coughed and acted as though she couldn't breathe. But he knew better than to fall for it, and Derrick only tightened his grip.

Barely able to get the words out, she finally asked, "So, why did you have to kill the old lady?"

Wondering if Penelope was trying to set him up, he turned her head to the side and barely whispered in her ear, "Because I could, and it was fun. I'd always wanted to bang an old lady to see what it was like."

It would have to be enough, Penelope thought, hoping Detective Black's tech could enhance the sound from the hidden mic in her coat. She took another look at Baylee and hoped they'd both make it out of this alive. She should've known better than to think the Detective and his crew would come to her rescue in time. I guess I'm going to have to do this myself, she thought.

"I wonder," Penelope said.

"You wonder what? Haven't I explained enough to you?"

Penelope knew with the gun still pressed against her, it probably wasn't the smartest time to make a move. But she had to do something, Baylee still hadn't opened her eyes, and Penelope had a bad feeling she was running out of time.

"I wonder… did you ever see this coming?" Without giving him a chance to register what she'd said, she quickly dug her nails into the pressure points on his arm, and elbow jabbed him in the sternum, causing him to loosen his grip. A mule kick to the groin loosened it even further and made him bend slightly forward. This gave her the perfect opportunity to slam her head back into his face. Hearing a cracking sound, she knew she'd broken his nose. Swiftly, she spun around, not giving him a moment to recover. She was now face to face with Derrick and his gun.

"Not exactly like you remembered, huh? Well, I'm not the same girl anymore. I'm done letting you or anyone else push me around."

"Is that right? Well, it could definitely make things a little more interesting. But unless you can move faster than a bullet, I'm not too impressed."

Aiming the gun at her, Derrick watched as her eyes dilated the way he loved. "See, I still hold all the power, Penelope. Why can't you just accept it?"

"You think I should accept the fact you kidnapped my best friend and put a girl in the hospital? Oh, and let's not forget the poor neighbor lady you killed just for the fun of it. Are you serious right now?"

Penelope knew she should watch what she said since he was the one with the gun. But she thought, if he hasn't killed me yet, he probably won't.

Derrick shook his head and said, "See, this is why we've had so many problems. You need to learn to keep that mouth of yours shut. None of this had to happen; it's all your fault."

"My fault?" Penelope asked, stunned she used to believe all his lies.

"Yes! Your fault. I had everything under control until you went and filed for a divorce. The old lady would still be alive if you hadn't done that. So, it's on you." He smiled at her with his evil grin.

"No, it's not; it's on you. I'm not going to let you turn this around on me again. You need to learn there are consequences for your actions too."

The sound of a scream registered in her ears; at the exact same time, she felt the bullet enter her gut. There had been no time to react. Instinctively, she pressed her hand to the wound and only then realized, the scream she'd heard only moments ago had come from herself. She pulled her hand away and saw it was covered in blood.

The impact had knocked her back a few feet. But she was still standing, which meant she still had a chance. Not having time to come up with a solid plan, she did the first thing that came to mind.

Screaming, she grabbed her stomach and bent over in pain. She kept her eyes averted and waited for Derrick to come closer. She knew he'd want to get in a couple more jabs before he was done.

"Come on, Penelope. I thought this was supposed to be the new and improved you? What, you're not as tough as you thought?" Laughing, he reached for her shoulder to give her a good shove.

Grabbing his wrist with her left hand, she twisted and pulled down, while using her right foot to kick the gun out of his grasp. It took him off balance for a moment, and that was all she needed to get the upper hand.

Ignoring the pain and pushing through, she used her momentum to circle around behind him. Penelope used the heel of her boot to kick him square in the back, landing him face-first into the ground.

But he recovered quickly and spun to charge her like a bull. His head hitting its mark, square in her stomach where the bullet had gone. He tackled her, and they both went down. He grabbed a hand full of hair and slammed her head into the snow-covered ground. Pulling a knife from his boot, he held it under her chin, making sure she didn't move while he spread her legs wide. She heard the sound of a zipper, then he said.

"I told you once; I'd never let you go. I'd kill you first. Well, it looks like you've left me no choice. But before I do, I might as well screw you one last time. Do you have anything left to say," he asked.

Penelope spit out a mouth full of blood and turned her head to get one more glance at Baylee. Knowing there was nothing left, she could say to change Derrick's mind, she closed her eyes and thought. Real-life wasn't like the movies. She guessed the good guys didn't always win.

Penelope opened her eyes and saw Derrick holding the knife high above his head, ready to stab her. Then suddenly, a gunshot blast sounded in the distance, and she heard a scream erupt from Derrick. Turning her head, she could see the knife he'd been holding was now a few feet away, along with what was left of the hand he'd been holding it with.

She realized quickly he was unarmed, she pulled her right leg up and kicked Derrick square in the chest, knocking him backwards off of her. Looking down at herself, she saw she was covered in blood, and after a moment, she understood why.

"You, this is all your fault!" he screamed. Getting up from the ground, he ran towards her. "Look, my hand is gone! I'm going to make you pay for this. Anything I've done up until now is child's play, compared to the pain I'll inflict on you."

Derrick was tackled to the ground only inches before reaching her. As she listened to him rant, she realized it was finally over, and he would suffer the punishment he deserved. She had no pity for him and turned her attention back to what really mattered, her best friend, Baylee.

When her eyes briefly met one of the detectives, they both knew she'd done what she'd set out to. Suddenly Detective Black assisted her to her feet and helped guide her over to Baylee. Leaning in the trunk, Penelope kissed her friend's cheek and realized just how cold she was. "We can't let him win, Bay, hang on."

"Come on, Penelope, we need to get you looked at. You've lost a lot of blood yourself," Detective Black said.

"I'm not leaving her!" Penelope said. Then without warning, everything went black.

Chapter 22

The room's wallpaper was a pale yellow, and Penelope had counted all the little flowers on it a hundred times. After a week in the hospital, she was running out of things to keep herself busy. However, the nurses were friendly enough to help her into a wheelchair and roll her into Baylee's room to visit often.

Hearing a knock on the door, Penelope watched Dr. Laura Morris walk in. "How are you feeling today?" she asked, while she looked at her tablet.

Penelope smiled, "Better thanks. Can you tell me if there's been any change with Baylee Reed?"

"I'm sorry, but I'm unable to discuss another patient's status. So, let's discuss your test results that came back this morning, instead."

"That's okay. How does everything look, Doctor?" Penelope asked.

"The blood work looks good. It seems your body is accepting the blood transfusion without any complications. You're lucky they got you here in time because you had lost a lot of blood," the doctor said. "I need to take a look at the bullet entry point, to make sure it's healing properly." Walking over to the bed, she pulled down the blanket and carefully lifted the gauze covering.

"Everything seems to be right on schedule, there's still a little swelling, but that's normal. How's the pain level today?"

Penelope looked up at her and replied, "About the same as yesterday. As long as I don't move too much, I'm fine."

The doctor smiled, nodded, and said, "That's good to hear. I'm going to have them run the blood work one more time, and if the results are the same, I see no reason to keep you here any longer. I'll go put in the order, and I'll come back and check on you later."

"That sounds good, doctor. Thank you." Penelope watched Dr. Morris step out into the hall. Moments later, another knock sounded on the door, and she assumed it was the nurse coming to take more blood for the tests the doctor had told her about. But surprisingly, it was Detective Black who stepped through the door.

"How are you doing, Penelope?" he asked.

"Better, thanks," she told him. "I'm hoping you have some news to share with me?"

"As a matter of fact, I do," Black said while pulling a chair up to the bed and taking a seat. "Derrick had his arraignment and was denied bail. So, he'll be awaiting trial behind bars."

"That's good to hear," she said with a smile as she thought of how much Derrick hated not getting his way.

"Also, the audio department was able to enhance the data from the mic we gave them. So, it looks like Derrick will be spending quite a long time behind bars. My tech specifically wanted me to tell you...hang on, I wrote it down," he said, pulling a piece of paper out of his back pocket. "They were able to magnify it enough to hear even a whisper. I'm not exactly sure what he's talking about, but he said you'd want to know."

"I do, and please tell him I said thanks. Have you heard anything about when the trial might take place?"

"No, nothing yet, but I'll keep you updated when I hear," Black said.

"Thanks, I'd appreciate it."

"So, how's Baylee doing? Any change," he asked.

"No, not yet, but I'm hopeful. The doctors all say, she could wake up any day now, because the swelling on her brain has gone down significantly."

"That's great news." He stood, "I better be going, and let you get some rest. I'll check on you again soon, just to make sure everything is going okay."

"All right, sounds good. And thanks again for everything you did, you went above and beyond what was required, and I really do appreciate it."

"You're welcome," he said. "I guess I'll see you later." He turned, opened the door, and was gone.

Penelope pushed the button on her bed for a nurse, and moments later, one walked in to see what she needed. The nurse agreed to help her out of bed and into a wheelchair but told her she couldn't visit Baylee right then because her parents were already in there.

"Oh, the Reeds are here?" Penelope asked. "Can you please take me there? I'd really like to speak to them. I can wait in the hall until they are ready to leave."

"Let me check with them first. They're very private people, and I was told to make sure they stay happy and respect their privacy."

The nurse left, and while Penelope waited, she thought, the Reeds were probably one of the top contributors to the hospital. It was no wonder everyone wanted to keep them happy.

A short while later, the nurse finally returned, but to Penelope's surprise, she had Ella Reed with her.

"Hello, Penelope. How are you, darling? I thought I would follow this lovely nurse back to your room and then accompany you back to Baylee's," Mrs. Reed said.

"I'm glad to see you, Mrs. Reed. How's Baylee doing?"

"She's still the same, darling, but we are all hopeful, of course."

"Yes, certainly," Penelope said. "I'm so very sorry. You know I never wanted anything like this to happen to Baylee."

"I don't blame you, darling, and you shouldn't blame yourself. You know Baylee wouldn't."

Penelope gave her a thankful smile and said, "I appreciate you telling me that. Some people might think differently because the man who hurt her was my ex-husband."

Ella leaned over and patted Penelope's shoulder, "This is how I see it. You were doing your best to get away from him, to start over, and he wouldn't allow it. None of this is your fault. It's all on him. But you never answered my question. How are you doing, Penelope? Have they told you when you'll be released?"

"Actually, the doctor said if my next test results come back good, then I can go home. But...," Penelope stopped herself. She knew she shouldn't ask. It wasn't the right thing to do. The Reeds almost lost their only daughter.

"But what, darling? I understand; you don't want to go home, do you? You want to stay with Baylee?" Ella asked.

Penelope didn't quite know what to say, glad that Mrs. Reed knew how she felt. She looked into her caring eyes.

"It's not my place, I know. You're her parents, and it's your place to be there. But she is the only family I have. I have no one else," Penelope said, feeling ashamed, she hung her head.

"Don't you do that, Penelope darling," Ella said, and using her finger lifted Penelope's head high. "Don't you hang your head, like you have anything to be embarrassed about. Baylee considers you her sister, and so it shall be."

"Are you sure?" Penelope questioned. "I know she's in intensive care and is only allowed one visitor at a time."

"Absolutely, I will talk to the nurses and hospital staff. I'm sure we can come to an agreement. When we aren't here, I want you with her, and I know you'll keep us updated. If anything changes, I want to hear right away. Please have the nurses inform us immediately." Ella told her.

"Yes, yes, of course," Penelope said, with tears streaming down her chin.

"Well, let's go see our girl and tell her the good news. Shall we, darling?" Ella took the lead, as the nurse pushed Penelope down the hall.

Once they went through the door to Baylee's private room, Penelope noticed the lights were dim, and the air was stale. Mr. Reed stood by the window, talking softly on his cell phone, staring out across the city around him.

"Push Penelope over to the bed, please," Ella asked the nurse, as Mr. Reed turned and acknowledged their presence.

Baylee still looked so pale, but the swelling had gone down, and the bruising had turned to a light shade of green. But it was still the same Baylee, and Penelope was happy to just sit there and hold her hand.

"Excuse us for a moment, Penelope," Mr. Reed said as he finished his call. "Mrs. Reed and I are going to step into the hall, but we will be back shortly." He went over to Baylee's bedside, leaned over, kissed her cheek, and whispered, "Love you, Princess; I'll be right back." He turned, walked over to Ella, took her hand in his, and together they left the room.

Penelope sat beside Baylee's bed and remembered she'd heard somewhere it was good to talk to people who were in a coma, so that's what she did. At first, she explained to Baylee everything that had happened at the abandoned paint factory. Penelope told her how Derrick had drugged her, and he'd killed the downstairs neighbor and everything in between.

"Please open your eyes, Bay, you know you want too. You've always said a girl needs her beauty sleep, but this is a little overboard, even for you, don't you think?" she teased. Squeezing her hand, Penelope hoped she'd feel Baylee squeeze back, but she didn't.

Not letting herself get discouraged, Penelope said, "Hey, do you remember when we were kids, and your dad let us put a tent in your backyard? Oh, we thought we were so brave until he snuck out in the middle of the night and scared us by making shadows and scratching on the mesh vents." Leaning closer to the bed, she whispered, "You were so scared you peed a little, but I promise, I've still never told a soul. Your secrets are always safe with me."

Hoping Baylee was hearing her, and would recall all the good times they'd shared, she continued. "Oh, here's a good one! Remember when we snuck into the back seat of your dad's car, and he had no idea we were there and took us nearly all the way to a business meeting in Wisconsin? Oh, man, I thought for sure we were going to get into big trouble. I know, I know, it was my fault we got caught, but I couldn't help it. If you would've been the one to drink two large sweet teas, you wouldn't have been able to hold it either. I had to ask him to stop, so I could pee. Your dad was so cool about it. I couldn't believe he rescheduled his meeting and took us to the Dells instead. Those were good times, don't you think?" Penelope again waited for a response, but Baylee only quietly laid there.

Penelope stopped reminiscing, looked around the room, and wished it was brighter, more like Baylee's personality. She'd hate being in a dull place like this, but when she finally woke up, at least she'd see all the pretty flowers and gifts people had dropped off to wish her well.

Finally, when the Reeds hadn't returned, Penelope located the nurse call button and pressed it. Moments later, the same nurse that had brought her here came into the room.

"Can I help you?" she asked.

"I'm sorry to bother you, but could you turn up the lights and maybe open a window? It's so dark and stuffy in here," Penelope said.

"The lights are no problem, but the windows, I'm sorry to say, don't open on this floor. It's for safety reasons," she said, turning up the lights. Then the nurse walked around the room to make sure all the flowers had enough water, then straightened Baylee's covers.

"Is there anything else I can do for you? Are you ready to head back to your room yet?"

"No, but thank you," Penelope responded politely.

"Okay, let me know when you're ready," the nurse said and walked out the door. She'd left it open enough to help with the airflow, but Penelope realized she could overhear the Reeds talking in the hallway.

"William, Please," Ella cautioned.

"What do you want me to do, Ella? That's my little girl in there, and I refuse to let her go back to that apartment. It isn't safe."

"You know how much Baylee loves her independence. She'll feel we're trying to control her life again," Ella told him. "You can't just make these decisions on your own. She has a right to say what she wants."

"But she can't! Can she, Ella? She's in a damn coma, and the doctors have no idea when my baby's going to wake up. So, it's settled, we're moving her to the apartment on East Chestnut." William rubbed Ella's shoulders to help calm her, and continued, "She'll need round-the-clock-care and later, therapy. This is the best decision, trust me."

Penelope tried not to eavesdrop, but she couldn't help but overhear what was being discussed. They were planning to move Baylee away from her. She desperately needed to think of a way to keep that from happening.

"Come on, Bay, you need to wake up. I don't think I'll be able to stop them. I can't do this alone. Open your eyes Bay, come on, you can do it. You have, too." With tears dripping from her eyes, Penelope leaned over and rested her head on the bed, so distraught she didn't hear someone enter the room.

With her eyes closed, she was startled when someone leaned over and gave her a hug, but the scent of perfume told her it was Ella Reed.

"Now everything has been taken care of, hasn't it Darling?" Ella said, looking to her husband.

"Yes, it has, and I think Penelope will be pleased, don't you, dear?" Mr. Reed said.

Lifting her head, Penelope stared at them with tear-filled eyes. "Please don't take her away from me! I don't know what I'd do without her."

"Whatever are you talking about?" Ella asked. "We have no intention of splitting you two up. I think Baylee needs you just as much as you need her. Darling, will you please explain things to poor Penelope."

Penelope cringed at the words 'poor Penelope', but let it slide since she knew Ella meant no harm or disrespect.

Mr. Reed pulled a chair up to the other side of Baylee's bed and took a seat as he explained, "Ella, and I have decided that you will stay here with Baylee until she wakes up. Once that happens, you both will be taken directly to Baylee's apartment on Chestnut. It's much safer there, and I've already arranged for around-the- clock-care and rehabilitation for you both." He picked up Baylee's hand, kissed it, and held it close to his face. "My Princess might be upset I've done this, but I hope you'll help her to see that it's the best decision for you both."

Shocked by what she was hearing, Penelope said, "I don't know what to say. This isn't what I was expecting. I was so afraid you were taking her away." She looked from one to the other and said, "Thank you. I do appreciate your kindness and will always do my best to look out for Baylee."

Ella placed a hand on Penelope's shoulder and said, "We know you will, darling. Now, remember, you promised to let me know of the slightest change."

"Absolutely!" Penelope said. "Thank you again. I'll call for a nurse to take me back to my room now, and let you spend more time with Baylee."

Standing up, Mr. Reed said, "No need for that; I'll help you back, myself."

Pushing Penelope down the hall, he said, "I have something I've wanted to tell you for years, but it's never felt it was the right time."

"Oh," was all Penelope replied.

Finally arriving at her room, he pushed her wheelchair by the bed, pulled up his own chair, and spoke. "I wanted to say, I'm sorry. Back when you girls were little, I knew what was going on at your place, with your parents. I made a choice to look the other way, and that was wrong. I should have done everything in my power to help you. I was young, and I worried more about my own career and how it would look to get involved than help to remedy what you had to deal with on a daily basis."

"Mr. Reed, it's okay. It was a long time ago. I don't blame you for anything. You did what you thought was right for your family, and going back to 'what if's' never help anyone. It could have turned out; differently, you're right, but have you ever thought about how it could have turned out worse for all of us?" Penelope asked.

"I don't see how it could have been worse. You poor child. You were so innocent, just a victim, helpless to change what was happening right in front of you. The images from back then, haunt me, still to this day." He said, standing up and going to look out the window.

"Mr. Reed, you can't predict the future. But maybe I can set your mind at ease. What if you would have gotten involved, and it set my father off? What if he would have hurt Ella or Baylee? You know as well as I do, what he was capable of. What I'm trying to say is, you may have regrets, but don't we all? Now, do you understand what I meant by it could have been worse?"

Mr. Reed turned and walked to Penelope, "Here, let me help you out of that chair. You know, you're pretty wise for your age."

"I sometimes doubt that, but thanks," she said, as he helped her into the bed.

He pulled the blankets up and tucked in the sides, just like she imagined most dads did at night for their daughters. Looking up into his eyes, she said, "Thanks for the help, and the conversation. I hope it made you feel better about everything. Don't you worry about Baylee; she'll come around. I know she will. We all know how she likes to make an entrance," Penelope said, smiling.

He laughed and said, "That sure sounds like something my Princess would do. Thanks for listening, Penelope. I do feel better, and I'm glad to know Baylee has you looking out for her."

"We have each other," she said.

He turned to go, then looked back, "By the way, I've already taken care of everything for you to be transferred to her private room. The bed should be here by tomorrow."

Before she could thank him again, he was gone, and the door closed quietly. Thinking about everything that had happened today, she closed her eyes to rest.

The next morning Penelope was awoken by a nurse who pulled open the curtains to let in some light. "Well, good morning, Penelope. How are you feeling today? I have good news for you, your test results came back, and Dr. Morris has already filled out your release papers."

Barely awake, Penelope stared at her without saying a word.

"It's release day, why aren't you excited? Let's get you up and dressed. Then we can move you over to your friend's room. Everything is set and ready for you there," the nurse urged her along.

With the information finally sinking in, Penelope smiled and said, "I'm ready to go."

"Hold on, young lady, I think you're forgetting a few things."

"Not really. I can take care of anything I need to do, once I get there."

The nurse walked to Penelope's bedside and lowered the rail. Pulling the covers back, she smiled and asked, "Have you tried to walk on your own yet?"

"No, but I'm willing to try. It would be wonderful to be able to go to the bathroom by myself." On unsteady legs, Penelope stood and took a step toward the bathroom. The nurse stayed by her side just in case, but she managed to finally reach her destination.

Once Penelope was dressed, and all the paperwork was done. She decided she'd eat breakfast in Baylee's room. So, with the nurse's help, they made their way in that direction.

Pushing through the door, Penelope looked at Baylee, still lying in bed and wanted to cry. Why hadn't she woken up yet, she thought. The doctors said she was doing better, and the swelling on the brain had gone down significantly, but seeing her with all the machines hooked up was jarring. She tried to keep a positive attitude and said, "Honey, I'm home."

The nurse stopped, looked at her, and started laughing, "Good for you; it's good to keep things fun. I think it will help her. I've seen some crazy things in my day, and believe me, she knows what's going on in this room."

Penelope stepped over to Baylee's bed and took a seat on the edge. "Do you really think so?"

"Yes, I really do. You just keep up that positive attitude and don't give up. She knows you're here, and you'd be surprised at how much of a difference it can make. Now, I'll let you get settled, and bring in your breakfast, in just a few minutes," the nurse said, wheeling out the chair she'd used to bring Penelope in.

"Well, here we are again, Bay. Just the two of us. I can't believe how amazing your parents are to let me stay with you until you wake up. Isn't that great?" She wanted so badly to hear Baylee respond.

Hours later, after eating breakfast, and catching a short nap, Penelope heard someone yelling in the hallway. Curious as to what the commotion was all about, Penelope slowly made her way to the door.

"But I'm a friend, I just want to make sure she's okay and to give her these flowers," said a familiar voice.

"I'm sorry, sir, but you're not on the list, and this is a private room. No one gets in without permission," the nurse said.

Struggling to open the door, Penelope knocked from the inside to get the nurse's attention.

"Wait here, sir. I'll be back with you in a moment." The nurse didn't move until he stepped back from the door. Then she opened it to see what Penelope needed.

"Is everything okay?" she asked.

"That guy out there is Emerson Burns, and he's a friend of mine and Baylee's. I give permission to add him to our visitor's list."

"I'm sorry, but you don't have the authority to make that call. I was given very strict instructions."

Cutting her off, Penelope said, "Look, I understand, but I promise it will be okay. I take full responsibility for him. If you would call Mr. Reed, I'm sure he will agree to let me add and remove people from the list."

"All right, I'll go give Mr. Reed a call. You can come out and speak with the gentleman in the hall until I get permission."

"Thank you," Penelope stepped out of the room, and immediately Emerson steered her to a chair and helped her into it.

"I've been so worried. No one around here will tell me anything." Emerson said, clearly frustrated.

"I'm sorry, Emerson. I didn't realize you were coming," Penelope said, trying to comfort him the best she knew how.

"Is Baylee going to be ok? It was all over the news, but of course, they never give enough details."

She looked at him and the pretty flowers he was holding and said, "I'm sorry, but Baylee's still in a coma. The doctor said she could wake up any time now. We just don't know when, but I'm sure it would be good for her, for you to visit. The nurse is calling Baylee's dad now, to give me permission to add people to the list."

"Oh, thank you. I'd really like to see her."

The nurse walked up beside them and said, "Good news, Penelope, you were correct. Mr. Reed gave you permission to adjust the list. So, it looks like Mr. Burns, here, will be able to visit Baylee after all."

"That's great news. Thank you so much for calling," Penelope said, and turned to Emerson, she smiled and asked, "Are you ready to go in?"

"I'm more than ready, let's go." Emerson stood and went to assist Penelope, but she held up her hand to stop him.

"You go, first. I'm going to find a vending machine and get a snack. The exercise will do me good."

"Are you sure?" he asked. "I can go with you if you'd like."

"Don't be silly, I can manage. They did officially release me, you know."

Emerson smiled, "I'm glad you're doing better. Now it's Baylee's turn." He placed his hand on the door, looked back at Penelope as she slowly headed off down the hall, and went in.

Going inside, Emerson went to her bed, bent over and kissed Baylee's forehead, then took a seat in the chair next to her. He held her hand and spoke softly. "Where's that feisty girl I met not so long ago? I've missed her. Come on, Baylee, open those beautiful eyes of yours."

He stared at all the machines hooked up to her, unsure of what the numbers on the monitors meant. But somehow, he felt reassured by their steady rhythm of beeps. "I'm so sorry this happened to you. I wish I would've been there. You could bet your ass, he wouldn't be so lucky as to walk away."

Realizing he'd forgotten to give Baylee her flowers, he bent over, picked them up, and said, "I brought you these; I thought they might cheer you up. I see you have plenty of admirers sending them, but mine seems to be the only purple roses in the room." Not sure what to put them in, he lifted the lid on the water pitcher and dropped them in. He'd remember to bring a vase next time.

He once again took his seat, just as the nurse walked in.

"Excuse me, sir, I need to ask you to leave for a few minutes, while I evaluate her."

"Okay, no problem," he said, and stood to leave.

Out in the hall, Emerson looked over and saw Penelope sitting by the nurse's station. "What are you doing out here?"

"Not much. I thought you'd enjoy some time with Baylee, so I stayed out here and ate my snack. How did it go? I thought the flowers were beautiful, by the way."

"Thanks, I hope she likes them once she wakes up."

"I'm sure she will. They are her favorite color, after all."

Moments later, the nurse walked out and gave them the all-clear to go back in. But before Penelope followed him, she stopped and asked if he wanted more alone time with Baylee. Following him in, she watched as he told Baylee goodbye, and gently placed a kiss on her forehead. He promised her he'd return soon to check on her.

Hours after Emerson had left, and it was only the two of them, Penelope sat on the edge of Baylee's bed and read out loud part of a book she'd been reading. She hoped Baylee would wake up and tell her to stop because she'd already read that one, but it didn't happen. Unwilling to be discouraged, Penelope patted Baylee's leg and said, "So, aren't you going to ruin it for me and tell me how it ends?" She laid the book down and continued. "I called your mom earlier, to give her an update. She and your dad are coming by in a little while to see you." Penelope looked at the clock and realized the Reeds could be there anytime."

Carefully climbing off the bed, she walked over to Baylee's bedside table and pulled out a hairbrush. "I know you'd want to look your best, so I'll do your hair, and get you back to looking like a Princess. How's that sound?" After finishing everything, Penelope gave Baylee a light spritz of her favorite perfume.

"Now, you look and smell fabulous, just the way it should be." After putting all the supplies away, she turned and said, "Now, let's go through all the cards you've gotten. I'll make a list of who sent what, so you can send out your thank-you cards later."

Penelope was touched by how many people really loved her friend. Baylee always made an impression on everyone she met. There were dozens of lovely bouquets, a few cute balloons, and even more cards.

"Bay, I wish you could see how many people are pulling for you to get better. A lovely vase filled with bright daffodils from someone named Eve. The gorgeous purple roses are from Emerson, of course." Continuing through the rest, Penelope explained what everything looked or smelled like. She told Baylee who they were from and made notes as she went along. Reaching for a lovely spray of white roses, Penelope located a full-size card taped to its side. She opened it and nearly dropped the flowers to the floor. Reading it out loud, she said, "I'm thinking of you and wishing you well. Speedy recovery for the best woman who was ever in my life. Sending you all my love, Adam."

"Why is Adam sending you flowers? Is there something you haven't told me?" She turned to Baylee for an answer, then remembered, she wouldn't be getting one. Penelope sat the flowers back on the shelf and continued on. Picking up the last bouquet, she was startled when the door opened, and Baylee's parents walked in.

"Penelope, how's our girl doing today?" Mr. Reed asked as he walked in.

"Sorry to say, there's been no change."

"That's okay; she just isn't ready yet," he responded, walking over to Baylee's bedside. He leaned over once again, kissed her cheek, and whispered in her ear. "How's my princess today? Father's right here, baby."

Ella walked to the other side of the bed, took a seat, and held Baylee's hand. A tear leaked from her eye, and she quickly wiped it away.

Penelope finished writing the final note and said, "I'll give you some time with her. I'm sure she's missed you both."

"Thank you, darling," Ella said.

Penelope smiled, nodded, and quietly slipped out the door. She was feeling better today than she had, so she decided to take a walk and make a call. Pulling her cell from her pocket, she dialed and put the phone to her ear.

"Hello, Choices Make Changes. You've reached Grace, how may I help you?"

"Hi, Grace. It's Penelope."

"Oh Penelope, how are you, dear? You weren't at the last few meetings. I've been worried."

"I'm sorry to worry you. I've kind of had a lot going on. Would it be okay if I came by to see you tomorrow?"

"Yes, absolutely. I have time open at 11:00, would that work for you?"

"Yes, thank you. I'll see you then." Penelope hung up and immediately called Emerson.

"Inner Strength, how can I help you."

"Hi, is Emerson there?" she asked.

"This is, Emerson. Penelope, is that you?"

"Yes, it is. Don't worry, Baylee's the same. I was hoping you could do me a favor."

"Sure, what's up."

"I have an appointment tomorrow at 11:00. Do you think you could come and sit with Baylee until I get back?"

"I'd love too. Thanks for thinking of me. I'll be there around 10:00."

"Great. It will good for Bay to hear your voice. Plus, I'll know she is safe until I get back. I'll see you then." Hanging up, Penelope took a deep breath and tried to relax. She hoped tomorrow's appointment with Grace might help ease her mind.

After resting against the wall for a few minutes, Penelope headed back to Baylee's room. She needed to think of a way to get Baylee to wake up. If what the doctors were saying was true, and Baylee could hear her talking, then maybe telling her something shocking would bring Bay back to her, she thought.

Finally, reaching Baylee's room, Penelope cracked the door a little before entering. She didn't want to interrupt Baylee's parent's time with her. She heard them saying their goodbyes, so she took a seat outside the room to give them their privacy and as much time as they wanted.

Moments later, the door opened wide, and Mr. and Mrs. Reed walked out, holding hands, with tears in their eyes.

"Watch over our girl, Penelope. We'll be back tomorrow to visit with her." Mr. Reed said, pulling his wife closer.

"I will, and I'll let you know if anything changes."

Ella turned and buried her head into her husband's shoulder as he led her toward the elevator.

Penelope waited until they were out of sight before turning to go back into the room to see her friend.

"How was the visit with your parents?" Not waiting for a response, Penelope walked over and sat on the bed with Baylee.

"I talked to Emerson, and he's going to come for a visit again tomorrow. I thought you'd like that. I don't know if you've heard, but your parents have hired a full-time therapy staff to come and take care of you once you're released." Penelope had hoped she'd get some kind of a response, but there was still nothing. Hoping this next one would do the trick, she tried again.

"Oh, and you won't believe this. Your parents also moved you out of your apartment and into the one on Chestnut." Penelope knew Baylee didn't want to live in the city, she'd heard her say it enough times. Yet, the news hadn't even caused her to flinch. Baylee loved her parents, but she also loved her independence and hated being told what to do.

Well, that was a bust. Out of ideas, but determined to come up with a better plan, Penelope decided the answer might come to her during sleep. She might dream up the answer to all her questions, how to wake up Baylee, how to get through the court proceedings she was sure to follow. And let's not forget what should her next step be, where should her life go from here. She needed direction, and maybe a dream would show her.

Chapter 23

The following day, Emerson arrived right on time, and Penelope was happy to see him.

"Another gift? Emerson, you're going to spoil her," Penelope said.

"It's a little teddy bear. I thought she might like to sleep with it. I sprayed some of my cologne on it, and hoped it would make her think of me."

Penelope looked at him and said, "I'm sure it will, and I can make sure it's with her every night."

"Do you think it's dumb? Like something a high school kid would do?"

"No, not at all. I'm willing to try anything, and I'm glad to see you are too." Penelope winked, then her phone rang. Answering it, she smiled. "Hello."

"How's it going? Has Baylee woke up yet?" Detective Black asked.

"No, not yet. But she will. It's nice of you to call and check on her."

"I called to check on you both. I know this has to be rough on you. Do you need anything?"

"No, I'm okay. But thanks for asking."

"Well, if anything changes, please let me know. I have to go now, but I'll be in touch."

"Okay, thanks again for calling," Penelope said, not knowing what to think. She'd assumed she wouldn't hear from the detective anymore since the case was closed. The only time she thought she might see him was during court, once the trial started. She hadn't known any cops like Black. The police she knew, hadn't seemed to care about the people involved. They cared more about the crime itself that had been committed. Maybe she shouldn't have grouped them all together in her mind. The jury was still out; she'd have to think about it for a while.

"Sorry, Emerson, I didn't mean to be rude that was Detective Black, calling to check up and see how things were going."

"That was nice of him, I guess. So, is this Detective Black single?" Emerson asked, with concern in his voice.

"No need for you to worry, Emerson," Penelope told him, smiling. "Baylee only has eyes for you. Now I have to take off, or I'm going to be late for my appointment. You have my cell, right?"

"Yes, I do. You're in my contacts. I promise I'll call if anything changes. Thanks again for thinking of me."

"It's what she'd want," Penelope said as she walked out of the room. Not healed enough to drive, she hailed a cab and headed for CMC.

Upon arriving, she walked straight to Grace's office, knocked on the door, and took a seat in the little waiting area. A few minutes later, Grace opened her office door and motioned for Penelope to come in.

"It's good to see you, dear," Grace said, making her way around her desk. "So, tell me, what's on your mind? You said you've been busy; would you like to talk to me about it?"

"Yes, I think I would."

Penelope gave Grace the play-by-play of everything that had occurred with Derrick. She told her how Baylee was still in a coma, and she wasn't sure how much more she could take. "Derrick knew exactly how to hurt me."

"Yes, he did, dear. But he hasn't won yet. After everything I've heard, Baylee is a fighter. She will fight and come back to you and to those who love her."

"Thank you for saying that. I don't know why you saying it seems to help me feel better, but it does."

"I'm glad. Now let's talk about you for a moment, shall we?"

"Me? I'm feeling better every day. The bullet went straight through, and it didn't hit anything major. They had to give me some blood and stitch me up, but I'm going to be fine."

"It's good to hear, dear. But not exactly what I was referring too. Have you thought about where you want to go from here?" Grace asked.

"I guess I'm moving to an apartment on Chestnut with Baylee when she gets out of the hospital. But I don't think that's what you meant, was it?"

"No dear, it's not. I'm talking about your future, down the road. Where do you see yourself in 5 years?

"Honestly? I don't know. The Detective in charge of my case, the one who helped me, called earlier today. It caught me off guard. I'm not used to a cop caring about what happens after the fact."

"Don't you think they should care?" Grace asked. "Don't you think they should worry or wonder about the victims they've helped?"

"I guess I do, but it's not what I've grown up expecting. It makes me wonder."

"Wonder what, Penelope?"

She knew Grace was watching her, waiting for something. For some type of reaction, maybe? She wasn't sure but said, "Makes me wonder why there aren't more cops and detectives like him. It might make a real difference in someone's life. You know?"

"Yes, I do know, and I completely agree with you. This world could definitely use more good guys. Maybe even people who understand what someone is going through, or perhaps someone whose been in their shoes," Grace said.

"Right. I wish I would've had someone like Detective Black around when I was a kid. It might have made all the difference. It might even have changed the outcome."

"How so, dear?"

"I don't know, everything always felt the same, nothing ever changed. The cops would come, then they'd leave without doing anything. Or worse, they'd take Daddy Luke to jail, and he'd come back even meaner."

It's a cycle, dear, even for the police. Think of how many times they'd been called to your home. They probably felt the same way you did. Just another domestic call, where no one ever leaves and ends it."

"But that's not fair, the police have more power than a kid does. We didn't have a choice, we had to live with him."

"Yes, you did, because unfortunately everyone around failed. The system failed, the police failed, the schools failed, and your parents failed. But you wouldn't have to fail. You could be the one to make a difference in a child's life. Be there for someone, even though no one was there for you."

"I'll have to think about it. Let it stew and see what turns out from it. Thanks for taking the time to talk to me. But I need to be getting back to Baylee." Penelope said and stood to leave.

"It was nice seeing you again, Penelope. I hope to see you again soon. Please keep me updated on your friend." Grace followed Penelope out of her office.

"I will, and thanks again. I'll try to be at the next group session." Penelope felt much better after talking things over with Grace. Walking outside, she hailed a cab and headed back to the hospital.

On the ride and still, in the elevator, Penelope kept replaying the conversation with Grace. Knowing what someone was going through because you'd been there could make all the difference. She felt something inside was trying to tell her something, but she couldn't put her finger on it.

Penelope stepped off the elevator and walked to Baylee's room, she couldn't wait to tell her everything she and Grace had discussed. She pushed through the door and then stopped, remembering Emerson was there. "I'm sorry to interrupt. I can come back later."

"It's cool. I was reminding Baylee of the date she'd asked for."

"Really?" Penelope eyeballed him with her left eyebrow raised. "She asked you out?"

"Yes, she did. Something about how she'd lost a bet, but it shouldn't have counted because you cheated?" he laughed.

"Well, we did have a bet, and she lost, but I didn't cheat. I thought I'd have to fight her a little more to comply with our agreement. Guess not?" Smiling to herself, Penelope made her way to the bed and sat down once again on the corner.

"I'm not complaining," Emerson told her. "I'll admit, though, I was shocked when she walked in. Then even more shocked when she asked me out. I wouldn't say we had gotten off to the best start."

"Yeah, I heard." She tried not to laugh, because she knew a little more about that encounter than he did, like how Baylee faked her injury. "But you both left on a good note? Right?"

"I suppose so," he said as he reached over and adjusted the blankets covering Baylee. "If she only knew how many times she's popped into my head since that night."

"How many times," Baylee asked in a soft, weak voice.

"Baylee, you're awake!" Penelope cried. "I'm going to go get a nurse." Not waiting for any reply, she left the room to find someone.

Looking up into Emerson's eyes, Baylee once again asked, "Are you going to answer the question, Blue Eyes? How many times?"

Emerson smiled down at her and shook his head. "More times than I could count, but I promise once you're out of here, we'll have plenty of time to discuss it." He leaned over and kissed her forehead.

Penelope pushed open the door, with a nurse in tow, and made Emerson reluctantly tell Baylee goodbye, promising to return soon.

Penelope called Baylee's parents while several doctors and nurses were checking her over from head to toe. They quickly arrived, and the joy on their faces said it all. They had their princess back, and for the time being, their world was set right again.

Late in the evening, since visiting hours didn't apply to the Reeds, they left for home. Promising to be back in the morning.

Finally alone, Penelope handed Baylee her Christmas present.

Baylee looked up questioningly but smiled.

"It's your Christmas gift, silly girl. You slept through the whole holiday. So, open it now, please," Penelope told her.

Due to all her injuries, Baylee took it slow as she unwrapped it. Once all the paper was removed, Penelope watched as tears slid down Baylee's cheek.

"Why are you crying? Don't you like it? I tried to get you something meaningful, but it's hard shopping for the girl who has everything, you know."

"No, of course, I do, I love it!" Baylee said, as she lovingly stared down at the bright purple picture frame. One slot held a picture of the two of them together as kids. The middle picture was of them, taken only a few months ago, while the third slot had no picture, but a card that read, 'Our Future.'

"It's the best gift you could've given me, thank you," Baylee told her, through a teary smile.

"I'm glad you like it, now we need to fill the third spot," Penelope said, then handed Baylee a tissue from the box next to her bed and smiled, happy her friend had come back to her.

Several weeks later, Baylee was finally released from the hospital, and they were on their way to the new apartment on Chestnut. Baylee made herself loud and clear she wasn't happy; this decision was made without her approval. Penelope thought she'd convinced Baylee to see the logic in moving. Once in the elevator, she explained the apartment was still hers, not her parents, plus did either of them really want to go back to where so much had occurred. It was safer with around the clock security, and they wouldn't need to worry about anyone sneaking in. This way, they'd be roommates with a full-time staff and rehab team to help them both heal faster. Penelope helped Baylee inside, where they were greeted by staff Baylee's parents had hired. Penelope wasn't sure if Baylee had agreed to it for her own safety, or for Penelope's, but either way, they were together.

"Can we please, get back to a little normalcy around here," Baylee said. "I'm so sick of living in a hospital room."

"Normal? Who wants normal? Normal is boring, and you have to admit our lives are anything but boring. Wouldn't you agree?"

Baylee laughed. The sound made Penelope's heart swell with joy. It was good to have Baylee back and on the mend.

Epilogue

A year later, Penelope looked back on what had happened and was thankful she still had her best friend by her side. They had both testified in Derrick's trial, it was hard to do, but together they got through it. He was sentenced to life in prison, with the slight possibility of parole. But at least he was out of their lives, for now.

Baylee had finally been able to return to the paramedic job she loved. But it was never proven Derrick had been the one responsible for the missing medication. Baylee hated the look of suspicion she kept getting from her coworkers and had been considering going a different direction in her career. Emerson was still in her life, and although they hadn't made any firm commitments, Penelope was glad Baylee had him.

As for herself, it had been a long hard road to get where she was. Once Pen realized what her gut had been trying to say, she knew what she needed to do. The factory job paid for her to take college classes and continuing education. She studied hard for years, and with Grace and Baylee's help along the way, always caring, always supportive. At last, she graduated and could say she was proud of herself, her accomplishments, and the values she stood for. She felt she was finally the right woman for the job.

Penelope now stood for those who needed her help, for those who could no longer help themselves. Now, she was Detective Penelope Fitch, one who always stood for what she felt was right, and fought hard for what she believed in.

Derrick and her father had been wrong about her. There had always been a strong woman inside, she just needed to learn to trust her.

THE END

Coming Soon

In the next installment of the Penny Series, Penelope takes charge and best friend Baylee is at the top of the suspect list! To get your sneak peek visit my website www.michellebachman.com

I love hearing from my readers! Follow me and leave a comment on any of my social media sites.

Remember you're not alone. There are many of us out there who have been in a similar situation. It is possible to break free. To be the person YOU want to be; not who you're forced to be.

The National Domestic Violence Hotline established in 1996, has been serving those in need for 15 years. Its lines are open 24 hours a day providing support through advocacy, safety planning and resources to help those affected by domestic violence.

The National Domestic Abuse Hotline Number is:

USA*********1-800-799-7233 (SAFE)
TTY*********1-800-787-3224
UK**********0808 2000 247